A Match Made in Spell

FATE WEAVER
BOOK ONE

REGINA WELLING

A Match Made in Spell

Copyright © 2016 by ReGina Welling and Erin Lynn

All rights reserved. No part of this book may be reproduced in any form by any electronic or mechanical means including photocopying, recording, or information storage and retrieval without permission in writing from the author.

ISBN- 978-1-953044-00-6

Cover design by: L. Vryhof

Interior design by: L. Vryhof

http://reginawelling.com

http://erinlynnwrites.com

First Edition

Printed in the U.S.A.

Contents

Chapter 1

Being wicked is a choice. At least I hope it is.

Most families try to hide their sins away from prying eyes; mine erected a statue to commemorate theirs. Okay, that's not entirely true.

Homicidal witches turn to stone, immediately and irrevocably. The murder of one of our own is the one crime for which, in our world, there is no redemption. I don't know who makes the rules; I only know it happened to my grandmother.

Nobody is sure exactly what went down that day, but when it was all over, my mother, Sylvana, was gone, presumed dead, leaving nothing behind but the charred mark of dark magic on the earth. Only the trees bore witness to the vile act that orphaned me.

However it happened, my walk to work every day took me right past a life-sized reminder of everything I never wanted to be. On the afternoon when everything began to change, I was running late to work, and my Nikes hit the pavement in speed-walker mode, so I only managed a handful of steps before something odd caught my eye. A flash of color blazed against the granite.

A blood red rose with thorns the size of a baby's thumb sent a flicker of ice up my spine and set the hairs on the back of my neck vibrating. A cloud of scent enticed me to lose myself in its sweet thrall, to test a finger against a petal to see if it was as soft as it looked.

As much as I preferred to ignore this particular piece of my history, Clara drew my eye every time I passed by. That rosebush hadn't been there the day before. Trust me; I'd have noticed considering it was a month and a half too early for the delicate petals to thrive.

Immortalized in stone, my grandmother stared balefully back at me. No artist would ever be that skilled with a hammer and chisel; tendrils of hair whipped by wind or fire were picked out in exquisite detail around the face that haunted my dreams. Feral eyes, fixed on something in the distance, pierced through the granite. The fierce grimace of concentration that curled back her lips couldn't hide that she had been a beautiful woman. No hooked nose or warts marred the perfection of her face.

Even if Clara Balefire *was* evil to the bone, they'd been lovely bones. For that, at least, I was thankful, since those same bones had been handed down to me. It was uncanny how much I looked like her. Another fact I chose to try and ignore.

Anyone who knew Clara points out how we could have been twins. Funny how no one ever mentions my mother. Speak the name Sylvana Balefire and those witches quickly find a stain on their shirt to fuss with, or a reason to bolt for the nearest exit.

Not that I have a lot of contact with the witch community. Whether it's because they know something about why my wicked grandmother murdered her poor, innocent daughter or they don't, I've never been certain.

They're probably afraid my defect will rub off on them.

Powerful witchiness runs in my family. With a last name like Balefire, how could it not?

My mom called me Alexis, which means protector. Alexis Balefire. Protector of the ritual flame. It's a lot of name to carry, so I shortened it to Lexi. Alexis is a fighting goddess who wears armor, carries a shield, and wields a sword. Lexi is the cute girl next door who wears designer clothes, carries a purse, and wields a lipstick.

That's who I wanted to be; or, rather, that's who I was destined to be. Call me shallow if you must, but saving the world isn't on my to do list. I'll settle for saving people from the perils of loneliness, and at least I'll be able to sleep at night knowing I'm not in danger from any falling houses. Wicked witches never meet their ends in a calm and peaceful manner, of that I'm sure.

But Balefire isn't just my last name; it's also my responsibility. Don't laugh, but an ancient Balefire lights up the fireplace in my living room, and since I have no other family to speak of, it's my job to feed it enough magic to keep it burning. If the fire goes out, bad things will happen in the witch world. Crazy, right?

Only one problem, though. The powerful magic running in the blood of my family passed right over me and, barring a miracle, at midnight on my rapidly-approaching twenty-fifth birthday, my fate would be sealed.

Witch or no witch. Soon the decision would be final, and I had little hope of it turning out the way I wanted. Looking at it from the glass half-filled perspective, not getting my magic would take away the worry of following in my grandmother's wicked footsteps.

But who wants half a glass of anything?

And being wicked is a choice I'd never make. I hoped.

What little power I did have showed itself in a heightened sense of intuition—one that applied almost exclusively to interpersonal relationships. Which is just a fancy way of saying I'm a matchmaker with a particular proficiency for recognizing potential love connections when I see them.

With no other skills to my credit, I used my limited powers to open up FootSwept Matchmaking, where word of mouth gets me as much business as I can handle, and allows me to help people fall in love almost every day. Who wouldn't love a job like that?

My office sits on the corner of a tree-lined block of storefronts backed by a larger section of converted factory spaces. Fumbling in my purse for the keys, I glanced up at the broom and stars logo painted on the front window just above the slogan, *Get Swept Away*. A nod to witchery only those in my closest circle understand. Once the door slammed behind me, I fired up the coffee pot, then opened my battered day planner to check my schedule.

I know, I know, I was a busy business woman in the 21st century; you'd think my entire life would be uploaded onto the cloud, but I was still attached to paper and lists. Somehow, the act of tracing the words, pressing pen to paper and leaving a physical mark on the page helped turn my intentions into actions. I don't think anyone else would understand my system, but it worked for me.

Not more than two seconds after I had settled in at my desk with a mug of steaming coffee, the phone began to ring and didn't stop for the next two hours. Business tends to run fairly steadily, with spikes of increased activity around the holidays. Other than the week directly after Valentine's day, my schedule is rarely overwhelmed; but lately, it was as though the entire city had become lovelorn—and nobody seemed able to sort it out for themselves. Not that I was complaining—but I don't like to rush through my work, and an increase in demand meant I'd have to turn clients away if I couldn't fit them into my schedule.

I slugged the last half of my coffee in one swallow, made a face at the now-tepid brew, and when a client I didn't recognize stepped through the entryway, hit the button to send all calls straight to voicemail.

"Are you the..the one? The matchmaker." The harried woman asked in a tentative voice. Her eyes avoided meeting my gaze, and her cheeks blushed a delicate shade of crimson. She scanned the office for the trappings she expected to find. A computer and a camera set up to record a dating video. Finding neither, her eyes fixed back onto the edge of my desk.

"I am. My name is Lexi Balefire. Can I help you?" I used my most welcoming voice and moved from behind my desk to lean down for a bit of eye contact. Thinking she needed a less formal setting, I led her to a cluster of armchairs occupying one corner of the room.

She sighed and sat down. "Probably not, I'm completely hopeless!" A tear formed in the corner of her eye, and she looked down at her trembling hands. Blond hair hung limply halfway down her back, and she wasn't wearing a stitch of makeup. On one wrist rested a beautiful, engraved silver bracelet, and the sandals on her feet looked like quality leather to me—but the rest of her outfit was clearly composed of bargain bin pieces. Frugal and smart, my instincts screamed, but self-effacing to a fault.

"What's your name?" I asked gently.

"Oh, I'm sorry, how rude of me. I'm Mona. Mona Katz. It's nice to meet you, Lexi." Despite her obvious discomfiture, the grip of her handshake was firm and when she smiled, her face transformed into something lovely.

I smiled and returned the sentiment. "Now, tell me your story," I invited. This was the most important part of my job. Listening to the client is what activates my…magic might be the wrong word, but I can't think of a better one unless it's intuition. Magical intuition.

"Well, I seem to just have the worst luck with men. Every one I've gone out with has some problem I think I can fix. They always start out nice but end up being jerks."

At least she'd come to that conclusion on her own. One less problem for me to solve.

"I know I'm not the whole package or anything; I'm just a plain-Jane pastry chef with a decent salary and an average body. I can take care of myself, but…I'm lonely." Mona blurted, finally looking me in the eye.

That one glance confirmed my instincts were, as usual, spot on. There was strength in her, and grace as well. It was too bad she couldn't see it for herself; Mona Katz had a self-image problem, but her priorities were in the right place.

Most of the time, people hold *themselves* back from love—and they usually don't realize they're doing it.

Squeezing her into my packed schedule would require a shoehorn if I was going to take her on. I already knew I would. The force was strong with this one. Forgive the movie reference, but that's the best way to describe how I work. It's actually quite simple.

They talk, I listen, and eventually I get the buzz, the tingle. A tugging feeling that originates right behind my belly button, and if I follow the pull, it will lead me right to the perfect match. I'm almost never wrong. My friend and business partner, Flix, says I have an internal GPS, and it's always set to romance. I tell him he's being cheesy, but it's as good a description of my methods as any.

The average amount of time it takes me to locate a match is two hours—longer if I have to go outside the city. Mona's match was close. I could tell by the caliber of the sensation I was feeling. Really close, actually.

"…utter disaster when I found out he was still married." On a roll, Mona continued to tell me about the last time she had dated anyone.

In the early days, with a match this close, I would have dragged her out into the street to engineer a first meeting right there and then. I've learned a lot in the last few years. No one wants to believe true love is that easy to find. They expect more pomp. More circumstance. I've learned to give it to them.

"And he was cheating on both of us. It was devastating." I saw the ghosts of her sorrow reflected in Mona's eyes. She hadn't just been beaten up by love; she had been burned, stomped into the ground, and then buried.

A boost of confidence is exactly what this woman needed, and I was more than prepared to give it to her.

I leaned back in my chair and looked at her thoughtfully for a moment, deciding that directness was the best option in this situation. "Mona, please don't take this the wrong way, but I think maybe you aren't giving yourself enough credit. You're a smart, attractive woman—don't roll your eyes, it's true—but you have to believe that for yourself if you want someone else to see you that way. Will you trust me to help you?"

She nodded hesitantly, and I went back over to my desk, pressed a button mounted beneath it, and marched over to a door in the corner most people assume opens into a closet. And while technically they're correct, this isn't where I keep my magic broom.

Indicating for Mona to follow me, I led her down a short hallway and into a large room, then spun around quickly to observe her reaction—this was my favorite part.

Incredulity and delight vied for first place as her

gaze bounced from the racks of clothing and accessories to the Wall of Shoes, as I liked to call it, and finally lit on a stunning man leaning against a barber's chair and wielding a pair of gleaming gold scissors in his manicured fingertips.

Flix was pure manly perfection, personified, and he knew it. To regular humans who could not see past the glamour to his true face, he resembled a Greek god. Apollo or Adonis, too beautiful to be real. It was a damn shame the faeries on his mother's side of the family considered him an ugly duckling.

And if he was ugly, what order of magnitude would be considered handsome? Probably too much hotness to handle. But I will admit I'm curious. Who wouldn't be?

Being only half of something was one of our common threads; Flix was half faerie and half human, and I was half human and half witch—which made neither of us one thing or the other. We also both loved old movies, the more chick-flicky the better.

Still, I was pretty attached to the whisper of power I did have and had wished to be a real witch on every star in the sky, plus twenty-four years of birthday candles, and about a thousand stray eyelashes. Meanwhile, Flix, who had magic in spades but no higher purpose to use it, would have done anything to be a regular human.

"And what do we have here?" His melodic voice exaggerated for effect, rang out. "A beautiful Goddess, somewhere underneath all this..." he waved a hand theatrically and grimaced, "frump. Sit down, my love, and let me work my magic." Any hope Mona might have had for a match between Flix and herself was dashed as it became clear that his tendencies leaned in the opposite direction.

Mona quietly accepted her fate and spent a solid hour chewing on the inside of her lip as Flix yanked unapologetically at her hair, painting strands into individual squares of aluminum foil and applying several colors of dye. While that was setting, he turned his attention to her face. With gentle hands, he applied soothing balms and makeup of his own creation before combing, cutting, and teasing Mona's hair into submission.

While she was being poked and prodded, we learned that Mona was actually quite an accomplished pastry chef, and had recently taken a position at one of the best-kept secrets in town: Crumb, a bakery specializing in unique wedding and specialty cakes. We also learned that part of Mona's problem on dates might be that she didn't stop talking. Like, *ever*.

She told us about every dog she had owned since the puppy she got on her fifth birthday. And then went on to provide exquisite detail about the last four wedding cakes she'd made.

I sensed the incessant chatter was a nervous habit and hoped getting her a little more comfortable in her own skin would give her that bit of confidence she seemed to need.

When Flix finally, with a flourish and a self-satisfied "Voila!", whirled her around to face the mirror Mona's mouth dropped open in disbelief.

Flix had worked with her natural hair color to create a dramatic multicolored effect, darker at the roots and fading subtly to golden blond at the ends. Layers framed her face, and long bangs swept across her forehead, enhancing her high cheekbones and bright blue eyes. Though he claimed not to use his magic on our clients, I sometimes wondered if he had a secret cache of faerie dust hidden in his apron pocket; but maybe he was just that good.

"I…I can't believe it." Mona breathed, looking back and forth between Flix and me as if wondering who to thank first.

"It has been my pleasure, my dear. All I did was make you look more like *you*. The natural beauty was there, it only needed to be released. Feeling good about your appearance has more to do with displaying who you are on the inside! Now, let's see what our Lexi can do about locating your soul mate."

Flix deposited a kiss on each of her cheeks, causing them to flush pink once more, and took his leave. With a noticeably lighter heart, Mona turned her head this way and that to get a good view in the mirror of what he had done.

"Does everyone get a makeover when they come

here?" I could tell Mona was hoping she wasn't a special case and that this was just how things worked at FootSwept.

Putting people together was serious business, and the last thing I wanted was to make any of my clients think that finding a soul mate hinged on such superficial things as appearance. I firmly believe that love comes from the inside, not the outside. Let's face it, though. By the time most people get to me, they've been through the dating wringer, and a little pampering soothes the battle-weary soul.

"Everyone gets what they need." I hoped my answer was diplomatic enough. "Would you like to pick out something new to wear?"

"Is it part of the fee? I don't want charity." The vehemence in her voice suggested that she might have had to rely on the generosity of others in the past. "I have a great job. I can afford to pay."

I laid a hand on Mona's arm, "I'll let you in on a little secret. I have deals with nearly every clothing store in town. They give me a rock bottom discount price in exchange for sitting in on job interviews to give insights on which applicants will make the best employees. The clothes are part of the service, but it's up to you whether or not you want to choose an outfit."

When Mona hit my closet full of goodies, it was with a spring in her step. No woman could resist picking through that many pairs of boots.

"You hang onto those clothes for your date, and I'll work *my* magic. I'll call you in a few days, and we'll take the next step." I promised, sending her on her way and locking the door behind her. It was well past my official closing time, but I had no intention of heading home just yet, so I pressed the button under my desk again, and Flix appeared before me as if out of the ether.

"Glass of wine before you head for home?" He guessed and pulled a bottle of my favorite red out of his back pocket. "Or do you need a place to crash?" His affected accent was gone in the absence of paying clients, and he was back to being my regular old Flix. If you can call a sexy faerie man *regular* at all.

"An adamant *yes* to the former, and a regretful *no* to the latter. I'm going to have to bite it and see what havoc has been wreaked since I left this morning." Did I forget to mention that Flix isn't the only faerie in my life?

Most of my kind only have one faerie godmother—they're sort of like guardian angels for witches—but my sordid past had left me with three, and trust me, that's two too many. What's more, being sisters, they didn't always get along.

Witches rarely, if ever, meet their Fae benefactors and I was probably the first in history to live with one, though since the house we all occupied belonged to my grandmother, technically they lived with me. The four of us made an odd family, but it was the only family I'd ever known.

Hinting that I might be old enough to be on my own made them laugh, and not in such a nice way, either. I guess, compared to the few thousand they'd admit to, my paltry twenty-four years seemed about a minute long to the godmothers. Probably why they treated me like a child half the time.

Flix handed me a glass, and I swirled it around for a moment before taking a longer sip than necessary.

"With Vaeta back from the underworld, it's been a little on the cray-cray side at my place. They've crammed a hundred years-worth of fighting into the span of six months, and they have no consideration for the fact that some of us need our beauty sleep."

If that sounded like envy, it wasn't. Much.

"I finally had to beg Terra to put a quiet charm on my bedroom."

Topping off my glass again, Flix quirked an eyebrow at my tone. "And how did that work out?"

"She made it so I can't hear anything at all when I'm in there; not my alarm, or my phone, or even my mp3 player. It's just completely silent now, which is even more annoying than the racket, and she won't lift the spell. But *I'm* the one acting childish?"

I ranted on while Flix finished off the bottle. "Not to mention, business has picked up exponentially lately. I'm even getting walk-ins these days."

"It's just a phase. In another month you'll go

through a dry spell and be crying on my shoulder that no one needs you." An elegant shrug dismissed that worry, and Flix changed the subject back to the faeries.

"Vaeta still not fitting into the whole sister dynamic?"

He didn't seem surprised. We didn't talk much about his Fae heritage and I wondered if he identified with Vaeta since she was the household outcast at the moment. A feeling he knew well enough from interactions with his extended family.

"The other three think she's an idiot and are not shy about stating their opinion." That statement earned a raised eyebrow. We usually avoided the subject of his family, but what little he did say made me think they were a two-faced bunch of snobs. Sneaky with their condemnation of him and his status as a halfling.

Don't tell Flix, but there were times I would have traded a handful of sneaky faeries for the filter-free bunch I lived with.

"She's been in the underworld, I guess, for almost a hundred years. Lured by some demon with romance on his mind and poetry on his tongue, if Evian is to be believed. Vaeta is the romantic of the family."

Flix quirked a smile.

"Okay, romantic is the nicest word anyone has used. I believe the word nymphomaniac has come up a few times, but the upshot is that she ended up in hell because of a dude."

Is it ironic that half my business comes about because some woman has experienced that very same thing only metaphorically?

Absently flicking a finger to clean the wine glasses and return them to the cabinet, Flix said, "I've heard my mother talk about that type of thing. Demons have a taste for Fae, and once on the hook, it's hard to get back out of the underworld."

My one and only brush with death occurred on the day Vaeta returned because she'd gone for the dramatics when setting up a reunion with her sisters.

"I'm not sure it was all that hard. She made her way into a nexus, lured and kidnapped a guardian angel to get the right mix of people there to open the portal, and then tripped out the door after tossing around a bunch of magic."

While I recounted the story for at least the third time, my fingers moved toward where my hairline arched over one eye. I touched the tiny scar where I'd hit my head on the edge of a mist-shrouded prison cell in the portal where Vaeta had made her stand.

Since her return, Flix hadn't been coming over as often.

"She says the demon was her captor, but all that time, her sisters thought she had chosen to turn her back on them. Which, I guess she kind of did, or she didn't realize she was in so deep until it was too late. Terra, Evian, and Soleil have been in my house for what feels like my entire life, and have literally never mentioned her. It's beyond strange that they could just pretend like she never existed. I mean, she's their sister, and I know it was painful, but…it seems cold."

Flix was silent for a long moment. "I imagine that kind of betrayal seems unthinkable to someone who has never experienced the way families can hurt one another."

I knew Flix's family wasn't the most loving, and if I could, I'd take all that pain away. It did irk that he seemed to have forgotten I knew exactly how easily families can hurt one another.

On that note, we closed up the shop and I headed home.

Chapter 2

Falling dusk verged on snuffing out the last pretty pink light of a spectacular sunset as I rounded the end of the block. All thought of raiding the fridge for leftovers—Soleil was a spectacular cook—and the hope of a quiet evening evaporated in a hot second. Flashes of light bright enough to rival any dance club shot out of the downstairs windows. Quite festive in a bizarre way that boded no good.

The faeries were at it again.

From the front, my house looks like a regular northeastern colonial. Clapboard siding, six-pane windows with shutters. Nothing fancy, and not nearly big enough for three larger-than-life faeries, so they added a little. Okay, a lot. The new addition is bigger than the original house and, being in the back, not visible from the street. Somehow, the yard is still larger than any of the others in our neighborhood. I suspect that's Terra's doing.

Half of me wanted to go inside and assess the situation, the other half wanted to grab a flight to someplace far, far away. Aruba. Cozumel. Antarctica might not be far enough.

The sound of a throat clearing behind me broke my reverie. "Looks like quite the party."

The voice was male and deeply resonant. Above my head, a streetlight flickered to life just as I turned toward a man who stood with my cat in his arms. Salem blinked back at me defiantly.

What's more, the little traitor was purring up a storm. Odd, considering how up until now, my cat had always hated the mere sight of any male who ventured onto the property.

"Do you live here?" The question drew my attention away from the cat and back to the man holding him. The streetlight highlighted a shock of curly blond hair that just brushed the top of his collar. In the subdued lighting, I got the impression of warm, brown eyes and a quirky smile. Cute. The fingers of one hand stroked and soothed Salem's head.

"Salem." I juggled my purse and the bag I was carrying to reach for him. "That's my cat, where did you find him?" I eyed the feline with suspicion. In all of Catdom there couldn't have been a lazier example than Salem, who rarely ventured past the sunny flagstones of the back patio. The furball returned my gaze with a blink

I swear was deliberate enough to qualify as a wink.

"Sitting in the middle of my dining room table. He must have slipped in when I came home. I'm Kin, by the way. Mackintosh Clark. I just moved into the gray house at the end of the block."

"Lexi Balefire." I smiled up at him. "I'm sorry for the cat invasion. He's…really, Salem? Are you wearing catnip cologne?" Salem knocked my purse to the ground when he squirmed away from me in an effort to get closer to Kin.

Kin treated me to another lopsided grin. "What can I say, I'm irresistible."

The comment earned him a raised eyebrow from me.

"Well, welcome to the neighborhood." An ominous booming noise issued from the house. "Really, you'll love it here. If you'll excuse me, I need to uh…" How was I supposed to end that sentence? Play referee to four fighting faeries? Get inside and stop my house from blowing up?

"Should I call someone? I could go in with you to make sure it's safe." His concern was touching, but taking him inside was number three with a bullet of the worst things I could do right now. Numbers one and two involved initiating a level of bodily contact that was premature, given I had only met him five minutes ago.

Tempting, though.

"No, it's fine. One of my…er…roommates

is…um…" Nothing, and I mean nothing came to mind as a plausible explanation, so I went for the crazy option. "A lighting designer. She's probably just experimenting with some new strobe effects or something."

It sounded lame, but Kin swallowed it hook, line, and sinker. And then he threw me a twist.

"I'm a musician. Do you have her card? I might ask her to design something for me." That explained the calluses I'd felt when his fingertips brushed against my hand.

"Not on me. I'm sure I'll see you around, though." He retrieved my purse and hung it awkwardly over my shoulder.

"Count on it." I got a warm smile while Salem received another chin scratch. Kin did the gentlemanly thing and waited to see me safely inside. Exactly what I wished to avoid. I managed to squeeze through the door without giving him a look at whatever fresh hell waited for me on the other side.

Speaking of the inside…well, I'm not exactly sure how to describe it. I put Salem on the floor, then picked my way around a swamp in the middle of the foyer. Muddy water oozed across the tiles until a border of spiky grasses contained the fetid sludge—compliments, I was certain, of a clash between Terra and Evian, whose elements were earth and water.

Four fighting faeries. Sounds like a kick-ass name for a girl band, right?

The bwarping voice of a bullfrog lifted me half off my feet. I shot a dirty look at the swamp denizen squatting on a rock. He glared back at me malevolently, flicked out his tongue, and snatched a buzzing fly from the air. I hoped neither of them would turn out to have been one of my faerie godmothers transformed, and continued into the family room to check out the light show.

I had to admit; this was a new one—probably Vaeta's influence. At least a dozen bubbles floated around near the ceiling; some filled with water, some with tiny flashes of lightning, some with both. The faerie version of disco balls. My nostrils flared at the ozone scent of scorched air. Magic hung over everything like a wool curtain, itchy and suffocating. No wonder Salem had run for the hills.

I'd do the same if I had a choice.

The house was quiet except for the occasional outburst from the warty frog in the entryway. I was starting to feel that scene-of-the-crime hush. The one that comes right before the forensic team swarms in. As I headed for the kitchen, I worried at what I might find.

Before I got that far, though, I had to pass through an obstacle course of fallout. Icicles stretching down from the hall ceiling like stalactites dripped to create ever-widening puddles that made for treacherous walking on slick tiles. I ventured past the downstairs bath and noticed everything in it was entirely covered with glowing moss.

It was too much to take in all at once. Weird things were happening all around me.

I found the four of them in the kitchen amid the shambles they had created. The range, covered in dripping ash, looked like a post-apocalyptic movie prop. The kitchen counter had sprouted daisies. Half of them were still cheerfully intact; the rest had been flash-charred, and when I touched a gentle finger to one blackened petal, the tiny flower collapsed in a pile of dust.

The table hovering near the ceiling with its chairs circling around it conjured the image of a demented game of Ring Around the Rosie. A flour devil erupted from the canister and flew out the window.

But everything else turned to background noise as I took in the tableau before me.

Four women stood as though frozen in various states of disarray. Even wet and covered in a mixture of mud and powdery ash, they were impossibly beautiful. Fae to the bone.

Evian, faerie of the water, drew my eye first. Hair, the color of a Caribbean sea, flowed with liquid grace around a face set in concentration. One hand, tipped with mirrored nails, gripped a swirling ball of water that was aimed at her sister, Soleil. Water and fire, a volatile mix, and the most likely reason why the entire house felt like a sauna. Evian's other hand gripped Vaeta's arm just below the elbow.

A study in shades of gray, Vaeta appeared to be in the throes of whipping up a miniature tornado. Probably not the first of the day, given the chaos in the kitchen. The little whirlwind had picked up some soil, undoubtedly deposited there by Terra, whose affinity was with earth. The dirty cloud spinning around Vaeta's feet made me think of Pigpen from the Peanuts.

Growing up around women who fell out of bed looking like warrior princesses had forced me to develop a healthy self-image. I learned early on not to compare myself to anyone. Right now, though, I would have won a beauty contest against the lot of them. Hands down.

The surprise of my entrance seemed to have put a crimp in the battle, and I found myself staring at four shame-filled faces. Half of me wanted to rail at them for the havoc they had created, the other half to laugh because they reminded me of children caught stealing goodies from the cookie jar. And I was the one considered a baby in this house. Right.

Sometimes less is more. I let my steely stare and raised eyebrow indicate my opinion of what they'd been doing. Deliberately surveying the room, I took in the enormity of the disaster, made eye contact with each of them in turn, shook my head in disgust, and headed for my section of the house. On my way out of the kitchen, I heard one of them mutter, *She started it*, followed by a vehemently hissed, *Shut up*.

Out of curiosity, I paused to see if I could overhear anything that would tip me off as to what had caused the battle. Half the time it was nothing more than a stray comment from one sister to another and taken as a grave offense. Nothing ever stayed just between the injured parties, though. Sides were taken, and the whole thing escalated until no one was even sure who said what, or why they were fighting in the first place.

"No, you started it," I heard Vaeta hiss. "You called me an airhead again."

"That was Soleil, not me," Evian retorted as the negative energy started to ramp up again.

"Stop acting like children."

"Shut up, Terra. Nobody died and put you in charge. Yet."

A crash drew me back to the kitchen. In the six months since Vaeta's return from the underworld, I had refereed this same argument more times than I wanted to count. You'd think beings who have lived for centuries would have a better handle on methods for dealing with their emotions. You'd be wrong.

This time I combined the glare with a wagging finger. "That's enough for one day. Apologize to your sisters." I included each one in the command. "And then clean up your mess. If you leave it for me again, I'm going to start rethinking our living arrangements."

These were the only mothers I'd ever known, but lately, it felt like opposite day had taken a turn for the weird.

Lost in thought, I didn't realize my feet had carried me beyond my own suite of rooms until I was standing in front of my grandmother's bedroom door. Equal parts fascination and dread fought for supremacy as they did every time my hand touched the knob. My wildest imagination failed to produce a scenario where the woman who had slept in this room might have resorted to killing her own daughter.

A deep breath, a twist of the knob, and a shudder as I passed the threshold were familiar experiences. I'd come in here hundreds of times over the years, hoping to find something that might provide insight into my family's sordid past.

I trailed a finger across the dust-free dresser—one perk of living with an earth elemental, no dirt dared mar any surface Terra deemed a clean zone. Of course, the opposite was also true. If I annoyed her enough, she took great pleasure in recalling her vast array of faerie cleaning benefits from my rooms, or worse, sending all the dust in the house to coat everything in my bedroom.

Not exactly a shrine, this room remained as it had on the day my family fell apart because I couldn't bring myself to change anything that might eventually provide me with answers. The only two people who know what really happened that day are gone. One innocent witch dead and the other wicked one turned to stone.

The frantic cries of an abandoned witch baby must carry a potent message to the Faelands. Terra, hearing mine, rushed to fulfill her duty and ended up dragging her sisters into taking care of me. None of them had any idea how long-term that care would become. No one has ever told me differently, but I assume it has taken all three of them to amplify my latent magic enough to sustain the Balefire.

That's my theory on why they stayed even though I'd long passed into adulthood.

To their credit, while the sister's child-raising methods have been unorthodox, they have done their level best never to make me feel like a burden. My adopted family, wonky as it is, is a loving one, even if faerie love isn't exactly the same as human. Their maternal instincts took a while to kick in, and by the time the faeries figured out what to do with me, it was a couple of weeks before anyone went looking for clues to what happened to my family.

All that had been left in the clearing was a lifelike statue depicting a witch gone over to the wicked side, and a blackened scar on the ground. Mother killed daughter and paid the price for her sin.

The only thing missing? A body.

With no other definitive evidence of her death, I spent years fantasizing that despite the granite proof, my mother, Sylvana, had escaped. As the years passed, so did the childlike hope. And still, here I was again, looking for something—anything—that might bring knowledge or power.

Of the two, power was the thing I needed now. Ever since my fourteenth birthday had come and gone without bringing on my Awakening—the term we use for when a witch comes into her full magic—my fellow witches had begun treating me like a lost cause.

The whispers and sympathetic looks increased each year as they trooped past me on their pilgrimage to secure a bit of the Balefire to light their home fires at Beltane. Worse, though, were the long, speculative looks into the magical flame as if each witch were assessing its color and intensity.

Talk about being measured and found wanting. My yearly trip to the bottom end of my self-esteem. Happy Birthday, Lexi Balefire.

I didn't need the added pressure of knowing they were counting on me to maintain the status quo. You'd think one of the nicer witches would have at least tried to help, but they avoided me like my lack of magic was contagious.

I pulled my wandering mind back to the task at hand and opened the trunk at the foot of Grandmother's elaborately carved, four-poster bed. As many times as I'd done this, I should have stopped expecting to find anything new, but hope springs eternal, I guess.

A layer of blankets came out first to reveal several

neatly-stored boxes. I pulled them out one by one. The topmost one contained a selection of baby clothes that looked ancient. I handled them gingerly as I pulled each piece from between layers of folded tissue paper and laid it aside, then ran my hands through the box to check for anything I might have missed.

Next was a carved box with exquisitely wrought hinges and clasp, stuffed to the brim with love letters from wannabe suitors. Despite my grandmother's wicked ending, scanning through the desperate pleas of numerous men made me wish I had known her. She must have been something in her day. I hastily, and none too neatly, shoved the contents back inside and moved on to her dresser drawers which, save one, held nothing but clothes.

The bottom drawer was where Clara kept her photograph albums. I leafed through them, hoping as I always did to find just one picture of my mother where her face had not been burned or cut out. Someone had taken out their vengeance on Sylvana's image in a big way. My grandmother, I could only assume.

The poster woman for cackling evil.

It was the same throughout the house—evidence that someone wanted to erase her memory. Did she take after her father? Or was her face as uncannily similar to my grandmother's as my own?

Who would I ask? The witches who barely acknowledged me on the one day a year I couldn't be completely ignored? I had no one to talk to about my past, and not even the love of faeries could overcome that kind of loss.

Fury rose in me while I methodically searched every nook and cranny of the room for something that might trigger the latent power inside me. My family history might be shrouded in intrigue and scandal, but one thing the Beltane fire-seekers agreed on was that my bloodline had produced the most powerful witches of every generation. Every generation except for mine.

How humiliating.

Chapter 3

I love what I do. It's a great job on the best of days. Today, however, wasn't shaping up to be one of those.

It all started with a phone call before I'd had my second cup of coffee, and now I was running, literally, to the office to deal with a panicked former client.

It's a fifteen-minute walk to work, one that I enjoy in all seasons because I don't like to drive. Today, however, I almost wished I had grabbed a ride from Flix, in his leather-covered convertible sports car that was completely ludicrous considering he could flit across town in half a second.

What I wouldn't give for the ability to teleport, but only full-blown witches could claim that type of power. Now, it was hotter than Hades—unseasonably hot—and my blouse was sticking to my armpits in a most unattractive way. I flapped my arms to air them out as I approached the office, and was surprised to find I had an audience.

Harry, the former client who had filled my voice mailbox before breakfast, shuffled back and forth on the front steps with wild-eyed panic written all over his face, and I was grateful he was too preoccupied to notice my unladylike behavior.

"Lemon doesn't love me anymore, and you need to do something about it." Way to build suspense.

"Calm down and come inside. We'll sort this out." I put on my most soothing tone. Harry had been one of my more difficult clients to match. It wasn't anything about his looks—he was actually a handsome guy—it was his name that put women off. That and the fact that he liked to introduce himself James Bond style.

Tart. Harry Tart.

It didn't have quite the same ring to it.

I got him settled into a chair, plied him with coffee—decaf, he was already keyed up enough—and let him pour out the whole story.

"She says I'm imagining things, but I'm not. Something is off with her. *Way* off."

"Could it be nothing more than a case of wedding jitters?" It wasn't every day you found a woman willing to saddle herself with the name Lemon Tart for the rest of her life. Maybe Lemon was having second thoughts.

"It's more than that. She's giddy over the wedding one minute, and then the next I feel like she's got one foot out the door. You said we were soul mates. You used the word destiny. I love her, Lexi. You have to help me." It all spilled out of him in a flood of pain and accusation.

This kind of thing rarely happens with the couples I put together. I have an inch-thick scrapbook of wedding photos to prove it's not just an ego thing; when I make a match, it pretty much stays made. Who am I to question why? All relationships have their ups and downs, but true soul mates have what it takes to weather any storm. Fortunately, troubleshooting those hurdles is not usually my department.

"Isn't she supposed to be picking out the wedding favors this afternoon?" Lemon's addiction to social media went well beyond the fanatical. Every step of her march toward wedded bliss had been recorded in infinite detail over half a dozen websites and a shared calendar. I knew her schedule as well as my own. Most of her friends probably did, too.

"If it will make you feel better, I'll stop over there and talk to her. We'll see if we can get to the bottom of this." I patted him on the arm, and he grasped my hand like a drowning man.

"Please. I love her." Simple honesty. Misery poured off the man in waves. I offered a few more soothing platitudes and sent him out the door just as Mona Katz stepped inside. A glance at his expression took a little shine off her smile.

"Everything okay? He didn't look like a happy

customer." The new haircut had done its job. I noted the change in Mona's posture, the tilt of her head, and the way her gaze remained steady. A flowing maxi skirt and basic tank looked comfortable and natural on her petite frame, and she had elevated the look with a couple of bangle bracelets, a turquoise necklace and matching earrings, and a cropped denim jacket with the sleeves rolled up.

"Some people need to take the rocky path to love. It's nothing to worry about. Are you ready to meet some men?"

Another huge lesson from my first few months in the biz: people need the show. Mona's perfect match was three, maybe four blocks north of here at this very minute. We could walk out that door, and my gut would lead me straight to him. A done deal.

One that would backfire on me six ways to Sunday. Anything that comes too easily inspires doubt, and so, while I planned to let my gut take me to her soul mate, we'd have to make a few stops along the way.

"Now? I thought we were going to just..." Mona flapped one hand and pressed the other to her heart. "Look through something, I guess. Like photos or profiles." A common misconception. "I didn't wear my date outfit!"

"Trust me." This was quickly becoming a catch phrase for me. "My methods might seem unorthodox, but I get results. We're going for a casual lunch, and you look gorgeous. If you didn't, I'd offer you another trip in there," I jabbed a thumb in the direction of the closet door, "but it's completely unnecessary."

"Okay," she replied on a choked breath.

"Relax, Mona. Finding love should be fun. If it isn't, we're not doing it right. We're just going to make one or two stops along the way." I practically dragged her out the door.

Impeccable timing let us bump into Lemon on her way out of one of my favorite specialty sweet shops. It would have been hard to miss her; I knew Lemon had decided long ago to embrace her off-beat moniker, and the bright yellow pantsuit she wore was the exact same shade as the drops of sweet-and-tart candy that bore her name.

Even more impeccable timing let me rescue a box of wedding favor samples before they hit the ground. "I'll carry this one for you. Where are you parked? This is Mona, by the way. She's a new client. Mona, Lemon."

I met Lemon's harried expression with a cheerful smile as I looked around for her car. Bridezilla on steroids, Lemon scorned the very idea of hiring a wedding planner. "Mind if I take a peek?" Not waiting for an answer, I popped the box of favors open and tried to hold back an amused snort.

"Nice to meet you, Mona. You're in great hands

with this one; she introduced me to my Harry and now look at us." Her expression turned sickly sweet for a moment and then she snapped back to attention. "You get it, right?" Lemon asked, referring to the contents of the box. "It's not too much, is it?"

Painstakingly crafted candies in the shape of a lemon tart were a cute way to give the nod to the funny coincidence of her new name.

"They're uniquely you." My seeming approval opened the floodgates. Lemon gushed about how perfectly everything was coming together while she wrestled in her bag for car keys and popped the trunk lock.

"Just put that right here next to the napkins." The back of Lemon's minivan looked like a bridal expo gone mad. This wasn't the vehicle of a woman who had lackluster feelings about her upcoming nuptials. "Don't you just love them?" Lemon pulled open the box to show me her choice of wedding colors. Half the napkins were a delicate yellow, the rest a charcoal gray; all were printed with the date and an image of the bride and groom's faces gazing sweetly at each other. I recognized it from the engagement photos that had been plastered over her social media for the past couple of months.

I looked closely at her face. Shining eyes and a mile-wide smile didn't track with the way Harry described her recent demeanor. This was a woman deeply in love and looking forward to her big day, not one who had a foot out the door.

"I take it all is well, and you're not getting cold feet?" I asked, feeling for the emotion behind it rather than just watching her reaction. I can always tell when someone isn't honest with me—it's great as long as they're not saying they like my hair or my outfit when the warning bells go off.

Lemon laughed easily. "Of course not; I couldn't be happier unless a wedding fairy came along and offered to pay for the whole shebang." Her words rang true; I couldn't figure out what Harry's problem was. Maybe the stress of a big-budget wedding was taking a toll on him. Either way, I'd have to save it for another day.

"See you soon, Lemon. Don't wear yourself out."

She snorted and rolled her eyes, grinning from ear to ear. "I'll try."

Mona talked a blue streak while we picked our way through several blocks of tiny shops and quaint restaurants in one of the trendier, almost hidden areas within the city, and I tuned back in just as she was extrapolating on the qualities she'd like in her perfect match.

"…hope he wants to have kids soon; I'm nearly twenty-five, which is most of the way to thirty, and I don't want to be raising kids until I'm in my sixties.

He's got to love to travel, and know how to ride a horse, and be able to bake." I tuned back out.

People always think they're going to get a person who fulfills every detail of their fantasy, but that isn't usually the case. In fact, it seemed to me the old adage of *opposites attract* was more accurate; the give and take make those relationships much more interesting, and people tend to get less bored than when they settle for an identical version of themselves.

"Here, this is our stop." I pointed to an old, hulking stone building fitted with a set of antique stained glass windows; The Coffer used to be a bank, but had been converted into a pub, and was one of my favorite haunts.

"Our goal is to get you comfortable meeting new people and learn a bit more about what you're looking for. Your job, for this afternoon, is to judge. I need to know what your first impressions are, and what you like and don't like. I can find all the qualities you want on paper rolled into about a dozen different packages, and none of them would be the right person for you. It's about more than that, and today we're going to suss out what goes in the "necessary" column, and what goes in the "would be nice" column. Does that make sense?"

Mona nodded, her eyes still wide as saucers, "Yes, I suppose so. I'm ready, let's do this."

I led her past the small crowd milling around out front. Instead, we walked up to a side entrance labeled "Deliveries Only" and flashed a smile at the man wielding a clipboard and wading through boxes.

Mona looked nervously at the muscled bouncer and back at me. "He's a teddy bear underneath," I told her under my breath.

"She's with me, Carl" I tossed him a wink and slipped inside, Mona on my heels.

"Wow, this place is great, I've never been here before," Mona exclaimed, taking in the atmosphere. An expansive, mahogany bar dominated one whole side of the space, centered around the original vault that had once housed the prized possessions of many of the city's richest residents. Now, its only treasure was enough alcohol to drown a whale.

"It's a personal favorite; most of the patrons here are regulars, and we like that it's a hole in the wall. Literally. So don't spread around my secret hangout, okay?" I smiled at Mona conspiratorially and received another wide grin in response.

"I won't. So what now?" She tugged nervously on her necklace.

"Now we grab a bite to eat and take a peek at the goods," I ordered us each a burger and fries, and we settled into two seats at the end of the bar to survey the room. "You tell me if you see anyone interesting."

Mona made an effort at nonchalance as she looked around the place. I followed her gaze. "Socks and sandals guy, big no; the blond guy in the middle of that group is handsome, but he's covered in football paraphernalia, so that means no Sunday brunches; and the one at the other end of the bar is cute, but he's with another woman." She threw her hands up in a gesture of frustration. I smiled to myself and launched into my well-rehearsed speech for picky clients.

"See, you've just negated everyone in here with one glance. What if that football guy loves Sunday brunch and is content to DVR his games. What if he turns you on to football and it becomes your new Sunday ritual? Maybe he teaches your kids to play ball and coaches their pee-wee team?" I asked with a raised eyebrow.

"Perhaps the woman at the end of the bar is that guy's sister—wait, no, definitely not, or at least I hope it's not." Not with his tongue now dancing with hers in a very steamy public display that made Mona giggle, and I couldn't help joining in.

"Okay, so he's out, but maybe socks and sandals guy is amazing in every other way, and only needs a bit of fashion advice. Or you could learn to live with that little flaw, in exchange for him overlooking some habit of yours."

If I ever found a man who could handle meeting my family, he could throw his wet towels on the bathroom floor anytime. That's my bar for relationships and it's pretty high.

"The point is, you never know, and you're not going to love every single thing about your mate—nobody does, believe me. If you did, you'd be bored inside of a year. Look, that guy who just came in—he's cute, and he's heading this way. Be open-minded." I hissed the last part at her under my breath. "And make eye contact."

Bless her little heart, Mona took my advice and cast a glance toward the attractive man dressed in khaki pants and a blue and white button-down shirt. Okay, it was more than a glance. It was a *come hither* look that almost crossed a line into *run away* territory.

He approached the bar, his gaze drawn to Mona's with equal parts fascination and fear.

"Whoa, back it down a notch and give him a nice smile."

She did, and then cast flirtatious glance at him from beneath lowered lashes.

"Better. Here he comes. Now relax and breathe."

Mona breathed into a cute giggle as he asked for her name and what she did for a living, and then I tuned out, knowing that even though it wouldn't work out, the experience gained would be well worth the effort.

My job is a double-edged sword. Sure, I get to help people come out of their shells, encourage them to open their hearts and recognize love, and I get to watch them ride off into the sunset together. All before going home alone, to cuddle with my cat. Sometimes, it really puts a run in my proverbial pantyhose.

Chapter 4

After work that evening, I was just passing Taste of India and deciding if an order of tandoori chicken was in my future when someone called out my name.

"Lexi Balefire." I knew what vile creature stood behind me before I even turned around.

"Serena Swampgrass. I thought I detected the scents of dog shampoo and regret." Loathing dripped from my tongue.

"That's Snodgrass." The L'Oréal blond drew herself up to full height, which brought her up to my chin level, and her beady little eyes snapped fire at me while I stared her down.

"What do you want, Serena? Are you looking for your perfect match? I could take you to the reptile cage at the zoo and let you pick out just the right snake. Only don't eat any live mice in front of me, I might throw up on your shoes, or maybe inside that hunk of plastic with the knockoff Gucci label you call a handbag."

Red-faced and spitting, my (almost) lifelong enemy ignored the sidelong glances from patrons leaving the restaurant while she treated me to a killing look.

"You'll rue the day, Miss High and Mighty." Rue the day? Who says that? I honestly have no idea what I ever did to piss her off for life. We've been like oil and water since our grade school days when Serena suddenly stopped being my best friend. Maybe it's because I'm taller, or maybe she's just mean down to the bone. More likely, she decided my limited magical abilities weren't up to snuff; there are more snobs than you'd expect among witches.

Clenching my hands at my sides, I stifled the desire to yank her hair out by the roots and prove just how dark they actually were.

"Run along home before it's too dark to find that rock you live under. There's nothing for you here but more trouble." I kept my tone even. Instead of leaving, she moved closer.

"Get away from me, Swampgrass. I'm warning you."

"Or you'll what?" Serena countered, "Turn me into a frog? You'd need magic for that, and we both know you don't have enough to light a candle, much less keep the Balefire going. Come Beltane, I'll become the new Keeper, and everyone will know you for what you are: a complete null. Your name will be mud. Literally. Lexi Mud. I like the sound of that."

As if she hadn't spent the last decade spreading stories about my family's sordid past throughout the supernatural community. Without her blackballing me, I might have found at least one witch friend with guts enough to ignore my history. Bitch.

A frown wrinkled my forehead. What on earth was the daft wench prattling on about?

"Ah. I see you had no idea." Serena leaned toward me with a vicious smile on her smug face. "No one with so little knowledge of her own heritage should be in charge of the sacred fire."

Tending the Balefire was more than a job in my family. It was a calling—a birthright handed down from generation to generation. The notion of Serena taking over made my blood boil, but I resisted the urge to punch her right there on the street with so many witnesses.

"Let me enlighten you." Tossing her head back, Serena talked down to me in a condescending manner. "The window opens for a witch to Awaken on her fourteenth birthday." Well, duh. Of course, I knew that. "And it closes on her twenty-fifth."

My heart lurched toward my shoes. Time was running out. And I'd had no forewarning.

Serena echoed that thought. "Your time is almost up, and when you fail to Awaken, the Balefire will pass to the next closest witch, and I intend to make sure that witch is me."

And now I knew why Serena had chosen to live within such a short distance from my house, even though she should have moved out of her parents' place years ago. All this time she'd been waiting for me to fail, and I'd had no idea.

With a barely concealed effort, I wiped the shocked look off my face and hissed, "Don't start sweeping your chimney just yet." It was a lame comeback that fed into Serena's triumph almost as much as when I brushed past her and got an elbow to my ribcage. She made it look like an accident, but I knew better.

Acid washed into my stomach in a bitter flood of anxiety. If Serena was right, I stood to lose the final legacy from my dysfunctional family dynasty. For about a second, I felt a profound sense of relief. Maybe it was better to let it go. All of it. The family name, the responsibility, the history.

If I didn't have to tend the Balefire, I could take a trip. See the world. Be gone longer than a week and not worry about keeping the home fires burning. Let Serena deal with the parade of witches coming to thrust their twigs into the fire.

Never mind a trip, I could sell the house and move someplace new. Somewhere where no one knew my name or any of the shameful details of my past. The idea of a fresh start briefly appealed—before my sense of family pride kicked back in.

Yeah, my grandmother was a murderous witch. So what? I didn't come from boring people, but I did my best to bring happiness to others. Call it atonement, call it my gift, call it George. I really didn't care. Serena would take the Balefire over my dead body.

But never hers, because stoned witches make lousy Balefire tenders, and following in my grandmother's footsteps on the path to wickedness was not on my menu.

After the dust-up with Serena, the dog-faced witch, I decided to blow off my plans for the evening and go home at what, for me, constituted an early hour. Another part of my job includes running recon on client matches to figure out the best scenario for a meeting.

Over the years, I've worked at perfecting the meet-cute. After all, these are the stories my clients will tell their grandchildren, and I'd bet half my shoe collection most of them won't include making a call to a matchmaker.

That being the case, I've pulled off some doozies.

Bar meetings are classic if a bit boring, but sometimes they're the only way to go.

For my sports-minded clients, I've practically sold my soul to secure adjoining seats at the big game. One time I shoved a client right into the lap of her intended, who was just trying to enjoy his coffee and donut. It could have gone horribly wrong, but I still rate that one right up there in my top ten.

Meeting over a cat who strayed where he didn't belong could have edged into my number one spot if I thought anything would come of Salem's antics.

Serena had driven all the happy out of my day, and now, instead of scoping out Mona's intended, all I wanted to do was go home, pull a pillow over my head, and scream out my frustration.

That was why, when I normally would have stomped right past Clara's rock-hewn form, I stopped and gave her a piece of my mind.

"I hope you're happy, with your stone face and your stone hair, and now I don't have a mother or a grandmother, and Serena wants to take the only thing I have left," I rambled. "What if Terra hadn't heard me crying? You think of that when you were all pissed off and throwing the magics around? No, you didn't."

We witches are a stoic lot. Crying is for sissies, which is why I wasn't doing it. Not even a little.

"Did you ever think I might need my family? My real family. But no, you just had your little temper tantrum and burned my life to the ground." Swinging my arm to make a point brought my hand into contact with one of the wickedly sharp thorns flanking velvet red petals.

Blood welled from the puncture, and I watched

with detached fascination as a single drop grew until it trembled and slid around the curve of my finger to hover and then fall. Right onto my grandmother's bare stone foot.

For the space between two heartbeats, the world stilled.

"Now look what you've done." I drew the sore tip of my finger into my mouth to suck on the tender flesh. Why do we do that? It's an odd instinct. With that thought in my mind, I turned away from my grandmother's burning gaze and went home.

Chapter 5

My sour mood had resulted in a night of restless sleep and an even later than normal arrival at work the next morning. I've never been much of an early bird anyway, and it's a good thing, too, considering most of my clients end up meeting their matches well after normal business hours.

Driven, an up-and-coming nightclub had started hosting open mic nights on Wednesdays as their version of a hump day pick-me-up. Apparently, that night, Driven was the place to see and be seen, because I got the tingle while I did my daily meditation with my client list. It's rare in my business to get a twofer, but sometimes the fates smile.

Mona and my newest lovelorn soul, an earnest young man named Tom, joined me at FootSwept for an impromptu excursion.

"What am I supposed to do, again?" Tom shoved

dark-rimmed glasses back into place. Behind the lenses, his eyes were a lovely shade of baby blue and framed by a thick fringe of lashes.

"Just have fun and follow my lead. Trust me, okay?" I rubbed a soothing hand down his arm; the poor thing was almost vibrating with anticipation. He rewarded my solicitous behavior with a face-transforming smile.

The right woman would peel him like a grape—shuck off that nerdy exterior and find the prize inside the Cracker Jack box. Without the glasses, and with his dark hair mussed up a little, he would turn into the total package. Underneath all the nervous tics and uncertainty beat the heart of a lion. All he needed was the right woman to see it.

"You should, you know. Trust her, I mean. Going out with Lexi is the best. It's worth twice her fee just for the experience." Mona's assertion worried me a bit. I know life's supposed to be all about the journey, but I only get paid at the end of the trip.

On the way out, I hit the button under my desk. Flix would find me wherever I was, and something told me I'd need the backup.

Mona practically danced the three blocks to Driven. Sweet girl, but all it had taken was a makeover and a bit of light flirting to turn her into a party monster.

We elbowed our way to the bar where I paused to take stock of the packed room.

Extra tables crowded with chattering women filled the area where the dance floor bordered a small stage. Total chick fest. My gaze landed on the chalkboard listing the roster of acts and scanned it for the presence of male erotic dancers, which might explain the gender imbalance. Nothing.

One name on the list sounded familiar: Kin Clark. My new neighbor whose front porch had become Salem's infatuation. The little traitor spent half his time lounging on the front steps of the gray house on the corner these days.

I wondered what Kin's act would be as I tried to recall if he'd mentioned what he did for a living during our brief encounter. All that did was get my heart rate up when I remembered the touch of his hands on mine.

Hands. Callused hands. Oh, that's right, he played the guitar. Lucky guitar.

Given the buzz in the room, I decided that tonight was probably not the best night for arranging a romantic first encounter for either Mona or Tom. The place felt too crowded, too amped up for what I had in mind.

Call me a romantic, but I love the idea of giving my couples a fun story of how they met. Just because one of them had asked for my help didn't mean that I wanted to figure highly in their history. Most people only need a little confidence and a nudge in the right direction.

"Hey Lexi, the usual?" Carlos poured cranberry juice into tonic water and added a twist of lemon.

Alcohol dulls my romantic radar, so I didn't partake during working excursions. I gave him the subtle sign that Tom and Mona's drinks would be on my tab.

"Busy tonight." An epic understatement, to which Carlos responded with a huge grin while filling more drink orders.

"Is he here yet?" Mona tried to keep a low profile as she scanned the room. That secret place inside me that tuned in to locate a perfect match opened up just enough to overwhelm me with what she was feeling.

My breath caught hard enough to draw Mona's attention and she looked at me with concern.

"Everything okay?" Her hand landed on my arm and intensified the experience.

An onslaught of trepidation equaled by a sense of eager anticipation rolled over me in a wave of conflicting confusion. I've heard it said that our worst fears and our deepest hopes are often the same.

Mona was living proof of that theory. Her most desperate desire to be seen and loved scared her half to death because that which has been seen cannot be unseen and she feared that living her dream meant baring her most vulnerable places.

"Fine," I lied. I wasn't fine at all. Not just because I'd never connected to a client that intensely before, but because her emotions so closely mirrored my own. Maybe, I thought, everyone who is single feels that way to some degree.

If so, I was ashamed to say that I hadn't taken parts of my job seriously enough in the past. The longing in us both bordered on pain and shook me down to the ground. The longing of lovelorn souls felt heavy on my shoulders.

What a lousy time for an existential crisis.

Pulling myself together, I focused in on Mona until my thoughts were steady again, then gave her arm a squeeze and shifted my plan for her first encounter. That night would be my chance to have the matches in the same place, just to make sure my radar was functioning properly. Later, I'd work out a plan for bringing these couples together—one that Mona would never forget. She deserved my best efforts.

"I'm not sure—it's busier than I expected. Is it okay if this doesn't happen tonight? It's so loud in here; I can't even think."

Relief flooded Mona's face. This was a little too much for her. Besides, her intended was nowhere to be seen, even if I could feel his presence in the club. Maybe he was working backstage or something.

Turning to ask Tom the same question, I found him gone. This is why I don't do multiples that often and when I do, I drag Flix along for support. It's a lot like herding kittens. Scanning the room, I saw Tom almost immediately—Flix, apparently, was running late. Probably primping.

Head bent low, Tom was engaged in an earnest

conversation with the woman I had brought him there to meet. Just goes to show you that proximity is a powerful thing. He glanced up and caught my grin. I gave him a nod and watched his eyes widen slightly. He swallowed hard, then treated his companion to a heart-stopping smile.

The way my stomach flipped over at the sight of them told me my work with him was done. My gut always knows a good match when it sees one. Well, that didn't sound quite right, but you know what I mean.

"Why don't we grab a table and listen to a couple of the acts?" With Mona requiring a more delicate meeting, it would help if I could get a look at her match ahead of time. Plus, I was curious to see Kin Clark's performance.

"Are you kidding, the place is packed, we're not going to get a table." She indicated the lack of seating with a wave of her hand.

Did I mention I came here a lot? I held up two fingers for Carlos to see and nodded my head toward the far end of the bar. He gave me the high sign in return.

"Follow me." I led Mona through the crowd and toward a spot near the corner of the stage where an empty two-top table about the size of a postage stamp had magically appeared—if you consider the dishwasher and bouncer dragging it from some shadowed corner as magical.

Did I also mention I matched the owner up with his

financial partners in order to make his dream of opening Driven come true? My talents are not limited to romance, and now I get the VIP treatment. Tonight that meant a tiny table in the front corner of the room.

My butt barely touched the seat when the spotlight picked out a lone figure standing on stage with a guitar. A shriek so shrill it could cut glass erupted from the table to our right. You could have knocked me over with a breath when I recognized the screamer. Lemon, the almost Mrs. Tart, dressed in a bright yellow tube top and a skirt so short I doubted she could bend over without exposing London *and* France, bounced in her seat, her focus trained on the stage.

I followed her gaze just as the spotlight softened enough to make out the man's face. Kin played his fingers over the strings, and half the place went wild. The female half. You'd have thought Elvis was making his triumphant, albeit spectral return, the way they were acting.

Don't get me wrong, Kin sounded good, and had the moves, too. A little wiggle and thrust of his hips against his guitar sent the women into a frenzy. At one point, he even turned around and gave the crowd a nice shot of his rear assets. Every twitch, every toss of his head sent screams rocketing toward the rafters.

He was fun to watch and attractive enough to make even my jaded heart go pitter-pat, but I wasn't feeling the compulsion to throw my panties on the stage. Lemon looked like she might faint, and I was beginning to wonder if Harry had been right about her.

This looked like more than a simple fangirl episode.

A disruption behind us drew my attention, and I sighed with relief as Flix made his way through the crowd, which, with a wave of his hand, parted like the red sea. He glanced from the commotion on stage and back to me. "These women have lost their minds," he muttered into my ear. "Isn't that Harry's fiancée?"

"Yep. And if she doesn't stop jumping up and down she's going to be wearing that tube top as a belt." I snarked, unable to hide my disgust.

I turned to Mona just in time to see her tongue dart across wet, glistening lips, her eyes following Kin's every move. "You, too?"

Mona declined to answer. In fact, I'm not sure she heard me at all.

Slumping back in my chair, I watched the spectacle play out. Halfway through his third and final song, Kin laid down the guitar to sing *a cappella*. The house lights came up, and he stepped off the stage to make his way around the first and second rows of tables, crooning straight to one lucky woman after another.

As he got closer to where I sat, our eyes locked. He was even better looking than I remembered. He gave me a wink, then turned back toward the stage to strum out the final notes of the song. The place exploded with screaming applause while he walked off the stage.

"Was that him?" Mona asked fervently. "Oh, I hope it was."

"I'm sorry, but no. Look, we need to go, okay?" All I wanted to do was get Mona safely back into her car and send her home so I could slug down a couple aspirin against the headache brewing at my temples.

"But I just got here," Flix whined, dragging the pressure in my head up another notch.

"Well, you'd have been here earlier if you hadn't been combing each hair individually," I snapped at him. "Sorry, it's been a weird night."

My apology went unheeded for a minute. Nightclubs bring out the predator in Flix. I think his Fae half feeds off the energy and right now, I could see him drinking it in as his eyes roved over the crowd. He patted my arm, eager to immerse himself in the throng moving toward the dance floor where the bouncers were already clearing the extra tables. "I'm staying, okay Hun?"

"See you tomorrow," I said to his fleeing back.

I shrugged at Mona's questioning look, and we turned toward the door, but only managed about three steps before I felt someone grab my arm.

"Lexi? I thought that was you. How's Salem?" Kin asked, guitar still in hand, his breath heavy with exertion.

"Fine. He's fine. I didn't expect to see you here." I

mumbled, the blood rising to my cheeks so quickly I began to wonder if the energy from the women in the club had rubbed off on me after all.

"Oh, I gig all over town." Kin opened his mouth to elaborate when Mona practically drove her elbow through my ribs in her haste to introduce herself. "I'm Mona Katz," she purred and grasped Kin's hand like a drowning woman.

"Nice to meet you." He glanced quickly at Mona and back at me. "Can I buy you a drink?" Kin asked while hastily stowing his guitar inside a battered case covered with band logos and old concert ticket stubs.

"I'm not drinking tonight, and Mona and I were just leaving." I declined, "It's good to see you again."

"That's right. I have work in the morning. It was nice to meet you." Mona's voice returned to normal, and she shook her head as if she was coming out of a dream. "Lexi, you'll call me tomorrow?"

"We have to go." Practically dragging Mona along behind me, I slipped out the side door into the cooling night and assured her I would call her just as soon as I could. She scurried down the block to where her car was parked. Mind racing, I watched her pull away.

"Don't tell me that was your ride home." Kin teased, coming up behind me.

"Hmm? No, I walked. It's just…" I broke off. How was I going to explain her weird reaction to him? "Never mind. I'm sure I'll see you around the neighborhood."

Kin stepped in front of me before I could take another step. "At least let me take you home. My car's parked right over there."

"I'll be fine." With three faeries only a frantic wish away, I was about as safe walking the streets of my city as I had been in my mother's womb.

Safer probably. The wrath of faeries descending upon a hapless thug would be epic and instantaneous. Just ask Justin Watson, a third-grade bully who had cornered me in the playground so he could pull my hair. One second he was large and in charge, the next Terra appeared behind him and said *boo*. With a few sound effects added, mind you. Justin peed his pants and ran. Problem solved.

"I won't." Kin argued. "If I let you go wandering around the streets alone and something happens to you, I'll never forgive myself. I'll take to the bottle to soothe my self-loathing, and before you know it, I'll be sleeping in a cardboard box and muttering about the night it all went wrong. You don't want that on your conscience, do you?"

I suppressed a grin, "You could be a crazed ax murderer who lures women into a false sense of safety so he can hack them up and hide the pieces in dumpsters."

"I brought your cat home, didn't I? Besides, the only ax I know how to use has six strings. Death by guitar? I don't think so." The corners of his mouth turned up in a smile that weakened my knees.

I let him tough it out for a few more moments before nodding in agreement. A shiver ran up my spine, and suddenly, I didn't want to walk home alone anymore. Or have to explain to the faeries why I needed an escort. They'd never let me live it down. "All right. You do live on my street."

It was a valid point, though I'd be lying to myself and you if I tried to pretend my acceptance of his offer had nothing to do with Kin's flirtatious coaxing.

"Excellent." He led me down the block and stopped next to a shiny black, vintage car.

"That's pretty, what is it exactly?"

Kin grinned from ear to ear. "A '67 Chevy Corvette. Last year they made 'em in this style. My dad and I spent my teen years fixing her up, and he gave her to me for my college graduation. Sweet, huh?"

"Definitely. What's her name?" I went on a hunch. Any guy who refers to his car with a gender-specific pronoun usually has a special name for it.

Kin laughed easily, an infectious, hearty sound that elicited a grin from my own lips. "I call her Betty. Well, actually, my dad named her that, after Betty White. I'm not sure why, but he has a huge thing for her."

"How old is your dad?" I asked. Maybe he had a bunch of older brothers and sisters.

"Not that old, which is why I keep calling her that. It cracks me up every time I think about it. Now, Lexi

Balefire, tell me something about you. So far I know you're a cat person; you've got a really cool last name; and an in at one of my favorite clubs. Oh, and you have some pretty interesting roommates. You know they danced around barefoot on the lawn during that thunder shower the other day?"

Sounded about right to me, faeries love wild weather. I parsed his tone for anything that resembled attraction toward one of my ethereally beautiful godmothers, and found none. The fact that I even cared spoke volumes about how this man had already affected me, and then my stomach dropped into my shoes.

Cut right to the part where I can't reveal everything about myself. Usually, it didn't bother me, because by the time we reached that point I already knew who the guy's soul mate was and that there wasn't any future anyway. With Kin, it was the first time I didn't get any vibe at all. So either this guy had no soul, or he was doomed to wander the earth without a mate. Maybe we were perfect for each other.

Hope welled in my gut and I tamped it down as quickly as it had risen. Sure, Kin might seem perfect—attractive, but not obnoxiously so; funny but without the added crass most men seem to find hilarious; and confident without coming across as cocky. But everything in my life seemed to come with some sort of caveat, and I'd been burned too many times to ignore the possibility that he might, for instance, have a proclivity for S&M or even worse, a Yosemite Sam tattoo on his butt.

I realized I'd been silent long enough for Kin to start wondering if I possessed adequate mental faculties, and forced myself to respond to his question.

"Well, I run FootSwept Matchmaking. What you saw tonight was part of my work. That's why I wasn't drinking. Though I could sure use one now. Long day. Sometimes people just don't want to take the easy path toward happiness." A safe enough reply, I thought.

"You actually go out to get drinks with your clients?" He seemed surprised, "I'm impressed. Most dating services are all technologically advanced; you have to tell them every minute detail of your life, and then they run some algorithm to see who you're compatible with."

I stared straight ahead and deadpanned, "You seem to know a lot about it…"

Kin's face broke into a wide grin, "Hey, you can't make fun of me! I'm very unlucky in love, and a couple of years ago a friend dragged me along to his appointment. I went on about three dates, and that was as much as I could take."

I snorted. "Unlucky in love, my left foot! You had so many women panting over you tonight I'm surprised you didn't break your neck slipping on a puddle of drool. What's that all about, anyway?"

Kin let loose a rueful laugh, "Trust me, that only

happens when I play. In real life, nobody ever notices me. Besides, that's infatuation, not love. You should know the difference," he challenged.

"Touché. So what's your day job then, Mister Rockstar?"

"I work at WKIT's studio. I write music and lyrics for advertisements. And I'm starting my own recording company; that's why I bought such a big house, so I don't have to pay for commercial space. I want to work with unsigned artists, and eventually, open my own label. But that's long-term."

Impressive and unique. This guy just got better and better. If only I could figure out what his deal was. "Would I recognize any of your work?"

"It won't win me a Grammy, but I did write the jingle for Fleet's Treats."

Organic dog biscuits. Catchy tune. The guy had chops. The rest of the drive was spent with me tossing out a list of imaginary products and him thinking up jingles for them.

We pulled onto my block just as I was thinking that if I laughed any more I wouldn't be able to feel my cheeks in the morning, and I knew in a hot minute it was going to be a long night. The windows all along the right side of the house were fogged over, and 80's music—the only decade my fairy godmothers declared was worth listening to—thumped loud enough to rattle them in their frames.

"Oh, no," I muttered.

"Looks like a party, can I come in?" Kin asked hopefully. Absolutely not.

"There isn't going to be a party for much longer. They're going to wake the neighbors, and Mrs. Chatterly has the cops on speed dial. I swear, I leave for one evening and chaos ensues. I had a lot of fun, thanks for the ride home. I'll see you later!"

Before I could open the car door, Kin reached over and caught my face in his hands, pulling me to his chest in a kiss that made my head spin. His lips were firm but gentle, and the scent of his breath trailed a chill up my spine. He smelled faintly of cinnamon and something I couldn't identify. Whatever it was, it went to my head like a fine wine.

When the kiss ended, I felt a sense of regret.

"I've been wanting to do that for days." He sighed and pulled me in again.

With no warning, I lost all control, crushing my lips against his, my breath hitching in my throat. He responded in kind, and for a moment I was lost. Then I came crashing back to earth and realized what kind of freak I must seem like. The last thing I wanted was for him to think I was like one of those girls from the club, willing to give it up just because he was sexy as hell.

"Oh my God, I'm so sorry." I scurried from his car

before he could respond, cursing Fae-kind all the way up
the walk as the thumping music suddenly changed to
"Like a Virgin"—by no accident, I was sure.

Chapter 6

Muttering under my breath, I took a moment to notice that the fog on the windows had blocked out what I could only describe as a faerie fireworks show, which would have been difficult to explain in the presence of a normal guy like Kin. Who probably thought I was insane, so what difference did it make, anyway?

Inside, the sound of raised female voices signaled nothing good. There are days I wish I could just get my own place. It took me a second to figure out it was laughter I was hearing, and not fighting. What does it say about my life that I didn't find the realization comforting?

Before heading toward the family room and the voices, I peeked into the kitchen and found it spotless. That which is destroyed by magic can be restored by the same. At least it hadn't been my responsibility to clean up after them after the last battle. My breaking up the fight only resulted in a temporary truce, and everyone had been walking on eggshells ever since.

I stuck my head in the doorway to get a feel for the tone of the room before I joined my supermodel mommies. Depending on the day you asked, I'd tell you that my life has been both blessed and cursed by having them around every day. Of the three, Terra was the motherly one, but each came with her own brand of wisdom.

Soleil caught sight of me lingering near the doorway and said, "We've made up, and now we're celebrating. Come join us."

You'd think the honeymoon phase after a big fight would be the best time to ask the question burning a hole inside me, but there were no guarantees.

Still, I needed to know, so I plunked down on the edge of the chair closest to the fireplace, dispensed with the preamble and said, "Why didn't you tell me there was a narrowing window of opportunity for me to Awaken?"

As soon I heard them, I realized the words sounded like an accusation. Faeries take great offense to being unjustly accused. Offended faeries tend to toss around magic. I might have started Fae War #2,357. Well, if I had, I'd own it. I lifted my chin to show them the sadness in my eyes.

"Oh, honey," Terra's sympathetic drawl let me know I was off the hook. With her anyway. "None of us had the heart to cause you more pain."

"We planned to tell you…after." Soleil chimed in.

"You knew the Balefire would pass on to Serena Snodgrass?" I asked, hoping there was some other explanation besides the one that smug witch had given me.

"Oh no, we would never let that happen. Technically, it would pass to the next nearest witch, and as long as there was someone else closer than that silly little girl, we thought…" In her haste to reassure me, Evian had let something else slip.

"So you planned to bring in someone you thought was better qualified and you weren't going to tip me off at all?" One time in third grade, I walked too close to one of the swings just as a classmate pumped her feet forward and took a hard kick to the gut. This betrayal carried a similar sensation.

Three shamefaced faeries found somewhere else to look, rather than meet my gaze head-on. Vaeta's countenance remained carefully blank.

"We had our reasons." Terra glared at Vaeta as if cautioning her not to speak and her next comment put an end to the discussion.

"There's still time before Beltane, and I have a good feeling about it. I think this is your year."

Pointing out that Terra's cheer rang a little false would be unwise if I was reading her expression correctly, and I knew I was, so I let the topic go, but reluctantly.

Terra said, "Now, we're celebrating, and you are woefully behind. Have a drink and tell us about the man in the car."

I recognized the bottle she waved around and then passed to Evian—moss green cut glass that sparkled in the firelight. The lower half of the decanter was wrapped in leather and copper wire: Twinkleberry wine. Sounds like it ought to be made from sugarplums, right?

Well, it isn't. One sip of that stuff can send a mortal off to La-La Land for a couple of days. My half-witch heritage means I can handle a glassful.

One.

Don't ask me how I learned two was over my limit. That's a story I'm glad I don't fully remember. Suffice it to say that coming to in the middle of the backyard, three days later, without a stitch of clothing on hadn't been my finest moment. I have a fever dream memory of pledging my love to the full moon.

The far corner of our backyard housed Terra's secret stash of whatever otherworldly fruit she blended into the wine—I was almost sure there were no actual twinkleberries. The spot lived inside a faerie glamour that deflected prying eyes—even mine, and that's saying something.

A slightly tipsy Evian splashed the rest of the bottle into the delicate bowl of a crystal wine glass and handed it to me. More for form than anything else, I raised the glass to my lips for a small sip. It tasted like liquid sunlight and wiped out the vestiges of my long day. Settling into my chair, I prepared to listen to the sisters catch each other up on the last hundred years.

Soleil uncorked a second bottle, most of which she served to Vaeta, I noticed. I also noticed the sidelong glance she paid to Terra. Maybe there was an ulterior motive to getting Vaeta well and truly plastered.

With a second sip inside me, I decided I didn't really care.

I felt like I was sitting in the exotic bird cage at the zoo with the four of them surrounding me. Evian looked like she had been born of the water that was her element. Hair the color of a tropical sea tumbling almost to her waist; eyes the angry white of a whitecap wave; and lips of blue set off an arresting face.

In stark contrast, Soleil's short cap of fiery hair whipped around her head like the flame that provided her life force. Dark eyes and ebony lips were like burnt embers on her ivory face.

Terra's coloring changed with the seasons. Today, she sported her spring look. Mahogany hair streaked in shades of earth tones swirled around a stunning face. Lips of apple red smiled easily and often. The ultimate earth mother, Terra protected and nurtured the soil and all the creatures who lived upon it.

Of the four, her appearance was closest to human form. Only eyes the color of pink marble required glamour in order for her to pass among mortals without detection.

"What this party needs is a hot tub. Shall we?" Terra jumped up from her chair.

Evian dragged me out of mine just in time. Vaeta drew a breath and not-so-gently blew the furniture away from the center of the room. Terra waggled two fingers toward the floor, which rearranged itself into a shallow depression that Evian filled with water. Soleil provided heat, and Vaeta added bubbles. Some days living with faeries is just plain awesome.

Garments shifting to bands that barely qualified as coverings—we'd had many a discussion about modesty and propriety in this house, me lecturing them, not the other way around—the four of them descended into the heated water. I debated going upstairs for my bikini, then decided my underwear would do and followed suit. Delicious, fragrant heat soaked into my bones. Heaven.

Somehow the talk turned to me and my love life, or lack thereof.

"It always goes wrong somewhere around the third date. That's when I find out *the thing.*"

"The thing?" Vaeta lounged in the bubbling froth. Like the others, her beauty could steal the breath. Vaeta's look was never static. It shifted from palest gray to the blue of a winter shadow and back. Hair, eyes, and lips all a perfect match against skin so pale it was almost translucent. Watching the slow shift of color was all the more mesmerizing under the effects of faerie wine.

"Yeah, the thing. *The thing*," I repeated with a bit of a slur. "The reason I have to break it off. Nine times out of ten, I get the matchmaker vibe. You know, the little whatsit that says he's fated for someone else."

"And the tenth?"

"The tenth is when everything is going along fine and out of nowhere comes the *and there it is* moment. Like when he shows me one of those tacky photos of him against the black background looking contemplatively up at a double exposure of his cat, proving he's already in a co-dependent relationship. You know what I mean."

A chorus of faerie snorts met that comment.

"I know they get the same thing with me. You can see it when a guy asks what I do for a living. The word matchmaker comes out of my mouth and all they hear is evil, scheming destroyer of freedom. They start looking for the door and you can clock it from there. Before you know it, my date is hightailing it away from me like I set his pants on fire. Half an hour is all they can manage—tops."

Except for Kin, who hadn't batted an eyelash. But, that was neither here nor there. At least, that was the lie I told myself.

"Oh, darling, half an hour isn't nearly long enough. You need a man with some staying power." Vaeta giggled.

Drat my ivory skin, it blushes at the drop of a…well, a sexual innuendo for one thing. Asking the faeries about their love lives fell deep into the icky, too much information about your pseudo-parents territory. Not least because, from what I could tell, most faeries don't mate for life. There's enough love-the-one-you're-with mentality to make all of their dating advice suspect at best, and flat-out disastrous at worst.

Don't get me wrong, I'm not a prude or anything. I've had my fair share of men to help me pass the time, but you don't work with seekers of love every day without catching a case of the happily-ever-after bug yourself. The heat and excitement of a fling were fun and all, but I was beginning to want something a little deeper. Providing, of course, there was a man out there who rated high enough on the not-a-frog scale to qualify for the job.

Who was I kidding?

Imagine this. Say I found a man who isn't intimidated by The Job. The next logical step is to bring him home.

The disco swampfest was not even close to the worst thing I'd ever walked in on. We get a lot of interesting visitors at our house. You try hiding four faeries playing host to a gaggle of cavorting mermaids or a nymph on a unicorn from a man. The way I saw it was that if he's dumb enough to accept any explanation I might muster up, he's too dumb for me to want to date. I guess that left me in a weird place.

More, I was actively trying to bring on my latent witchiness, which, if successful, would add a whole other dimension to the situation. I'd seen Bewitched. I didn't want to marry a Darrin. Honestly, the way that man tried to keep a witch down just made my blood boil—and all under the guise of being protective. Bah.

Faerie wine buzzed through my head and stole all my angsty thoughts away while my family managed to spend a pleasant hour getting giddy with each other.

"What about tonight?" Evian waggled blue-green eyebrows at me. "Looked like you were getting cozy with the guy in the nice car."

"Kin? Nope. That's not going to be a thing. Not my type at all." I blatantly lied.

"Then why were you playing dueling tongues with him? Looked pretty hot to me." Soleil would be the best judge of hot, I suppose.

"Things aren't always what they seem." Already heated from the steaming water, there was no red left to blush my cheeks, and Soleil wasn't buying my weak protest.

"What's wrong with him? If he's good enough for a game of tonsil hockey, why not try a second date?"

Because I didn't hang around long enough for him to ask for one was the correct response, but not the one I gave.

The next morning brought a dozen men fully equipped with strobe lights and jackhammers to take up residence in my head. Navigating the stairs with one eye slit open and the other squeezed shut, I oozed into the hall leading to the kitchen. History with that particular brew proved the aspirin clutched in my hand would be of limited use in warding off a Twinkleberry wine hangover.

Food would help, even if the thought of it made my stomach flip over like a seal chasing a ball in a water tank. I knew without looking that my hair was standing up every which way—because I could feel every strand—and I probably had bags under my eyes drooping clear down to my chin.

Slumping onto a stool, I clapped hands over my ears to dim down the apocalyptic echo of Vaeta's cheerful voice.

"Here, drink this." She slid a glass of green goo in front of me. If I didn't think the act of heaving would kill me, I would have tossed my cookies right on the table. "My patented hangover cure."

I shot her a murderous glare that failed to leave her bleeding on the floor. Almost took me out, though.

"Drink it." Hating her for looking daisy fresh when I felt like a bag of week-old garbage, I did as she said. The goo smelled worse than it looked and tasted like something scraped off a frog's butt. I gagged it down as fast as I could.

Have you ever seen one of those stop-action movie clips in reverse? Picture a piece of paper going from crumpled to smooth. That's about how I felt during the next thirty seconds.

By the time it was over, I felt normal. No, better than normal, and I swear my skin was clearer. Vaeta could make an absolute fortune selling that stuff on the late-night shopping channels.

"Better?" She asked the rhetorical question.

"Like new. What was in that?" I rested my chin in my hands and watched Vaeta wave her fingers in a circular motion over a bowl of eggs that looked like they were whipping themselves. Interesting talent to have.

"Trade secret," she chirped. I nearly died. Vaeta was a morning faerie. Even hopped up on her kill-the-hangover juice, I wasn't wild about the way her fluttering around the kitchen made me feel like a slug. "If I told you what was in it, you wouldn't have taken it." She was preaching to the converted.

I lost a couple minutes in silent contemplation that involved trying to remember a portion of time the night before. The time between my joining in a rousing chorus of "Don't Stop Believin'" and the moment the sun fell on my face this morning with a thud was a total blank. That didn't bode well for me.

"Did I do anything weird last night?" Vaeta treated

me to an eloquently-arched eyebrow of foggy blue over an eye that gleamed with purple fire.

"Define weird."

On second thought, I'd rather not know. "Never mind."

A steaming plate of fluffy eggs dotted with bits of veggies and ham landed in front of me. Vaeta poured coffee before tucking into her own breakfast and eying me with interest. This was the first time since she had come back from the underworld that we had been in a room alone together. I had a thousand questions I wanted to ask, but none of them seemed appropriate, so I waited for her to break the ice.

"What have my sisters told you about me?" She opened with a conversational minefield and played right into my curiosity.

"Not a lot. Nothing bad, I mean," I assured her when her face darkened. "I think it was too painful for them." Probably true. It's hard to tell with faeries sometimes. They either keep their emotions under wraps or spew them out all over the place—often in physical form. There's not a lot of middle ground. The truth was that until Vaeta dropped back into our lives, I hadn't known she even existed, but that probably wasn't what she wanted to hear.

Vaeta snorted. "A diplomatic answer, how sweet. They've taught you well, little fate weaver."

It was my turn to snort. "Fate weaver? You mean

my matchmaking work? I wouldn't call it anything quite that dramatic. I bring people together, the rest is up to them. It's a step up from a dating service, but not by much. I have no control over what happens after they ride off into the sunset."

Of all the possible responses to that statement, a hoot of laughter was the last I expected from her.

"A dating service? You can't be that naive." The laughing stopped abruptly. "Or maybe you can. I see my sisters have kept you in the dark, and far be it from me to shatter your illusions." The next words she spoke in a contemplative voice, "Is that why you haven't claimed your birthright?"

I assumed she meant the full measure of my magic. "Oh, I've tried. Believe me. I'm beginning to think there's nothing to claim. Why else would I be little better than a null after all this time? The ritual doesn't work for me because I don't even have enough magic to complete it."

Another peal of laughter grated on my nerves. My last nerve, actually, if you want to know the truth. "Poor little fate weaver." I couldn't tell if her tone was condescending, but I suspected I was. "Tell Auntie Vaeta the whole sordid story. Who knows, a fresh eye just might see a clear resolution to your problem."

Amid reservations, I described finding the paper with the ritual spell tucked into a leather-bound notebook stuffed into the bottom of my grandmother's jewelry box on the day of my fourteenth birthday. What I didn't mention was that I was sure that notebook hadn't been in there before.

"The first time I tried the spell I was so excited. I knew…just knew it was going to work. Took my breath away, I wanted it so much. And then nothing happened. I was crushed." Vaeta made sympathetic noises. "It got to the point where I dreaded pulling out those ingredients because I knew I was going to fail."

"How long has it been?"

"A year. I give it a shot every year on my birthday. Just for form, you know?" Shoving the plate aside, I folded my arms into a cradle and dropped my head onto them. "It's never going to work. I don't have…I don't even know what. The skill, the delivery, or if I'm not meant to have magic, I guess." The words came out muffled.

The crack of a plate hitting the tabletop brought back a fleeting memory of the pre-hangover-cure headache. My head came up at near whiplash speed.

"Stop wallowing in self-pity. I swear, you remind me of Nero fiddling away while the smoke thickens around you." Her scorn cut me in places that don't bleed. "What do you think is going to happen if your birthday comes and goes this year and nothing changes?"

She responded to my duh look with a twist of the lips and enough pity over my limited mental faculties to tick me off.

"If you know so much, why don't you tell me?" Why is it everyone in my life felt the need to keep secrets? "I'm getting tired of being treated like a child."

"Then use your head and stop acting like one. Witches get faerie godmothers, right? What do non-witches get?"

"Guardian angels." An easy answer since I was already acquainted with one.

Vaeta waited for dawn to break over my addled brain.

"Are you saying Terra will find a new witch if I don't Awaken?" I couldn't believe I hadn't thought of that before. "Well, I guess it makes sense, but I'm not sure why it's that big of a deal."

The gentle breeze that always stirred Vaeta's hair whipped up to flip it around her face in angry lines. "Did Terra prepare you for nothing?"

I pushed my untouched breakfast across the table, crossed my arms, and waited for her to drop a new bomb on me. Seemed like there was a perpetual target on my head where she was concerned.

Slumping into the chair across from me, Vaeta let the wind die off and contemplated me for a moment before she said, "Once upon a time—"

What now? I was too old for fairy tales.

Okay, given my living arrangements, that wasn't even close to the truth.

Vaeta continued, "—Every witch had three faerie

godmothers to protect body, mind, and spirit. You may have read stories about a young witch who, under threat of a curse, was given into the care of her three faerie godmothers who raised her as if she were their own. She was a beautiful girl with a soul as pure as the feather on a dove. On her fourteenth birthday, she failed to Awaken."

The girl had my sympathies.

"Her faerie godmothers blamed themselves for not being able to help her touch her magic and they tried everything to help stir the power they sensed in her blood. Spell after spell, each year passed with nothing to show for the effort but frustration and pain. Until, the final year, her twenty-fifth, loomed and her godmothers knew it was all or nothing."

Moments passed while Vaeta sent my plate drifting to dump its contents into the trash.

"What happened?" It had to be bad, or she wouldn't have had such a sorrowful look on her face.

"They poured everything into one final spell, and risked all upon its success. But the girl was not meant to carry power, and when the smoke cleared, none were left alive."

As quickly as it popped into my head, I banished the mental image of Terra's lifeless body sprawled on the grass. "Terra would never try such a thing."

"Of course not." All the sorrow gone, Vaeta treated me to a disgusted look. "She's not an idiot, and even if she was, there are sanctions in place to prevent such tragedies."

"Then why did you tell me the story?" Airy faerie, indeed.

"So you would know what's going to happen when and if the time comes. If you don't Awaken before midnight on your twenty-fifth birthday, Terra—and I assume this goes for Soleil and Evian as well—will return to the Faelands."

My breath whooshed out like I'd been punched in the gut.

"I'd miss her, but it's not like she couldn't come back and visit."

And then Vaeta dropped the rest on me.

"She could, of course, but she wouldn't, because the bond of witch and faerie godmother would be broken."

"I like to think we have a deeper relationship than charge and protector. We're family. All of us." For me, it was just that simple.

Rising, Vaeta turned away, but not before I saw the glint of a tear in the corner of one eye. "And I'm sure she feels the same way, but you don't understand, Lexi. Once the bond is broken, all memory of the witch is taken away. Terra wouldn't come back, because she wouldn't remember she'd been here in the first place."

Shoulders rounded, Vaeta kept her face turned away as she tidied up the kitchen while I sat in shocked silence.

Come midnight on Beltane, I'd either be a full-fledged witch, keeper of the sacred Balefire which would grow mighty under my watchful eye, or I'd be alone in front of my darkened hearth.

"You have to help me," I whispered.

"You know I can't," she whispered back. "Not with magic."

"Then with knowledge. Isn't there anything you can tell me that might help?"

Her shoulders squared, and when she turned back to regain her seat, there was nothing of sadness in her eyes. Only a crafty determination that I hoped would not come back to bite me later.

"How do you think young witches learn to cast?" Vaeta demanded.

"From their mothers," I said tentatively. Slap me with the orphan stick. "But I've had your sisters in the house; I think I know how magic works."

Rolling her eyes, Vaeta waved a hand and everything turned into a scene from a Disney movie. The kitchen cleaned itself while I watched with jaded eyes. This kind of thing happened daily around here.

"Listen closely. This is important. Magic takes many forms, even if the outcome is the same. You know Evian's element is water and mine is air. Our magics are complementary in some ways. She could communicate with the water, enchant it to fill a glass."

Or a pond. I'd seen Evian pull liquid from a stone.

"I could do the same by asking the wind to give up the moisture it carries."

To punctuate the statement, Vaeta demonstrated by watering down my coffee.

"Different magic, same result. Magic does not beget magic. You keep assuming you have none. Have you ever considered this from a different perspective? Witches don't get magic at a given age, magic comes through blood. It is inherent. Touching that power is how a young witch Awakens. Every spell takes the right ingredients. Ones that must be blended correctly and with the proper intention."

It was a head-slapping moment for me. Could I really have been working with just one small incorrect element all this time? Was I making the whole thing harder on myself without realizing it? Seemed about right.

"If I showed you the spell would you help me figure out if I'm doing it right?" I asked with pleading eyes.

Vaeta shook her head, "You need a witch to help you."

Just peachy. Too bad all the witches I knew were either my mortal enemy or they thought I had non-magic cooties.

Please, I sent up a prayer to whichever goddess might be listening. *Help me find a witch with some answers.*

Chapter 7

"Harry, calm down." I sighed into the phone. At least I could understand his distress now, having watched Lemon act like a smitten groupie at Kin's Driven gig the night before. Still, understanding wasn't enough to drown out Vaeta's warning as it swirled inside my head on a loop.

I dragged my attention back to Harry with considerable effort. He wasn't wrong about his fiancée's behavior; I was nearly as disturbed by her little demonstration as he was, but that didn't make it my problem, did it?

Who was I kidding, anyway? I could cite business concerns as my motivating factor till the cows came home, but I wouldn't—couldn't—let Harry's happy future crumble into dust without at least attempting some sort of intervention.

I coaxed the details of the previous night out of him

with a few well-chosen words, "She came home smelling like a frat house basement, Lexi. I tried to get her to tell me where she'd been and who she'd been with, and she just got angry and defensive."

The sneaking suspicion that Harry hadn't been entirely calm during their exchange almost drove the image of Lemon shaking what the good lord gave her out of my mind.

"You didn't accuse her of anything, did you?" I ventured a guess.

Harry sputtered, "No, of course not." I didn't need witchly intuition to know he was lying through his teeth.

I was torn. On the one hand, I hadn't actually seen Lemon do anything except imbibe a few too many and get a little overly excited about a sexy guitar player. Just because there was a ring on her finger didn't mean her eyes were out of order. Half the club had mooned over Kin, and understandably so. It didn't give Harry the right to jump to conclusions.

On the other hand, I understood where he was coming from. The fact that he hadn't seen Lemon's display firsthand didn't negate the fact that she hadn't been acting like a happily engaged woman. The line was blurry for me, sitting squarely in the middle, though I'm sure it looked solid as a rock from where each of them were standing.

"I'll talk to her, Harry, but my advice is to relax and remember that you trust Lemon. You do trust her, don't you?"

As if there were an appropriate alternative answer to *yes, of course*, which was exactly what Harry replied with. Five more minutes of soothing platitudes and a swig of lukewarm coffee later, I raced downtown to intercept Lemon just as she was about to head to lunch.

"Chocolate therapy?" Sinclair Fuller, genius confectioner, reached for one of his signature white boxes with the word *Sinful* scrawled across in red lettering. "A six or a nine?"

Our scale of busy or stressful days was counted by the number of handmade chocolates needed to restore both body and soul. "It's probably closer to a twelve, but six will do." He gave me eight and then applied the "friends and family" discount. Chocolate and romance make a great pair, so I often sent business his way. In return, he supplied my weekly fix.

"Tough client?"

"Understatement of the year," I sighed, "Looks like I've got a return on my hands."

"How does that work? Here's my boyfriend, he's not sensitive enough to my needs, get me a new one?" Sinclair's smile softened the sarcasm.

"Funny, but no." Truthfully, I didn't know how it worked because this was the first time it had ever happened—and furthermore, it seemed as though

Harry's predicament was largely in his own head.

During our short lunch, Lemon maintained she'd only been enjoying an evening out with her girlfriends, and had prattled on about wedding details until I'd finally determined that perhaps both Harry and I had blown the whole escapade out of proportion.

She had either already forgiven him for his overreaction, or forgotten all about it thanks to one too many vodka sodas with a twist of, well, lemon. Either way, I felt like I'd wasted my day trying to put out a fire that had already dwindled to ash.

I nipped a bit of heaven from the box in front of me and took a bite. Salted caramel truffle dipped in dark chocolate, and then rolled in a crunchy coating. Sinful indeed. I cast a questioning glance at Sinclair. "What's the crunchy stuff?"

"Crushed ice cream cone. The sugar kind."

Best thing ever.

Visiting Sinful added extra walking time to my trip home, which was one way I rationalized my chocolate indulgence. His place was three blocks in the opposite direction from home. Better yet, Sinclair stayed open late. We had the night owl thing in common. Sinful opened at noon and closed at nine.

A glitter and flash in one of the shop windows caught my eye as I passed Hanover Street. Curiosity pulled me down the block for a closer look.

Nestled into the narrow space between a dry

cleaner and an insurance agency, the mystical supply shop, Athena's Attic, looked like it belonged—like it had been there all along. I knew better.

This is my city and I know her well; the streets, the businesses, the people. Witches may have a reputation for hovering over cauldrons in the dark of the forest, but I guess I sort of count as a witch, and I draw my energy from the bustling crowds.

It had been a week—maybe two—since I passed this way and in that location, there had been…I drew a blank and tried again. My mind fogged, then it cleared.

Why, of course. Athena's Attic. What was I thinking? I must have been having a mental moment. The pentacle etched into the window was as familiar to me as the blue velvet curtains framing an interior filled with intrigue and mystery. Apothecary cabinets with polished brass handles lined the wall opposite the window; their drawers filled with ingredients for making potions and powders.

Every time I went to a place like this, it was like spinning the wheel on the witchy lottery. Come on, baby. Momma needs a spell that will work.

Two weeks remained until this year's Beltane celebration on the day of my 25th birthday and my time wasn't just running out, it was almost up. I should have realized if there was a deadline for getting my magic, there was also one for the Balefire being passed on to a proper tender.

Humiliating.

I was no closer to my Awakening than I had been last year at this time.

Without the ability to fully access my magic, I didn't have enough power to keep the Balefire lit. According to the sparse notes in Clara's little handbook, Keepers of the Flame experienced a symbiotic relationship with the Balefire, with both witch and flame gaining strength in the transaction. Talk about being caught in a circular problem.

Where was a spot of divine intervention when I needed some?

Over the years I'd searched for a way, a charm, a form of meditation—anything that might provide a little something extra. Maybe enough extra to let me complete the Awakening spell. Potions, crystals, ritual candles, and spell books had eaten a significant portion of my discretionary funds and then begged for more. None of those things brought peace to the restless place inside that called out for the power I knew should have been mine.

Everything you send out into the world is supposed to come back to you in triplicate. Call it Karma, call it a rule of threes, I don't really care because I'm going to call it a steaming pile of dung. I send love out into the world every day. True love. None of that "happily for now" or "love the one you're with" nonsense. According to Karma, I should be getting good vibes back from the universe. All I get is a headache and a kick in the pants.

I'd begun to half-wonder if performing good deeds didn't count when part of the motivation was the desire to avoid turning into a wicked witch.

"Won't you come inside?" A smooth voice dripped honey behind me and I realized I'd been staring into the shop window for some time while I indulged in my private pity party.

"I guess." Color me enthusiastic. I must have been in here a thousand times looking for something that would help. Right? Then why couldn't I remember ever making a single purchase?

"Please." One word spoken gently and my resolve vanished like a teenager on laundry day.

The woman standing behind me was my polar opposite. Hair the color of a sunbeam, eyes bluer than sapphires, skin so fine it didn't look real. Anyone would remember meeting this woman. I didn't.

"I'm sorry," The more I tried to look away, the more I felt drawn to stare at her. "Do I know you? Have I been here before?"

A silvery laugh beguiled me even more. "Maybe. Or maybe we met in another life. Do come inside." Those blue eyes swept over me with shrewd assessment. "I've got just the thing for those aching feet." Until that moment I wasn't aware I had aching feet, but as soon as she mentioned them, my arches throbbed painfully.

"Come inside. We'll fix you right up. It's just an

herbal remedy. If I promise not to hex you, will you let me help?" A raised eyebrow and a quirk of the lips gave humor to what might have been a serious statement. She'd taken me for a newbie. Or worse, for a seeker—someone without blood ties to power, but looking.

Wondering if the rats had recognized the piper's tune of doom and gone along anyway, I followed the silken swirl of her dress into the shop.

"I'm Athena," she said. "Tea? Brewed from fresh leaves. Chocolate mint."

A favorite of mine and hard to resist.

"Okay."

Don't laugh, but the way she was looking at me reminded me of an Animal Planet documentary. I could hear the hushed voice of the presenter in my head saying, "It's the rare, skittish half-witch. Be careful not to spook her," with an Australian accent, naturally.

That bit of foolishness broke through the stasis.

"I'm sorry. Distracting day. I'd love a cup of tea." What could it hurt? "I'm Alexis. Everyone calls me Lexi."

"Alexis. It's a strong name. Did you know it means protector?" Her knowing that creeped me out a little.

"I did. Ironic, considering how badly I'm falling down on the job." At her blank look, I elaborated, "Do you know anything about Awakening spells?"

"So you're a blood witch, then." Her gaze swept

over me from head to toe. Standing awkwardly before her, I felt as if she had assessed everything about me. "And a late bloomer." I really wished she'd stop looking at me like that.

"The last of a once-great line. Probably better if it ends with me; at least I won't be passing down tainted genes," I said bitterly.

A sudden shadow cast Athena's face into sinister lines and for a fleeting second, the skin on the back of my neck lifted and crawled.

"You're the last Balefire. Keeper of the Flame." No getting away from my family history. My great, great and then some, grandmother brought the fire to America when there were barely more than a few settlements. Keeping watch over the ritual flame used to light the Beltane fire was more than just a job in my family, it was our identity.

Blood witches could recognize one of us in a crowd, so her knowledge of that aspect of my heritage didn't bother me, but the knowing look in her eyes sure did.

"For a few more days. Then I will become Alexis No Name. Loser of the Flame, which will then pass to, if she has any say in the matter, the scourge of witchkind."

Athena, without asking, doctored my tea just the way I liked it best. A splash of milk and a dollop of honey went into both cups along with the fragrant minty goodness. Apparently, she drank hers the same way.

Weird.

We settled into a pair of chairs that made up a reading corner in the area where she sold books. I eyed Athena warily over the edge of my cup. Years of dealing with people told me she was either one of two types. A) she wanted to sell me something and would do anything to get me to buy, or B) she was naturally curious to the point where the personal part of the term "personal information" meant nothing.

"Tell me all about yourself. What do you do? Besides carry on your family tradition."

Totally B.

To tell the truth, I hate answering that question. Hate it with a bloody passion. Once they hear I'm a matchmaker, more than a few people look at me like I'm a meddling she-spider who wants to trap them in a committed relationship. That faction is mostly men, by the way. Not all of them, though. Some of them jump to the conclusion I'm running an undercover escort service. You can tell by the way their eyes slide south the minute I mention my profession.

Women have more complex reactions. Some start to gush, some ask for my card—there are men who do that as well—and some mentally go through their list of friends for any hidden clues to tell them which ones might have used my services. The ones who are already in happy relationships get a twinkle in their eye that tells me their thoughts have turned to the day they met their own true love.

"I facilitate interpersonal relationships in the dating milieu." Milieu? What on earth made me say that? "Matchmaker." Just calling it like it is made me feel better.

Athena seemed unsurprised, which made me wonder why she asked a question to which she might have already known the answer.

"It sounds like fulfilling work. Is there any money in it?" People inevitably ask questions about my job once they learn I'm a matchmaker. This was the first time anyone ever asked me about the financial aspect rather than the romantic one.

"I make a living." My stiff posture and dismissive tone let her know this line of questioning was not welcome.

"A regular Cupid."

An apt comparison, I supposed, if not an entirely original one. Though, this was the first time it had been delivered with a hint of bitterness.

Since her statement required no answer, I sipped my tea without speaking. No wonder I didn't shop here regularly. The owner was a busybody.

Still, I couldn't afford to let any straws pass without grasping at them, so I said, "Have you worked here long?"

"Hmm? Oh, no. Not really."

Okay then. The awkwardness had gone on long

enough, so I came right out with the one question I dearly wanted an answer to. "Is there anything you can tell me about how to Awaken my magic? I've tried so many times and there's no one left to ask for help." Athena's face turned pensive, but she offered no suggestion.

A silence fell between us that grew so long it tumbled right into that awkward space where I wasn't sure whether she couldn't help me, or could and didn't want to. An eternity passed before I said, "Well, this was fun. I'll just be going now."

"No, please. One more question, is there no one, even a distant family member who could become Keeper in your place?" She hedged.

Jab another sore spot, why don't you. "No. No family at all. I was adopted." Technically a lie. "There's nobody to explain to me what I'm doing wrong; why I can't seem to access the path to my magic. I've done the spell over and over. I don't know what's missing. I think it has to do with not knowing how to focus my intention, but my…the people who raised me have a different frame of reference and are unable to explain." Or unwilling. I kept that last bit to myself.

"What spell?" She asked, curiosity lighting up her already too beautiful face.

I fished through my purse and pulled out my day planner. Tucked between two pages was a slightly crumpled piece of parchment. Handling it gingerly to keep from smudging the handwritten text any more than it already was, I laid the spell on the table. "To Awaken the Initiate" it was labeled, and as Athena ran a scarlet-tipped finger down the ingredients list, her eyes narrowed infinitesimally.

"Where did you get this?" She asked.

"I found it in my grandmother's things. Right before my fourteenth birthday. Why?"

"This isn't…" A frown marred the perfection of her forehead. "Never mind."

Again with the cryptic.

Athena read the spell aloud twice, giving each verse the correct intonation and cadence. She had me repeat it several times to make sure I'd remember the precise inflections.

"The initiate must prepare herself by completing a cleansing ritual for clear sight, followed by a drawing spell to call the latent magic into being. The list of ingredients is pretty standard." Pulling a sheet of lined paper from under the counter, Athena scratched down a couple notes.

"Modern conventions are nice, but a copper tub is best for Awakenings. No one has those anymore, so I'm making some changes to the list. Three pennies added to the water will mitigate the effects of the porcelain. Are you hooked up to the city water supply?"

"For the past ten years, why?"

"Chemical alchemy." I just stared at her.

"Chlorinated water. Use these." She tossed a foil wrapped packet at me. "Effervescent bath salts, a trial pack should do it. I make these myself. They have vitamin C; good for the skin and for counteracting chemical additives."

Athena went to work. Running a finger down the list, she collected ingredients from various shelves around the store, naming them as they went into the bag.

"Right here, this says to pound the dried dandelion root. Use a mortar and pestle, but don't grind it. You understand?"

I nodded. Despite the odd sense of mistrust I felt around her, I rose to stand near the counter and watch while she sorted through her wares with abandon. Finally, there was only one more item left on the list. Stone of Blood. Athena tapped her finger against the words scrawled on the yellowed sheet.

"Stone of Blood. That's bloodstone, right? Also known as heliotrope. Stone of blood sounds cooler, though." My comment was met with a blank look. Athena's mind seemed to be focused elsewhere, but I kept talking anyway. "Stone of blood. Bloodstone. What else could it be?"

Athena nodded absently.

"How would you recommend I charge the bloodstone? I've tried running water, sunlight, moonlight, and incense. Is there anything I'm missing?" Despite her strange reactions and constant questions,

Athena was helping me feel confident about my chances of making the spell work this time.

There was a pause before she answered. "Bloodstone reacts best to contact. Carrying it close to your heart is the best way. Let it touch your skin."

I grimaced thinking of the two-pound hunk of it sitting on my windowsill. Not the easiest thing to tuck into your clothing. My consternation must have shown because Athena patted me on the arm.

"Here, take this one. It will bring you luck." Her eyes locked on mine with intensity while her fingers unerringly picked the clasp of a heavy silver chain from among the pendants she wore around her own neck. She chose an oval cabochon of forest green flecked with brilliant red and polished to a slick gloss nestled in a simple silver setting.

Before I could say no, she rounded the counter and motioned for me to hold my hair out of the way while she slid the necklace into place. Her fingers felt both warm and cold upon my neck and I shivered under the sensation. "Please accept the Stone of Blood as my gift to you. May it help you keep the fire burning in your hearth."

"Are you sure? It looks old. I wouldn't feel right accepting so valuable a gift."

"Take it, Alexis." Athena's voice softened. "With my blessing." After all the intense looks, the cheeky smile she displayed next was welcome. "Besides, that bag of supplies is going to cost you a pretty penny." I settled the bill while she asked random questions about my home and family. Most of them centering around my mother.

"She died in an…accident when I was a baby."

Why such a simple explanation made Athena's jaw so tense, I couldn't explain, but it was time to leave.

"I really am running late," I checked my watch with exaggerated surprise. "Very late." This experience was getting a little strange, even for me.

"Alex…Lexi, I'm sorry if I've been a nosy Nellie. I don't intend to pry, it just seems to happen. A healthy curiosity coupled with wanting to know enough about my customers to give them what they need gets me into trouble sometimes." Athena flashed me one of those toothpaste smiles—the kind where a sparkle of light glinted off the white. "I hope to find your flame shining bright come Beltane."

I thanked her for all her help, but before I could cross the threshold, she grabbed me by the arm, her touch sending prickles over my skin and causing my hair to stand on end. My mind seemed to fog over, and when she spoke I listened without a trace of the skepticism I would normally display.

"The Full Milk Moon rises tonight; the seeds have begun to sow, and soon the life energy of the earth will move from darkness into light. Hold tight to the talisman with my blessing, and complete the ritual before the moon begins to wane—two nights hence. Infuse the stone; anoint the candle; gain your Sight. Only then will you see the way to what lies hidden within. Blood the stone two times to seal the spell. Follow your instincts and you will know what to do," Athena hissed. Then, suddenly, I was back to my normal self; her words curling away like smoke until they were entirely gone from my memory.

"You take care of yourself, Alexis." For a moment her eyes met mine, and I could identify genuine sadness in her gaze. What a total nut job. I stuffed the supplies into my enormous leather tote, right on top of the chocolates I would definitely be indulging in later, and decided that one more try at the spell couldn't hurt.

Chapter 8

I retreated to my bedroom, and was eternally grateful to hear the sound of my feet shuffling over the carpet after closing the door. Blessedly, I couldn't hear anything from the other side, which meant the silencing charm I had requested was working correctly.

Seemed like Terra, Soleil, and Evian had gotten bored with torturing me. Vaeta hadn't yet developed a reason to try, and I hoped I never gave her one; elemental faeries are temperamental, with the potential for creating destruction and chaos. Pinpointing Vaeta's intentions toward the rest of us might take some time—and a truce between the sisters that lasted more than an hour.

Reaching into my purse to retrieve the box of chocolates that promised to lift my spirits, I yanked out the bag of supplies from Athena's and stared at it while I chewed on a decadent glob of white chocolate filled with hazelnuts and pieces of chewy, dried strawberries.

Then I stuffed the whole thing underneath my bed. What was the point? I'd been down this road before, many times. And yet…the talisman Athena had given me hung heavy around my neck as I lifted my fingers to touch it.

Warm against my skin, the stone felt slick and full of power.

Bolting out from underneath my bed with far too much spunk for an animal his age, Salem made his presence known. Somewhere around my thirteenth birthday, when my greatest wish had been to become Sabrina, The Teenage Witch, I found the poor cat living in a potting shed at the edge of the woods behind grandmother's statue.

Salem didn't look any older than he had that first day—his black coat shined like silk, and the little patch of white on his forehead diminished his otherwise uncanny resemblance to a traditional witch's kitty—but I knew he wouldn't live forever, and my heart ached at the thought of losing him one day.

The little minx curled up next to my leg and purred. I laid back against the pillow and allowed the vibration to lull me into a sense of total calm; I always did my best thinking like this. At least I know if I never find love, my affinity for cats means I won't be completely alone in my old age.

I can see it now, the neighborhood kids will call me

a crazy cat lady, and tell stories about how I fly around on a broomstick. They'll avoid knocking on my door to beg for candy on Halloween. What fun.

Despite my best efforts, I couldn't stop thinking about the sack stashed under my bed. Indecision and self-doubt were becoming my best friends these days. My stomach flip-flopped back and forth so much I thought I might upchuck all that expensive chocolate.

The scene of me getting into the bathtub and performing the Awakening ritual played over and over in my mind. Exasperated, I got up and pulled the bag onto my lap. Annoyed at being displaced, Salem jumped onto my dresser and watched me with his favorite piercing cat stare as I smoothed a spot on the coverlet to lay everything out on the bed in front of me.

Was I really going to try this again? Every time the spell failed, I felt my confidence slip a little more.

It will be different this time, a little voice whispered in the back of my head. You've never done a cleansing bath before. Could be the key to everything.

I pulled out the bath ingredients first. Athena's packet of fizzy cubes landed on the bed followed by a small bundle of herbs tied with string.

A cloth drawstring satchel held a bit of roughly cut sea salt. Himalayan pink, to be precise. Carefully wrapped in paper were two small bottles of sandalwood and myrrh essential oils and three candles; one silver, one purple, and one red.

Yes, I was going to try again. All I had left to lose were the final vestiges of my pride and self-esteem, and really, who needs those anyway?

I grabbed my purse for the three pennies and then strode over to the big bay window on the south side of the room where I opened a secret cabinet beneath the window seat. There, nestled inside, rested a carved wooden box that held my most prized possessions: a tiny bronze bell; a piece of purple cotton hand-embroidered with a Celtic design that didn't correspond with any runes or symbols I could find (and believe me, I had looked); a censer; and two small knives, one with a white handle and one with a black handle.

This meager bundle of ritual supplies was the only thing I knew for certain had been owned by my mother. I had found them hidden in the back of the closet during the renovations. I liked to think Sylvana wouldn't begrudge me the space I gained when we expanded my small childhood bedroom by tearing down the wall leading into hers. Her ritual tools were the ones I used ever since I learned how to cast. Or at least, how to attempt to cast.

I pulled only the bell from its resting place and laid it on the bed with the rest of the supplies. Lastly, I donned a white robe pilfered from my grandmother's closet. White is the color of purity and seemed the appropriate choice for an initiation ritual.

Gathering up the various items, I carried the lot into

the adjoining, private bathroom, cleared all the bath products off the shelf around the big claw foot bathtub, and finally, as if compelled, scrubbed the porcelain until it shined and rinsed it with scalding hot water. Carefully, I placed the candles on the clean shelf, spacing them evenly in a line. While the tub filled with water I tossed in the pennies, added seven drops of the oils, and a generous handful of the salt.

Before settling into the heated depths, I lit the silver and red candles and turned off the overhead light.

Athena's bath cubes fizzed and frothed when they hit the water. They smelled like carnations. Combined with the fragrant oils, the sweet, yet spicy scent rose seductively with the steam. The sound of the running water relaxed me and helped tune out the jumble of thoughts vying for first place inside my scattered brain.

My heartbeat turned slow and steady with a few deep breaths and, feeling more grounded than I had in weeks, I twisted the taps closed, let the white robe slither to the floor and dipped a toe into the tub. A warm tingle ran up my leg, swirled around my calf and up the back of my thigh. I stepped all the way in and felt the same odd sensation travel up my other leg and then north, across my hip bones and around my back, finally tracing a path over my shoulders before settling into my chest.

Contentment and satisfaction seeped into my heart and bones and muscle as I sank into the water up to my chin, then gave the bell a little shake. Its tinkle sounded louder than it ever had before, reverberating off the walls to begin the ritual cleanse.

Moonlight shone through the open window and a light, unseasonably warm breeze played across the water's surface, creating ripples that twinkled in the glow. I began to hum to myself, a tune I couldn't actually remember ever hearing, but one that seemed familiar and beloved, as though it were a part of me, of my past.

As if in a trance, I reached for the pendant around my neck and pressed my index finger down on a particular spot in the silver setting. Pain seared my skin, and I pulled my hand away in surprise as a tiny droplet of blood swelled from my fingertip.

Instinctively, I knew what I was supposed to do—and what I had been doing wrong every other time I had attempted this ritual—and began to rub my finger over the unlit purple candle, anointing it with my own blood. I placed it back in its spot, struck a match, and touched the flame against the candle's wick.

The talisman around my neck blazed with heat but did not burn my skin, and the flames of all three candles turned bright red, then went out. I saw the smoke they left behind billow in the moonlight to create shapes that disappeared as quickly as they formed, and felt the talisman return to its normal temperature.

Encouraged by the way the stone had responded to the cleansing, I threw caution to the wind and reached for the rest of the ingredients needed to complete the spell meant to draw my magic to life. Long practice sped the process and soon everything was ready. Closing my eyes to remember the exact cadence Athena had used, I repeated the words that would (hopefully) seal my fate.

> Candle burn and flame grow bright
> I call upon the power of light
> Blood to blood and heart to heart
> From moon and star the power impart
> Awaken magic, come to me
> As I command, so mote it be

Then there was nothing. No sparks shooting from my fingers, no feeling of transformation. I rang the bell to signal the end of the ritual out of habit, rose from the tub and flicked on the light. A glance in the mirror confirmed what I already knew. It was just me, as I had always been. As I always expected to be. Plain old Lexi. Vowing to clean up my mess later, I slammed the door behind me and fell into bed without even brushing my teeth.

Chapter 9

Tears wet my pillow as I tossed and turned, knowing that time was running out and, despite Terra's "good feeling", if nothing changed soon I would be plain old Lexi forever. Finally, my eyes closed and my body shut down, pushing me into a deeper sleep than I had thought possible.

My dream self, however, still couldn't forget my troubles. She wandered out of my bedroom and down the stairs, searching for the key that would access my magic. I noticed that, in my current dream state, some of the areas of the house remained shrouded in a kind of fog, and if I tried to move in those directions I ended up back on my original path; in fact, only the older rooms, the sections untouched by faerie magic, were accessible to me.

When I entered those areas, they seemed familiar and alien all at once; wainscoting that I had painstakingly helped Evian whitewash when I was eight or nine was once again stained dark to match the chestnut floors. I recognized an antique sideboard that had been relocated to another room, resting in its original spot and holding an old, long-dead Christmas cactus. Killed when Terra's attempt to teach me some horticultural responsibility had ended in failure. It was my house, but it was as it had been in the past when Clara and Sylvana still lived—of that, I was suddenly, unquestionably sure.

With morbid fascination and complete control of my dream self, I made my way through each of the other rooms, examining every corner and crevice while I had the opportunity, and noticed that the mist curling around what was left of the present had receded as I became entrenched in the past.

My grandmother's room hadn't changed, so I returned to the one that might hold secrets about the mother I'd never have a chance to know.

The door looked the same as ever. Antique oak with six panels in the honey color of aged whiskey. As they always did, my eyes sought the familiar pattern of a face in the fine grain of the old wood.

When I was little, I thought the face belonged to a sprite that lived in the door and watched over me. What might sound creepy to others comforted me, and I found similar patterns throughout the entire house. Dozens of faces watched me wherever I went. Some kids have imaginary friends, I had wood elves. That doesn't make me weird, does it?

One deep breath, then another and I opened the door. I found myself standing in the middle of a teenage girl's—no, a teenage witch's—sanctuary. Eyes wide, I surveyed the room that was at once my own and yet, not mine at all.

Sylvana seemed to have been caught between two worlds. I knew the feeling. Posters of rock and roll gods shared wall space with woven tapestries depicting various symbols of Wiccan lore: a tree of life, the five elements, and even the goddess Athena in all her glory.

What looked to me like the entire night sky of stars spotted the ceiling, hand painted in intricate detail, complete with astrologically-correct constellations. I wondered if the godmothers had painted over this particular piece of artwork, or if at some point, Sylvana had grown tired of the sight and covered it herself.

Hunger to know her better fed the great, keening sense of loss that welled up in me. What kind of evil would drive a mother to kill her own daughter? Only a level of darkness I hoped I would never understand.

The vanity I had spent my own teen years preening in front of sat in a place of honor against the far wall, exactly where my bathroom door was now. Testing the limits of the dream, I reached for a tube of lipstick and it felt solid in my hand. Flipping it over, I read the tag on the bottom. Cherry Red.

Nice color.

Sprawled across the scarred top was a collection of makeup in a palette similar to my own preferences, and I wondered for the millionth time whether Sylvana carried the same coloring and features.

Instinctively, I opened the middle drawer and reached into a secret compartment near the back. My hand closed around a stack of photographs bound with a ribbon, and I knew that in a few seconds I could be gazing at the first picture of my mother I had ever seen.

I barely caught a glimpse of the first photo in the stack—a girl, her head turned from the camera, wild jet black hair cascading in curly tendrils to cover her face—when a noise echoing from the hallway diverted my attention. The tufted ottoman I had been sitting on went up in a cloud of dark matter, as did the rest of the room, and I was back out in the hallway again. Panicked, I jiggled the door handle to no avail and growled out my frustration and disappointment.

Twice more I heard the banging sound before identifying its origin. Whatever was making the noise was in the parlor. Full of curiosity, but still mindful of danger, I crept down the hall to take a look.

The twinkle of the Balefire and the sound of it crackling in the fireplace drew me closer, and I felt Salem's furry cat body entwine a figure eight around my legs. He let out an almost human yowl, looked me straight in the eyes and ran a few feet ahead of me as if beckoning me to follow. As I neared the hearth the fire's glow began to grow until it shone brighter than I had ever seen it during my lifetime.

It drew me in; I was mesmerized by the flame, and the raw power I saw reflected there. As if on a reel, I saw my life play out as it should have, in a matter of mere seconds; me growing up as a witch, tending the flame and wielding a magic broom, its willow binding bursting at the seams with fresh birch twigs; my mother running with me through a field of daisies, our dark hair spilling down our backs; dancing under a full moon, communing with a benevolent goddess, my heart full; and finally, me exploding with newfound power, my pure intentions solidifying as a vow to do only good with my gifts.

Okay, so maybe my dream life resembled a TV commercial for insurance or some such.

As soon as it began, the vision within a dream was over. Something in the flame caught my eye and I blinked away tears at the sudden brightness. Salem let out another ear-piercing yowl and curled himself around my crouching legs, back and forth, before trotting over to the fire grate and meowing again. This time, when I looked into the flame, I could clearly see a handle positioned in the very center of it.

What on earth was the reasoning behind that? For more than three hundred years a fire—fed by magic—has burned on this hearth. Handles are made to be handled. Isn't that how they got the name in the first place? Putting one in the only place in the house it could never be touched seemed like an odd choice to me.

Pondering of that conundrum only lasted a moment before an otherworldly force intruded on my consciousness. In total shock, I watched as my own hand reached toward the flame—reached right through it actually. I grabbed the handle and pulled.

Chapter 10

Shrill pandemonium sucked away the memory of my dreams long before sleep had time to restore either body or soul, leaving behind only a vague notion something important might have happened, but no detail of what.

I swear my eyelids made a sucking sound when they peeled open—not that I could hear it. My head swung around to orient my sight on the alarm clock I didn't remember setting. Batting it off the nightstand hard enough to send it scooting across the floor only served to unplug it from the wall while the noise continued unabated.

What the hell was going on?

Heart racing against the rush of adrenaline, I catapulted out of bed, tangled my feet in the sheets, and went down hard enough to score a carpet burn on my chin and knock the wind out of me. Not my finest moment. My one consolation was Salem being the only witness to my ungainly bed exit, and he wouldn't be telling the tale.

"What is that horrible noise?" So much for the silencing charm. My ears rang. I think my eyes rang. Another minute and they might have started bleeding.

Halfway to the kitchen, I realized the noise sounded a little bit like opera music. Twisted and insane opera music playing at a volume you would hear if you were standing right inside the soprano's mouth while she sang.

I skidded into the room like a cartoon character and came to a dead stop with my arms waving a little. There was a nymph in the middle of my kitchen.

A naked nymph.

Yeah, that's how you can tell them from other denizens of the Faelands—the nudity. I think I said something like *ack* and reversed my trajectory.

In the living room, Evian smirked at me.

"What? I…What is happening in there?"

"Dutch Elm disease," Evian explained without providing illumination.

"And the nymph is trying to scare the disease out of the tree." I could see how that might work.

Evian smirked, "Something like that. Rhenei is a Hamadryad. Her singing promotes healing and regrowth."

"To trees. Not to humans," I pointed out. "Is she

almost done?"

"Great Goddess, I hope so." Evian rolled her eyes.

"What happened to the silencing charm on my bedroom? You know most of my work is done at night. I'm not a sunrise girl." I grumbled.

"Just sharing the love." Evian joked. "Go back to bed, it will be quiet now."

Easier said than done. Salem snuggled up against the small of my back, but my mind would not quiet enough to be lulled back to sleep. Images from a half-forgotten dream—the kind that you just know was important—surfaced, then slipped away every time I closed my eyes. That maddening feeling of anticipating some nebulous event lured me out of bed. A few hours sorting through the closet in the office might drive the teeth-chattering emotions back into submission.

The unholy racket continued in the kitchen, and I needed coffee now. Like in an IV, stat. Northeastern spring mornings can bring brisk temperatures, but today no breeze cooled the warmth of the sun. I grabbed a warmer jacket anyway and detoured into the garage. Driving a car, while a skill I have mastered, is not something I do unless I have to. I can't explain why, but I feel like I'm climbing into the belly of a beast every time the car door closes behind me.

It might have to do with Soleil—the first one of my faerie godmothers to score a license—being the worst driver on the planet. I'm an orphan with safety issues, what can I say? Almost everything I ever need to do plays out within a reasonable walking distance from home anyway. For those days, like today, when I needed to roam farther or faster, I had Pinky.

Pinky is a vintage Vespa. Flix insisted she was a stepping stone to something worthy, like a Harley, but I loved her just the way she was. And right then, she was going to get me to coffee in half the time it would take to walk. Grinning, I slid into the bubblegum-colored helmet that matched Pinky's gleaming paint and plunked down on her vinyl seat.

She fired right up with a satisfying sound, so I zipped out the door and down the drive where I nearly ran over Kin Clark. Did I mention I'm not a morning person?

Kin managed to step aside in the nick of time and I brought Pinky to a gravel-spewing stop while my heart galloped on ahead.

"Are you all right? I'm so sorry. I didn't mean..." The words trailed off when I saw the look on his face. He wasn't mad, he was laughing at me. Apparently, my overly enthusiastic kiss from the other night hadn't scared him away.

I wondered if he had thought about it as much as I had; if he had replayed it over and over in *his* mind, finishing out what might have happened if we hadn't been interrupted. Oh jeez, now I was blushing—and wondering if he'd stopped by specifically to see me this morning.

"If it isn't Lexi Balefire and the pink rocket," his mocking lacked malice. "The least you could do is take me for a ride and buy me a coffee. After all, you almost killed me back there."

"I…um…okay." Under the helmet, I wore almost no makeup. A coffee date had not been part of my agenda. No graceful method of refusal popped into my mind, a fact I totally blame on being awake so early in the morning.

Kin slid on behind me, wrapped his arms loosely around my waist, and I forgot how to drive. Only for a second, until the warmth of his chest against my back relaxed my busy brain. Keeping Pinky at a sedated pace—you know, for safety's sake, not because it felt so good to be cocooned against Kin—I drove us into the heart of the city and parked in the alley behind my office. It was easier to walk from there than to find parking near The Grind.

Helmet hair. That's what you want to show a guy in the bright light of day. Kin didn't seem to notice and while I examined that thought for possible subtext, I tripped over an uneven spot in the sidewalk.

"I swear I'm not really a klutz." Kin's hand on my arm steadied me until I regained my footing.

"You're not usually up and around when I leave for work." How did he know that? Was he watching the house or something? That was either sweet or creepy.

"There was a..." Words failed me. *Singing nymph in my kitchen* was not a wise ending to that sentence. "...disturbance this morning."

"Sounded like someone was flogging a dying cat. I hope Salem hasn't met his maker."

"Oh, you heard that?" I made a note to remind the godmothers that disturbing the neighborhood wasn't the best way to win friends and influence people. Sometimes they forget that small things count.

"Heard it? No. It was more like a visceral experience," Kin joked, "I can hook you up with new speakers if you want. From the sounds of things, yours are totally blown."

I snorted. I couldn't help myself. "Thanks for the offer, but it wasn't a mechanical malfunction."

"Alternative music, then. Interesting. Like Peruvian throat singing? Maybe you could loan me the CD sometime."

"You wouldn't believe me if I did," I muttered and then changed the subject. "Do you need me to drop you at work after this?" He was too interested in things I had no valid explanation for. Most of what went on at my house went far beyond the realm of normal. "I don't have any clients today, so I'm headed into the office for a bout of spring cleaning." The perfect explanation for my lack of personal grooming. Nobody dresses up to clean their office, right?

"Nope, I have the day off." He gave me a crooked

smile. "Buy me lunch in exchange for my services and I'll give you a hand. You can't beat that for a deal."

I think I managed to keep my mouth from dropping open. Who volunteers for cleaning duty?

"Okay, I guess I can find you something to do." There are worse things than having a hot guy at your beck and call. Right now I couldn't think of a single one, though. "First, coffee." I needed it now more than ever.

"Lexi." I got the standard Cheers-style greeting when I walked through the door and before I made it to the counter in the rear of the store, my regular order was waiting for me. Not even caring about burning my tongue, I guzzled a few swallows and waited for the sweet, sweet burst of caffeine to clear my mind.

"Give the man whatever he wants, Pete," I pointed to Kin, "And I'm still waiting to see those photos of the new baby."

"Even better," the smile of pride on Pete's face warmed my heart, "Elena's in the back. Wait one minute, okay?" Pete disappeared and returned with an arm around his wife who cradled an infant in her capable hands.

"You want to hold her?" Elena's pride shone through the smile on her face. She didn't wait for me to answer but handed me the pink bundle topped by a tiny head covered with dark fuzz. I'm more used to setting up the circumstances that lead to making babies than actually holding them, so the whole transaction felt awkward and strange.

I shot a wide-eyed glance Kin's way, then looked down into innocent blue eyes that blinked back at me. One second was all it took to turn me from a fully grown adult with a fairly wide vocabulary to a nonsense-spewing baby-talker. I think babies are magic that way. The babbling lasted until the tiny face screwed up and turned red. A rumbling, liquid sound erupted from the area under my cupped hand and the powdery baby smell I'd been enjoying turned considerably less sweet.

A lot less reluctantly than I would have done a minute before, I passed the pretty pink bundle back to her mother and when her hand brushed my own the world flipped over without warning.

Kin told me later that my eyes rolled back in my head. I thought I was dying, right there in the coffee shop. Even hopped up on faerie wine I don't get the head spins. Dry mouth and a headache, sure, but I'm never disoriented. Fingers tightened on my arms as Kin lowered me into a chair and, in the same motion, pushed my head down between my legs.

From a great distance, I heard him calling my name, but I was too far down the rabbit hole to answer. Symbols written in sparkling blue light branded themselves across the inside of my fluttering eyelids. A heart, a lightning bolt, that circle with a line through it that means no, and a couple more glittering images paraded past my inner vision. As they did, I felt a sense of recognition, almost as if an old friend had finally come home. When it was all over, I basked in the sense of rightness—of balance—that came over me.

"Call 911." Kin's voice seemed unnaturally loud as his warm hand chafed mine. "I'm right here, Lexi. You're going to be okay." His tone belied the reassuring words. He was scared. How cute.

"No, I'm okay. It's okay." I forced my eyes open and waited for the blur that was his face to clear. "It was…my blood sugar must have dropped." I struggled to sit up, but Kin held me down. "Mackintosh Clark, you let me up right now. I'm perfectly fine."

Reluctantly, he obeyed, but his face was dark and worried.

"I think you should see a doctor. At least get checked out."

"No. Everything is fine. I feel perfectly healthy." I scrambled to my feet. "Though, I have to admit my pride is a little bruised. I left the house without eating breakfast. It's not a big deal." That last part was a complete lie.

Whatever it was that had just happened was more than a big deal—it was life-changing—of that I was certain, but I needed time to ponder the experience. Pete snatched the bag holding my breakfast order off the counter—a sesame bagel slathered with veggie cream cheese—and ordered me to eat.

"We're not leaving until you do." Kin stuck his chin in the air and stared me down with a cocked eyebrow until I took the first bite.

"Fine. I'm starving anyway." I replied with the same attitude as if I'd followed it with a petulant *I'm doing it because I want to, and not because you told me to.*

By the time I finished, the previous half hour seemed like a waking dream. One that triggered a fleeting memory of flame and caused my heartbeat to speed up a little.

Meanwhile, Kin drank his coffee and watched me like a hawk for signs of a relapse.

"You have seriously got to stop staring at me." Placing one hand on my heart, I raised the other in the air, "I promise to never skip breakfast again. Are you happy now?"

Reluctantly, Kin let it go and followed me back to FootSwept where I unlocked the door and let us in.

To be honest, it was a bit unnerving having him see where I spend most of my time; I've never had a boyfriend to speak of, and I would never bring a date to work with me, so Kin was the first person I was sort-of involved with who had ever come to my office.

He looked around in a manner I could only describe as *nosy* and then turned to me with both hands outstretched. "Where's the big mess. This looks pretty neat and tidy to me." FootSwept isn't a big business; I typically deal with no more than three clients at a time. I don't videotape them, or have them make testimonials; there's no wait list, and I'm not actually a dating service. Most of my work takes place around town, and in the space beyond the door I hadn't led Kin through yet. But it's my space, and I love it.

The main reception area looks more like a living room than an office. I have a fireplace, a cluster of cozy chairs, and a table that doubles as my desk. Abstract paintings and some pretty pillows provide a pop of color. The whole room is designed to put clients at ease.

"It's nothing like I expected." Kin wasn't the first person to say that.

"This is my favorite part." I opened the door leading to the closet and gave Kin the tour.

He let out a low whistle and sat down on Flix's gleaming barber's chair. "Well, I can see why. It looks like the back room of a department store in here."

"Yeah, if it exploded. That's why I'm here on my day off." I picked up a couple of hangers and Kin started handing me discarded items. "My last client was a browser. Or a tornado. She tore through here in about three minutes. Made it easy to see why she's having trouble finding a match."

"How does all this work, anyway? And who is that guy in the photo?" he asked, pointing toward the glamour shot of Flix with his chest bared that took up the entire back wall of the salon.

I laughed. "That's Flix, my partner. He works on an on-call basis; runs the salon, keeps the closet stocked, and manages what little PR we do. And he's my friend. As far as how this works, well, mostly I follow my instincts. I know a lot of people, and I do a lot of networking around town."

Usually, I avoided questions like that with a simple "trade secrets" riff, and even though there was no way I was going to tell Kin I used my witchy intuition to identify a person's true soul mate, it felt wrong, somehow, to brush off the question. Maybe I liked him more than I was willing to admit.

"So you what, polish them up till they look shiny and new, and then go with them to meet their future husbands? Or wives." Kin corrected himself.

I sighed. "Not exactly. Only about half the people I work with end up coming in here. It's the ones who come to me obsessed with the idea of finding someone—anyone—they can believe is the one. Usually, by the time I get them, they've spent time on the roller coaster of life with unsuitable relationships and have suffered all sorts of emotional damage.

"The clothes and the hair and the attention are worth at least a few good therapy sessions on overcoming low self-esteem. A lot of them end up with someone they already knew but were too scared to ask out. I'm more of an orchestrator than anything else. And I have a very high success rate."

If Kin picked up on my defensiveness, he didn't let on. "It must be nice to help people like that. True love is a rare and magical thing." It took everything I had not to snort.

"Have you ever been in love?" I can't believe I asked him that, but my mouth had a mind of its own.

"Not really." He shook his head, "I thought so once, but it didn't work out. People change. Some people were never who you thought they were, to begin with. What about you?"

"I'm exactly who I say I am. Open book." A total lie that was sure to bite my ass at some later date.

Kin laughed. "Good to know, but I meant have you ever been in love."

"Oh, that. No, never. Always a matchmaker, never a match."

I turned away from him and made myself busy with the hangers so he wouldn't see just how painful a question that was to answer. Seconds later, I felt the warmth of his body against my back.

"Maybe your luck is about to change." His voice grew husky and he gently spun me around to face him. I held my breath as he leaned in and kissed me.

Chapter 11

Thinking it best to stop the epic make out session with Kin before things turned carnal, I dropped him at his front door and refused his offer to come inside. He held the tips of my fingers until our arms were stretched between us, refusing to let go until the last possible second like a scene from an overly-dramatic movie. The dopey smile lingered on my face until I approached my front walkway and prepared for another possible disaster.

I tiptoed through the front door, sniffing the air for any clue as to whether the dark windows I saw from the street were a good thing or a bad thing. The acrid smell I anticipated was absent, and it seemed nobody was home. Maybe Evian had dragged the rest of them to her underwater grotto for an evening of…whatever it was they did there.

After briefly considering calling Flix over for wine,

chick flicks, and a second-by-second breakdown of my entire afternoon with Kin, I realized I'd have to bring up the incident at the coffee shop. What was I supposed to say about that when I hadn't even had time to process the implications.

Hell, who was I kidding? I didn't have enough information to even consider the implications, much less process any of them. Was it some sort of witch fit? A leftover from the Awakening ritual? Or a symptom of some sort of mania?

What else besides powerful magic ran in my family? Too bad there was no one left to ask. Besides, what was so scary about seeing shiny heart symbols? Probably the *almost but not quite a witch* equivalent of a migraine.

With no better explanation, I turned my thoughts to other things.

Inside my bedroom, I kicked off the uncomfortable flats that had rubbed a blister into my heel throughout the day and shoved them under the bed. Undressing quickly, I changed into a pair of super stretchy yoga pants and a soft cotton camisole and took a seat at the old, antique vanity.

Suddenly, the piece seemed out of place, crammed into a corner across from the foot of my bed. Some niggling part of my brain insisted that it would look better along the other, longer wall where the sun coming through the big bay window would provide the perfect amount of light in the mornings. Too bad the bathroom door was positioned right in that exact spot.

Like a forgotten dream or a ghost from the past, a different image of the room swam over the reality before the vision faded and everything looked normal again.

My own tired face, and dull eyes stared back at me from the gilt-trimmed mirror. The minute I walked back through the front door, the weight of my family legacy had crept over me like a pall. I couldn't stop imagining what would happen if I lost the faeries.

Or the Balefire.

Or my business.

If the magic in my blood powered my matchmaking intuition, would that go bye-bye along with everything else at a minute past midnight on Beltane?

What would I do then? Who would I be? Lexi Balefire, washout witch, that's who.

I opened the top drawer of the vanity and was about to shove all the various tubes of lip gloss and eyeliner pencils into it when that absurd, irritating feeling of Deja vu came over me. Reaching into the drawer, guided by the overwhelming feeling that there would be something different this time, I slipped my hand into the secret compartment in the back.

My fingers closed around a thick stack of photographs, and the feel of the rough edges made my heart skip a beat. I looked through the familiar images: me with Evian, Terra, and Soleil at a Halloween party when I was about seven, dressed as a witch in a black pointy hat, them in full faerie mode during the one night of the year when they could let the glamour slip; me and my poor prom date who didn't yet realize his soul mate was another boy from our history class; several more photos fluttered to the floor, all the same, me and my happy but misfit family.

A rush of emotions gnawed at me; disappointment mostly, but not directed anywhere in particular. It felt as though I was repeating actions I had already taken, and that something that was supposed to happen hadn't yet. A lousy end to a perfectly weird, yet partly wonderful day. I didn't know what any of it meant, and so I hastily finished removing my makeup, brushed my teeth and, grabbing a mystery novel, headed for my bed.

With no faeries around to yell at me about leaving crumbs between the sheets, I changed trajectory and went to the kitchen for a package of cookies. White chocolate with macadamia nuts would pair well with a glass of cold milk. Who says milk and cookies are for kids? I needed the distraction of living someone else's life for a little while.

Salem, who normally just curled up next to me and continued the nap he spent most of his time enjoying, was standing at attention on the edge of my bed when I returned. He let out a yowl and hopped down, ran to the door and began scratching at the frame.

"All right, all right, already. I'll let you out, silly." I

opened the door and he bolted halfway down the hall, then back, entwining himself between my legs and running on ahead again. That niggling feeling from before returned, but with a sudden intensity that made my eyes pop open in surprise. This seemed too familiar, and I could distinctly remember Salem acting the same way, though I couldn't pinpoint when, exactly.

I followed the visceral pull that had begun to build in my belly, the same one that guided me toward other people's soul mates, and wound up in the parlor, where Salem was perched in front of the fireplace, gazing at me expectantly.

"What is it?" I asked as if he might answer. When he didn't, I crouched down next to him, and as I got close to the grate the Balefire flame began to grow. Salem yowled once more and rubbed against my legs again. Suddenly, I remembered my dream from the other night and, without thinking, plunged my hand straight into the fire and felt it close around the mysterious handle.

I looked down at my hand, which should have been scorched to the bone, and wasn't even surprised to see it completely intact. Wondering briefly if I was still dreaming, I gave the handle a tug and heard a loud *thud* coming from the space behind the chimney. I stood up and watched in amazement as the wall began to shake and the entire fireplace rotated, creating an opening large enough for me to walk through.

Salem darted in and disappeared into the darkness. I followed, my heart pounding in my chest. My hands shook in time to the frantic beat, and my pulse tapped out the tattoo in my ears. If someone had said *boo*, I probably would have passed out.

It shouldn't have surprised me that an entire room could have been hidden here the whole time, even considering that Evian's bedroom was positioned on the other side of the fireplace, but I still couldn't contain my disbelief. I jumped at the sound of the wall closing behind me, and squinted as the dim light from the Balefire radiated from the fireplace that was now facing into the secret room. As I spun around to survey my surroundings, I wondered if the parlor now featured a blank wall where the fireplace had been.

What I saw when my eyes finally adjusted to the firelight left no doubt in my mind that I had just taken a giant step on the path to awakening my power. Sticking my hand in a magical fire was only the beginning. When my heart set to pounding again, it was with anticipation as much as fear.

An elevated, circular stone platform dominated the center of the room, spanning at least ten feet in diameter. A basic pentacle, one of the most recognized and frequently misunderstood emblems of witchcraft, took up the entire sphere. The five points of the star were spaced equidistant around a thick border meant to denote the link between the elements of earth, air, fire, water, and spirit, and I knew this had been where my family had practiced the craft for generations. But that wasn't even the most impressive thing about the space.

A glass dome roofed the area above the dais, providing a clear view of the moon and stars overhead. Across from my position at the entrance, I spied a wrought iron spiral staircase leading to an upper balcony lined with shelf after shelf of old, leather-bound volumes. Everything I could have ever wanted to know about witchcraft, hiding in a room of wonders behind the fireplace that held the very Balefire which I was bound to tend. Talk about irony.

The outer edge of the room was broken into sections, and I wandered through each one while Salem trotted along at my heels. One alcove featured an alchemy station, vial after vial of viscous liquids, strange ingredients, and a series of pipes and burners I couldn't even begin to understand. I examined several of the bottles lining the shelves around the space, passing over some of the more normal ingredients—the perfectly preserved lavender blossoms and the pastel pink rose petal dust—and wrinkled my nose at others.

What any white witch would need with spider legs and toad eyes I couldn't fathom, but then again, what did I really know about the ways of the wicked? The outcomes, sure, but the exact mechanics were beyond fuzzy. Still, the jar of dehydrated turkey gizzards was what really sent me over the edge, and I decided to reexamine this particular cache another time.

Further into the dark depths of the room, another area held a waist-high, heavy wooden table covered with partitioned boxes filled with every kind of gem and crystal imaginable. More boxes hung on the walls, displaying the biggest, most impressive members of the collection. I recognized many, dredging up the names of the more common, such as moonstone and lapis with ease, and somehow pulling the term shungite from my memory as I handled a small, shiny black stone.

It would take me weeks, months, or even years to pick through the treasures surrounding me, and it wouldn't matter in the least if I didn't figure out how to move forward and harness my power. The answer was close, I could tell, so I reluctantly abandoned a shelf full of runes and tarot cards positioned next to a table with a very large, clear quartz crystal gazing ball and returned to the center of the main space.

How had I missed the large pedestal positioned in the middle of the carved pentacle? Or the big leather-bound book laying open on top of it?

Trembling, I placed one bare foot on top of the dais and held my breath, waiting to be flung from the platform, an unworthy, powerless mortal. When that didn't happen I nearly ran to the pedestal and fingered the yellowed pages of the ancient volume I was sure was my family's Grimoire.

Now, some witches call this type of book a Book of

Shadows, or a Book of Magic; most are handed down through the generations, and others are created by solitary witches for their own use. They've all got to start somewhere, right?

Magic evolves just as any other science or art would, and any witch worth her ritual salt knows well enough to keep her Grimoire a secret from everyone other than her nearest and dearest. I couldn't help thinking greedily that there must be some pretty interesting spells in this one for my family to have erected an entire secret lair to protect the thing.

Except that when I looked closer, I found that all of the pages were blank. Of course; I had been given too much, too fast. Why would my luck change now? Angry, I flipped the book over. There was no title or author, only the likeness of a tree embossed on the cover—a tree with a flame where the leaves should have been.

Immediately, I recognized the symbol; heck, I looked at it nearly every day, except that there, on a pendant hanging around the neck of my grandmother's statue, it was carved into stone rather than leather.

My hand fluttered to my own throat, almost instinctively, and I fingered the pendant that had, in a matter of days, become a treasured object. At that exact second Salem, careening out from beneath a brocade settee near the fireplace, ran straight in between my feet and knocked me to the floor.

As my fist closed around the necklace I felt the same sharp jab I had the other night in the bathtub, and then the warm dampness of a smear of blood against my palm. Scurrying to my feet, I suddenly knew what I needed to do; my own blood had opened the door for me to See, so it only stood to reason that my own blood would activate the book.

I took a deep breath, placed my hand on the cover of the volume, and sent up a silent prayer. I heard a buzzing noise, and then everything went black.

Chapter 12

I woke up on the floor, my head cocked at an uncomfortable angle, and the edge of the dais digging into my hip. Seconds passed while I tried to remember where I was and I had to blink several times to bring my unfamiliar surroundings into focus. Like an image from a dream, the Balefire washed cleansing flame against the hearthstones. Brighter, stronger than I had ever seen before, the flickering tongues snapped and crackled.

Memories slid back in layer after layer. The spell had worked. Not like I expected, but then I hadn't really known what to expect. Presumably, most initiate witches already have access to their Book of Shadows when it comes time to awaken their powers, which meant that part of the spell hadn't been added to the list. Finding this place—my family's sanctum—was the last piece of the puzzle.

"What the hell just happened?" I asked aloud, and

nearly peed my pants when a deep, velvety voice behind me purred, "You've finally been Awakened."

I spun around, my hair whipping in an arc across my back, and stared at the striking man draped languidly over the chaise lounge where Salem had been sitting when everything went wonky. His skin was black as night and smooth as silk; in complete contrast to the shock of pure white hair dangling over one eye. The other, a vibrant shade of blue, sparkled with a mischievous glint that looked oddly familiar—I would have giggled had I known just how accurate that description was.

"Who the hell are you?" I revised my previous question, mouth agape, wondering how anyone could have gotten into the room behind me and not caring how rude I sounded. How long had I been passed out, anyway?

The man rose with catlike grace and perched on the edge of the chair, flicking the hair from his forehead to expose the other eye, this one bright emerald green, and raised one eyebrow.

"Salem?" I sputtered, feeling my blood pressure start to rise.

He walked over to me and looked me square in the face, then grinned from ear to ear. "Well, you got one right."

"But how? What? Wait, what's going on here? You're human? This whole time?" The implications begun to set in and I felt my stomach do another somersault.

"Not entirely. I'm your familiar—I assume you know what that means?"

Of course I had heard of a familiar; every modern day portrayal of a witch includes a cat as a companion, and I had heard tell of witches and wizards who could talk to animals—but I had never been told of a cat who turned into a man. Just one of the many secrets I hadn't been privy to all these years. It felt as though the short end of the proverbial stick had been crammed up my butt.

"So you've been in my bedroom, listening to me whine and cry all these years? That's a little creepy, you know. You could have given me some kind of signal or something, couldn't you?" I demanded.

Salem sighed, and rolled his eyes. "I've been waiting for you to access your magic. Took you long enough, didn't it? But, no matter, you've finally Awakened, and I'm going to help you learn to use your new powers."

"So you were there when I was crying because Bobby Nash dumped me right before the prom? And when I lost my virginity to that punk rocker dude with the squirrel tattoo and went through every dirty detail with Flix?"

My face blushed pink. "And you've seen me naked."

Some part of my brain screamed that this was a ludicrous conversation to be having with *my cat*, but somehow it didn't bother me as much as it should have. I was giddy with the sensation of magic in my veins but hadn't quite grasped the concept of that yet, and so was focusing on Salem instead. I had always thought he was nearly human, and now I could chalk it up to witchy intuition. Nobody needed to know that wasn't entirely true.

"First of all, *eww*. I am a cat, not a man, so you can relax. This form simply allows me to communicate and assist you more easily. Secondly, your life isn't as fantastically scintillating as you might think. Do you know how many angst-filled teenage conversations I have suffered through?" He cast a disapproving look in my direction. "And yet, I have still tried to steer you toward the correct path."

I weaved a little and let human Salem guide me over to sit next to him. His skin was warm to the touch, and satin smooth, and I could see where his lush cat coat had come from. Or maybe it worked the opposite way. A cloud of dust puffed out of the couch as I settled in, and I waved it away with a flick of my hand. It went up in a momentary shower of sparks, then flickered out and disappeared. Whoa, did I really do that?

Salem ignored my fireworks show, "Of all the witches I've guided through all of my lives, you've taken the longest to find your path. Now, will you accept my help or do you want to keep imagining all the things I might know about you? I'm happy to answer any questions you have for me, but you've got to start thinking that maybe it's a *good* thing I know you better than anyone else does."

"So, you'll answer *any* question I want to ask?" I hedged.

"That's my purpose, yes. What would you like to know?"

About a thousand thoughts whirled around my head; Why had it taken so long for the spell to work? What was I supposed to do next? Did he know the Easter Bunny? I latched onto one of the more inconsequential ones that kept ricocheting off the sides of my skull.

"What do you mean, *all* your lives? And how many witches have you…helped?"

"Well, see, cats have nine lives…" he began, rolling his eyes skyward.

"Don't get persnickety with me; how am I supposed to know that's true?" I crossed my arms and glared at him.

He shot me a glance, complete with raised eyebrow, that prompted me to shut my mouth and so, gritting my teeth as I did, I motioned for him to go on.

"I have been familiar to eight witches before coming into your service, which means you are my final charge. My life—lives—are tied to the life of the witch

I'm currently serving. When you die, I will also die and this time, I will not return. So please, if you've enjoyed my company at all, try not to meet your death too early." Salem's voice took on a foreboding tone.

"No pressure or anything! Wait, so how long have you lived over all of your lives? I know witches age slower than other people, but that hasn't seemed to affect me. And what will happen after you die?" I was bursting with wonder at this point. Question after question popped into my head, each one sparking another.

Salem licked his lips in a decidedly catlike manner and continued calmly. "Even witches age normally up to a certain point, and I don't know what happens after we die any more than you do. Is there a heaven for beings like me? I certainly hope so. I have lived 675 years over eight lifetimes. And you—"

"Hold on," I did some quick division and cast an inquisitive glance at Salem, who refused to meet my gaze, "that's an average of only about 80 years per witch—I wouldn't call that an extended lifetime. Soleil used to tell me tales about witches who lived a thousand years…or were those just bedtime stories?"

He stuck his nose in the air and his eyes settled on a point just above my head. "Your godmother told the truth, but not all witches survive that long. There is no normal, which shouldn't come as much of a shock to you. Everything you do comes back to you threefold—I am aware that you know that saying, but I'm not sure if you fully understand what it means. That phrase typically goes hand in hand with harm none, do what ye will. At least, that's how your kind chooses to put it."

This cat…man…whatever he was, slept at the foot of my bed for years, and while his circumstances had just undergone an enormous change, I knew him well enough to see he was trying to hide something.

"Of course I understand what that means; it's not exclusive to witches. Nearly everyone in the world agrees that you reap what you sow." I motioned for him to hurry up and get to the interesting part.

"Right, but humans have control over very little energy compared to the amount a witch can wield. How she treats herself and others, what she puts into the world, how she formulates and realizes her intention—all of those things require different kinds of energy."

Lectured to by a cat. Not even the most bizarre event this week. What does that say about my life?

"Intention plays a more substantial role in magic than you ever thought. The energy a witch can harness not only comes from, but also contributes to her life source, and the nature of that energy—may it be pain and vengeance or love and healing—dictates what kind of life she leads. It's a circular pattern."

If he said the word energy one more time, I was going to scream.

"That makes it sound like my lifespan is dependent upon whether I'm a good witch or a bad witch. Maybe that's why my mother and grandmother died so young—because Clara's intentions carried enough evil to kill them both."

Salem sighed, and his voice softened. "Lexi, I wish I had information about how you lost your family, but I was—well, it doesn't really matter where I was."

He dashed my hopes.

"Everyone—human, Fae, witch, demon, familiar—we all have good and bad in us. Now, there are witches who send what we would term "evil" out into the world and who manage to outrun karma; they might stay alive for centuries, but their souls turn dark."

Clara, obviously. Probably passed her darkness on to me, too. Blast the witch.

Choosing his words delicately, Salem added, "There are others who put out only good intentions and still manage to be," a hesitation, "relieved of the mortal coil before their time."

Curling my legs under me, I waited for an explanation of the odd turn of phrase, but Salem just kept talking.

"But most fall somewhere in the middle; it's not about reward and consequence—it's about being affected by what you create."

Sounded a bit new-agey to me, and somewhat esoteric.

"Even if I can't shed light on what happened, I've known you long enough to know you weren't born from dark people. There was more than enough good in them to have turned the tide another way." He patted my knee.

"It's up to you to decide what kind of life you're going to lead now; what kind of intention you're going to put into the world because it doesn't matter what happened before. You can choose a different path." His words calmed me, and I tucked the notion away for later reflection.

"Does this all mean that you've been familiar to witches who…were on the receiving end of some bad karma?"

Salem sighed. "Some of my companions could have made better choices, yes."

"What happened to them?" I was beginning to wonder why he was being so cagey.

"If you must know, one was killed during a quest for more power. One, tragically, stepped into the street at the wrong moment and was hit by a bus. And then there were a couple who were…blown up." He refused to meet my gaze.

"What do you mean, blown up?" My voice reached a fever pitch.

"Spells go wrong, things happen. Enough bad mojo, or a moment of inattention and KABOOM! But don't worry, I'm sure that won't happen to you."

"Great, that makes me feel so much better," I said,

going for offhand and carefree and failing miserably. Then I promptly burst into tears. Salem wrapped his arms around me and let me cry on his shoulder, making a soothing noise that resembled a purr while stroking his cheek against my head in an oddly comforting way.

A few minutes passed before I pulled it together enough to sniffle my way back to normal. The crying jag had worked wonders in making me feel well enough to further explore my surroundings. Mostly, now that I had a snowball's chance in the underworld of making something happen, I wanted to try out my new magic.

The Grimoire should have a simple enough spell for my first try, so leaving Salem still curled up on the couch, I approached what I now realized was probably a casting circle. None of the photos in books or the ones I had found online had ever shown anything quite like this one. The metal pentacle was set deeply enough into the granite circle that I wondered if the trench it created was meant to hold something. Oil or water, maybe, depending on what a spell required. A vision of a dark figure in the center with fire filling the five-pointed star flitted through my mind and I shivered with a sense of dread.

"What are you doing?" Salem drawled from behind me.

"Just looking. I thought I might…"

"I know what you want to do, and I don't blame you after all this time. Start with something simple." He padded over to one of the shelves and pulled out a stubby beeswax candle. "Light this."

"With magic? Sure. Um, how?" A movie montage of possibilities played in my head. Wiggle my nose? Cross my arms and blink? Wait, that's not even a witch thing. Flick my finger or maybe just blow the flame to life.

"Use your intentions. See the flame, feel the heat, and focus your magic on making it happen. The method is unimportant, it's the intention that counts." Salem held the candle out to me and smiled encouragement.

Okay, Lexi, you can do this.

Eyes closed, I pictured the candle sparking and catching fire. When I had the image firmly in my mind, complete with heat and the smell of melting wax, I opened my eyes and blew gently on the wick. I'm telling you it was the strangest sensation. I felt the fire flow out of me.

And then the candle blew up. Sparks shooting, wax melting, and Salem snarling an ouch that sounded like an angry cat.

"What part of hearing about my former companions blowing up did you fail to understand? Are you trying to freak me out?" He hollered.

"I'm sorry, I don't know what I did wrong." I held my hands up in surrender.

"Talk about using a five-pound sledge to drive in a tack. Holy cats, Lexi. Pull it back a little." Salem peeled the melted wax off his palm while giving me a dirty look. The second candle went into a saucer-style holder.

"Try again."

Five candles later, Salem was picking cooled wax out of his hair and I was close to tears.

"I'm done for today." Sweat dribbled down my back and I felt like I had run a marathon. This magic making business was harder work than I expected. Salem practically carried me upstairs and into my bedroom where I fell asleep before my cheek hit the pillow.

Chapter 13

"Something happened last night." I had to say it three times with increasing volume before the petty bickering stopped. Vaeta shot me an annoyed glance for interrupting her during a hot retort that I took for the faerie equivalent of *I'm rubber and you're glue*.

Evian, the glue in this scenario, turned all sweetness and light. "Tell us all about it, dear." I didn't miss the scorching glare she tossed at Vaeta or the *screw you* look Vaeta returned.

"It all started the other day when Serena…"

"What did that little witch do to you? I'll turn every hair on her body black and itchy." Terra interrupted, and while the visual of Serena looking freakishly hairy while continually battling the need to scratch was satisfying, I really wanted to get through my story.

"Shut up, Terra. Let the girl tell us what happened."

Soleil gestured for me to continue, which I did, but not without an exaggerated eye roll.

"Serena took it upon herself to explain what would happen if I couldn't muster up enough magic to keep the Balefire going on my own." My tone implied I was still a little miffed about getting the information from my biggest enemy and not my family.

"I told you then, that girl doesn't have enough power to keep a candle lit, much less the Balefire. We would never let that happen."

Caught between elation and annoyance, I selected a slice of pizza and doctored it with some extra parmesan and fresh oregano. Given the frequency of my favorite comfort foods appearing on the table lately, I flirted with the idea of waiting a day or two to drop the happy news bomb.

"I appreciate the sentiment. There's more, though." This wasn't going to be a short explanation, so I took a bite and waited for the four of them to do the same, and then blurted out, "I went to Athena's for new ingredients, did the Awakening spell, and it worked." I guess there was a short version of the story after all.

"Then you're…" Evian broke the stunned silence.

"Awakened to my fullest potential." Elated, I practically chirped and waited for the cheerful, happy noises to begin.

Crickets.

Even Vaeta sported a frown when she turned to

Terra. "But how? Wasn't she supposed to have…"

"Isn't that simply wonderful news." Terra pushed away from the table to stalk around in circles. The sting of sarcasm in her tone tipped me off that my godmothers weren't seeing things in a happy light.

"I thought it was, but apparently not." Unexpected anger welled up fast and hot. "Thanks a heap. It's not like I expected champagne and party hats, but a simple *congratulations* doesn't seem like it would be too much. You know, this is coming what? Only ten years late, so it's not like it's a big accomplishment or anything, considering how close it came to never happening at all. Carry on ladies."

I flounced away. Yeah. That's right, I said flounced. I knew it was a juvenile reaction, and I didn't care. Sometimes temper tantrums happen.

"Lexi…" Soleil's soft voice followed me out of the room.

Slamming a door that is subject to a silencing charm is about as satisfying as the sensation of a tickle in your nose that produces no sneeze. No sound, not even a muffled *whump* accompanied the visual of the door shaking into its frame. Knowing Terra slapped the charm on there just to gyp me out of the satisfaction of the slam, I saw red. Actual red. Until that moment, I didn't even know that was a thing.

For a few minutes, I stomped around the room, and then, thoroughly humiliating myself, I burst into tears.

Terra's ill-timed remark had tarnished my shining moment from sparkling silver to deepest black.

"They're not angry with you. You know that, right?" Two years of my life flitted away in an adrenaline-fueled rush when Salem spoke up unexpectedly. That was going to take some getting used to.

"I'm putting a bell around your neck if you don't stop doing that."

Gracefully, Salem rose from the depths of a fur-covered polka-dotted beanbag chair in hot pink that looked like it hailed from the Jim Henson collection and came to rub his cheek against mine in a catlike manner. I don't mind telling you I found the gesture both sweet and entirely unsettling. But, it worked.

The touch of his warm skin soothed away the hurt feelings and I gave him a scratch under the chin for his efforts. I know how that sounds odd and I'm sure it looked worse, but what can I say? My life has taken a left turn into Weirdsville lately.

"Why aren't they happy for me, though? I give them the best news I've had in a long time and all I get is a snotty response." Slumping down on the bed, I picked with restless fingers at the chenille fibers on the bedspread. Terra's reaction had cut me to the bone.

"Oh, sweetie, don't you understand? You just told the three women who raised you that you don't need them anymore. Of course, they're upset."

"I never said any such thing." At least I didn't mean to. "They're my family. Even if it was their job to take care of me, they've never made me feel like I was a burden."

Salem stared at me without blinking for a lot longer than a normal human could.

"You really have no idea how faerie godmothers work, do you?"

"Sure I do…" I started to defend myself hotly, then realized I might be overstating. "Vaeta told me some stuff, but no, I guess I don't know as much as I should. Tell me."

He settled back onto the beanbag, his favored spot. "Normally it's one faerie godmother per witch and they watch from a distance. Most witches will never even meet their faerie godmother in person because you have to screw up royally before one shows up…"

That much I knew.

"…And then there's the cost. With faeries, there's usually a price for their help, even when they are doing their job."

I wrinkled my nose at the new information. What kind of jinky system was I part of, anyway?

"But they haven't…they've never…" It was a new perspective and a lot to take in all at once.

"Nope."

"And they're…" I waved a hand to express words that wouldn't come.

"Yep."

"I owe them an apology, don't I?" I levered myself up off the bed to go eat a well-earned snack of crow. On toast. With a big slice of humble pie.

"A big one, sweets. Bring me a tuna sandwich?"

I waggled my fingers over my shoulder and opened the door to the sound of complete pandemonium. Turning around and hiding in my bedroom tempted me to the point of taking a step back inside where the silencing charm would wrap me in its boon of peace. Or it would have, if the charm hadn't dissolved the second I opened the door.

Unfortunately, this fight had been mine to start and that also made it mine to end.

Shouting, booming noises, an ominous fizzling sound, and fog greeted me at the top of the stairs. Faerie-geddon round 957, *oh goodie*.

The banister felt ice-cold and slick under my hand, and probably would be useless in stopping my descent if I lost my footing—which I did just two stairs from the bottom.

Way to make an entrance, Lexi—I thought as I windmilled my arms to regain my balance.

Following the path of destruction, I straddled a swath of quicksand in the lower hall, and picked my way through the kitchen. Surprisingly, the room looked pretty normal until the refrigerator burped and spit the chewed up remains of a Tupperware bowl at me.

The patio doors were open, which I knew was a bad sign. When the godmothers took the fight outside, it was an indication that the house wasn't big enough or connected enough to the elements to hold all of the chaos they planned to draw down on each other.

Thankfully, I could see one of them had had the presence of mind to erect a barrier over the backyard. Explaining to my neighbors the presence of dragonflies as big as a dog was one of those experiences in life that I could happily live without. Being buzzed by one hit low on my list as well.

Looking at the vista before me with objectivity, I thought the product of their freaking out had turned the backyard into a wonderland. Evian and Soleil had dressed a small stand of fir trees with the evidence of their emotions. Frost-coated needles mirrored the glittering blue fire reflection of a cloudless spring sky.

One large maple tree marked Terra's less-than-gentle touch with an all-season showing that ran the gamut from spring swollen buds on the lower branches, through the palette of summer greens, fall reds and golds, to end with winter barren fingers.

A confused chickadee scolded me in human speech as I passed below her nest.

"You peck your mother with that beak?" I shouted back. The little bird had a potty mouth.

I passed a snail big enough to ride on, and a thicket of enchanted dill weed that towered over my head and made me crave pickles. Faerie dust floated through the air like wafts of cotton candy caught by a naughty wind. When a cloud of it floated toward me, I hit the ground and rolled out of the way. I've had enough run-ins with that stuff to learn it's best to steer clear.

The flutter of dust passed over me to land on a pink granite boulder that was part of Terra's decorative border. I heard a noise like an enormous zipper whizzing closed and the boulder developed an eye. I decided I'd better find another place to be in case it had a mouth and pointy teeth, too.

The garden must have multiplied in size by a factor of ten, given how long it took to navigate to the area in the farthest corner where the shouting was coming from.

"Harpy."

"Hag."

Each outburst was punctuated by banging sounds and flashes of light. Of all the faerie battles I've witnessed in my day, the ones since Vaeta's return had been the most flamboyant.

According to mythology, all the elements were supposed to have an affinity for each other. Air feeds fire; fire brings light to nourish the earth and promote new growth; earth cradles water as it flows upon and within her breast. Water provides succor.

But water and earth can stifle a fire, and air can blow the earth from bare rock, leaving no soft or fertile place to create new life. And when the sun turns cold, water freezes on the ground. Such is the duality of nature, and such is the nature of life with four elemental faeries. That which they are can be used to both create and destroy—but never so severely as when they turn their power against each other.

Fifteen yards and a maze of vines dense with thorns were all that separated me from them when all sound ceased. The sudden quiet scared me more than thunder.

Bleeding from half a dozen thorny encounters, I rounded the last corner hoping they weren't all lying dead on the ground. They weren't. The only things missing from their mannequin challenge were the person with the video camera and Black Beatles playing in the background.

"Put those down." Each grim-faced faerie held some sort of weapon trained on one of her sisters. Triggering one would set them all off in a chain reaction of epic proportions.

"Please. Put the weapons away. Clean up your mess and then come inside." I said softly. "There's something I need to say."

Sanctuary. That was what I needed. Sanctuary and wine. And my best friend. I revved Pinky's engine and sped to the office, pressing the button for Flix several more times than necessary until he shimmered into view before my eyes.

Before he even had a chance to ask, I let every detail of the story unfold. I will not describe my celebratory hopping in circles in honor of my Awakening because that would invoke a less-than-dignified mental image.

Then I told him about the godmother's reaction.

"You should have seen the backyard. I had no idea Terra would take the news so badly. Or that she would stir the rest of them up and set them off like fireworks."

Or that her negative response would suck the air from my lungs and set my guts churning. Silly me, I thought she'd be happy for me. Big mistake.

One I covered with bravado and feigned annoyance.

"How am I supposed to keep up with Fae mood swings? One minute they're fighting to beat the band, and the next they're hopped up on Twinkleberry wine and enjoying a dip in a magical hot tub, laughing and giggling like teenagers."

On a roll, I slipped up and hit him with the truth.

"The biggest thing that's ever happened to me and not a whiff of congratulations. I can see why Vaeta went MIA for a century."

All that nervous energy bubbling up inside me needed an outlet, so I decided to rearrange the furniture. Around Flix, of course, since he refused to budge.

"You'd think they'd just be happy to have her back, not that you'd have known they missed her in the first place. It's strange, the way they just pretended like she didn't exist."

Sweat beaded on my forehead as I pushed the sofa the last few inches over the carpet. Mid-rant, I noticed Flix hadn't said a word. That never happened unless he was about to drop something profound on me and felt the need to save it up until it would make the most impact.

He sat in silence while I contemplated the new arrangement, then with a sigh, moved to put everything back the way it had been before.

Five minutes later, I dropped heavily onto a seat and stared at him until he gave in.

He raised a perfectly groomed eyebrow in my direction and said quietly. "I think what's strange is that you've lived with three faeries for most of your life and don't seem to know a thing about them."

"I know plenty."

Sullen was never my best look, but that never stopped me trying it on now and then.

"I know they act like children more than half the time. You don't, so I assume that's not entirely a Fae trait."

When he paused again, I felt like a chastised schoolgirl.

"Faeries—at least, full-blood faeries—age slowly." Not what I expected him to say at all.

"Well, duh, I'm not an idiot. I can see behind the

glamour, and they haven't changed in all these years." I shot back, feeling myself start to get defensive.

"It's not just about how they look. The Fae aren't human, and can't be expected to respond to situations in the same way a person would. It's a blessing and a burden, to live such a long life and their emotions are amplified. Vaeta leaving, seemingly on purpose, was a big blow."

"I'd figured that much out for myself, thank you very much." Some things are not that hard to understand. "The sisters felt betrayed. Even so, you'd think they would have at least mentioned her at some point."

Flix contemplated and shrugged. "It's one thing to have someone be taken, and quite another when the person chooses to leave. All that pain, and now guilt over whether they should have tried rescuing her sooner; all the negative thoughts, the times they cursed her for leaving. And now, when they finally feel like all the pieces of the puzzle are at least on the table, you've Awakened and their lives are up in the air again."

And if they hadn't kept certain bits of information from me for years, I might have felt more remorse.

"You're comparing my Awakening to their sister following her hormones into the Underworld? I'm calling BS on that. Seems like they should have been doubly happy since, from what Vaeta let slip, they'd have forgotten all about me if my magic went away."

Judging from the surprised way his eyes rounded, Flix hadn't expected me to trot out that piece of news. Everyone had been hiding things from me, even him.

He snapped his mouth shut and took a moment to frame the next comment. "Terra probably worried over you getting your powers since the day they showed up and to her, it's a double-edged sword. You don't get your powers, she has to leave. You get them, you won't need her anymore, and she has to leave. Only this time, she'll remember."

Faerie logic, I supposed. Flawed to the core since I hadn't planned on asking anyone to leave.

And then he dropped the big bomb on me.

"What you ought to be worried about is why Terra didn't sense your Awakening when it happened."

I mulled over that for a moment and decided it was too much for me to process just then. "Thanks for peeing in my already soggy Cheerios."

"So tell me how it feels to be Awakened. Is it everything you hoped for?" I detected a carefully veiled hint of sarcasm and maybe even a touch of jealousy in Flix's tone.

Anyone who didn't know him as well as I did might have missed the faint flavor of sour grapes. Given his insight into faerie godmother thinking, it made sense he might be entertaining similar emotions and that was why he recognized them so readily.

"It feels like asking for a pony for your birthday

and getting an Arabian with an attitude problem. I can't even light a candle without it turning into a catastrophe, but the Balefire is burning brighter than ever and that's what counts the most right now."

Trading one failure for another. Yay.

It didn't seem like my life would be taking a turn for the simple anytime soon. Oh, joy.

Chapter 14

This time I reached into the Balefire with trepidation; yeah, it didn't burn me before, but the way things had been going since my big Awakening had me second-guessing myself more than ever. I watched the flame dance across my hand and noticed that it wasn't invincibility that allowed me to touch but not be touched; it was more like a layer of magical plastic wrap, and I wondered if it was exclusive to the Balefire blood or if all witches could play with fire.

The lever creaked, and the fireplace spun around just like the last time, and I found Salem in his human form, curled into a smaller ball than I would have thought possible for such a large man, fast asleep on the sofa.

"Ahem." I cleared my throat until he roused, reached his arms and legs wide in a lazy stretch, and finally perched himself on the edge of the seat, looking at me expectantly. "Is this all you're going to do? Lay around and sleep? That doesn't seem any different from what you did before."

"Wow, you're cheerful. What happened?" He yawned lazily.

"I just didn't expect to feel powerless at this point. I thought I'd finally be *in* control, and that's not how it's going at all." I wailed.

"You've been given all at once what most witches spend years developing, including all of the emotions that go along with it. Now that the Balefire is safe, you can focus your attention on learning the basics." Salem replied calmly.

"Like lighting candles? Is there anything less volatile I could try? Maybe conjuring up some fluffy cotton balls. Anything that won't blow up would be nice."

"Every newly Awakened witch is eager to test the limits of available magic and rarely do they manage without experiencing a few growing pains."

Salem's words calmed me down. "I can't wait to see that hag, Serena Swampgrass' face when she shows up for Beltane." The thought filled my mouth with saliva and sent a delicious shiver of anticipation up my spine. "All these years she's done nothing but berate me and now she's finally going to get what's coming to her."

A dark thought or two curled up like smoke to play a few scenarios though my head. Each one ending with

Serena in tears until the ferocity of my response scared me into locking the urges away before I acted on them. Dropping down to that level might satisfy me in the short term, but I had a conscience. Didn't I?

"If you've moved on from distress to happy vengeance, can I broach the topic of food? You've never been generous with the table scraps, and while I enjoy Reese's Pieces, would it kill you to develop a taste for some salty snacks? I can finally eat like a human again, and I have some requests." I heard a rumble from low in Salem's belly and took the opportunity to enjoy a little alone time.

"You're allowed to leave the house, right?" Salem's look said duh, but how was I supposed to know the rules?

"My purse is in my bedroom. Grab some cash from my wallet and go get us some takeout. Whatever you want. I assume you know what I like. Order for me."

I swear his ears perked at the word *takeout* and he gave me a quick peck on the cheek before pulling the lever and letting himself into the parlor.

"Not all the cash from my purse, Salem! Salem?" Oh, whatever, let him have fun. After all, how long had it been since Salem had been able to go out in public on two legs? What trouble could he possibly get into?

I ignored the half dozen scenarios, each one worse than the last, that immediately popped into my head, grabbed the leather-bound Grimoire from its place of honor at the center of the pedestal, and settled into a cross-legged position, the book open on my lap.

This time, I noticed more pages filled with spells, but they were few and far between. It seemed I was only to be allowed access to the most rudimentary; those related to cleansing, anointing, and protection. An incantation for learning a basic glamour seemed about as active as I was allowed to get, and my hand immediately fluttered to my face where a tiny pimple had started to form on the tip of my nose.

At least, I hoped it was a pimple and not a wart. Either way, if I could get the Balefire up and running I should at least be able to glamour a simple blemish from my face.

A few simple ingredients were all I needed, so I searched around for six pink candles, the biggest, darkest amethyst I could find, a sage smudging stick that looked more than a bit withered, and then grabbed a medium-sized cauldron from a collection stacked near the alchemy station.

According to the blurb at the bottom of the spell, once I had the basics down, I wouldn't need to pull out all the stops every time. I looked forward to that day.

Feeling lighter than I had in years, I bounced around, placing a pink candle at each of the five points of the carved pentacle. Then, I walked deosil, or clockwise, around the circle, lighting each candle while calling to its corresponding element in turn.

"Persephone, Rhea, Ceres; Goddesses of the North. Hear my call and lend me strength from the Earth." The wick flared and the flame turned a deep shade of amber.

"Cardea, Aradia, Nuit; Goddesses of the East. Hear my call and lend me knowledge from the Air." A bright white flame appeared, followed by red and blue as I called the next two elements. "Vesta, Hestia, Brigit; Goddesses of the South. Hear my call and lend me energy from the Fire. Isis, Aphrodite, Marianne; Goddesses of the West. Hear my call and lend me wisdom from the Water."

A shower of sparks rained from the last in the outer circle as I spoke the words "Element of Spirit, I call to you. God and Goddess unite; lend me your balance and bless me with your light. I invoke thee!"

I returned to the center of the pentacle and lit the final candle—with a match because I wasn't taking any unnecessary chances. Each wick flared once more and burned bright. I used the middle flame to light one end of the bundle of sage, the amethyst grasped tightly in my fist, and my mind set with the intention of clearing my skin.

Keeping Salem's advice firmly in mind, I held back all but a trickle of the magic that flared in me and hoped it would be enough.

The sage burned at a much faster rate than I had expected, and the smoke billowed and grew dense around me, building and building until I couldn't see two inches in front of my face. I heard a loud banging noise and the fireplace rotating, and finally Salem's muttered expletive.

When the smoke cleared and I came face to face with my familiar, he burst into mocking laughter at the sight of my complexion.

"What? What happened?" Something didn't feel quite right.

"See for yourself." Salem looked around, spotted a hand mirror, and passed it over.

I cringed instinctively as I held it up to my face. What I saw brought tears to my eyes, and not just because it looked like I had come down with the world's worst case of the chicken pox. And the mumps. And an allergic reaction, all at once.

I'm Alexis Balefire, keeper of the flame, finally in control of my birthright. Well, *control* might be an overstatement, but I was still supposed to be an extremely powerful witch, and I was failing miserably at my first spells. "Tell me what you did."

I explained the actions I had taken during Salem's junk food run, holding back my frustration as he munched happily on a cheeseburger. "You probably don't want any of this, right?" Salem asked, pointing inside the fast food bag. "You know, greasy food and acne and all that..." I pierced him with my most withering stare.

"I did exactly what the book said to do." I wailed, miserably.

Salem finally softened at my distress and wrapped a comforting arm around my shoulder. "Even if you hadn't, you shouldn't look like a teenager in the throes of a hormonal imbalance. This is certainly more blow-back than I've ever seen from such a simple spell." Salem frowned while I huddled in misery.

"I wonder if it has something to do with how late you connected to your magic, or maybe you're just putting too much into it. Overpowering the spell. Let me do some research; see what advice my comrades have to offer. Assuming they stop laughing at the length of time I've been reduced to a diet of kibble long enough to answer my questions. Don't worry, we'll sort it out. For now, maybe don't try any new spells without supervision."

"Thanks, Salem. But what do I do about my face?" If I couldn't cast a reversal spell, then how was I supposed to fix this? No way was I going to work with pizza face.

Salem arched an eyebrow and nodded toward the rest of the sanctum. "I'm going to guide you through the process of making a magical balm that will clear that right up. It's not a glamour, but an herbal remedy. There's very little actual magic, and it's more passive than what you were doing before. You'll need to catch up on your potions and herbs. Most of what's in here is usable and like new; your grandmother was a whiz at preserving spells, I'll give her that. But eventually, you're going to need to replenish your supply of bases and catalysts."

I tuned out when Salem turned smug. Yes, I was hopelessly behind. Yes, I had barely scratched the surface of my magical education. Yes, I mucked up my first glamour and probably looked like a hopeless case, but at least I hadn't blown myself up. Yet.

Salem's history as a familiar didn't exactly inspire a lot of confidence.

Nor did his salve, which did not work as planned and it was two days before my face cleared up enough to show it outside the house.

Chapter 15

Kin's arms tightened around me as we swayed together; a soft, slow song with a lot of strings playing in the background. I felt warm and safe and cherished surrounded by him and a cloud of white. I curled my fingers in his hair to pull his head down, to claim his warm lips with my own. They tasted like wedding cake and champagne and future.

On a sigh, I slid deeper into the kiss. Tangled tongues set my heart racing, turned my knees to jelly, and made me crave more as I pressed closer, ever closer to the heat and warmth of him.

The sound of my text message alert broke the kiss. Who on earth would be texting me at a time like this?

I came out of the dream with a startled jerk and my phone beeped again. And again and again.

Reaching for the phone, I discovered Salem

snuggled up against my back. In human form and gloriously naked, no less. I slammed my eyes closed to keep from seeing anything I really didn't want to see and groped for the beeping device. We were going to have to talk about the ground rules.

Two taps silenced the noise but not the vibrations. Someone really wanted my attention and I really wanted to go back to sleep. If it was serious, they'd call instead of text, right?

The debate still raged within me when Salem nuzzled his head against my arm and started to purr. That launched me out of bed faster than a five-alarm faerie fight.

Rules. There were totally going to be rules.

My messaging app informed me that twenty-seven missives from Harry Tart had come in starting from the afternoon before and several from Flix as well. My calendar app notified me that I had also missed two meetings. Annoying.

Can't a girl have a day or two off when life gets weird?

Nothing good could come of reading my messages before I'd at least had some coffee. No one sends twenty-seven messages when things are going well, so I knew my day was already headed south.

Half expecting more chaos, I was happily surprised to hear the pleasant sound of harmonizing voices when I opened the door. Pausing for a moment to listen, I had to smile. If the faeries felt calm enough to sing, there was a good chance there would be pancakes waiting for me downstairs. With blueberries and maple syrup. Harry could wait another half hour. Unless there were waffles, and then he could wait even longer.

Flix poked his head out of the back room as soon as the door closed behind me.

"There's a Harry Tart looking for you."

I pressed my lips together hard to keep from laughing at Flix when he was in one of his moods, but the way he said Harry's name was hard to ignore. He gave me a long look and pointed to a sea of sticky notes covering the Biedermeier fruitwood table that doubled as my desk.

"I am not an answering service." Putting some extra force into his flounce, Flix turned his back on me and left the room by way of the connecting door. Plenty of past experience had taught me to recognize when he was in enough of a snit to want to be left alone. As much as I wanted to follow him and make things right, letting him brood it out was the better plan.

The worst part of working with a temperamental genius who was also my best friend was when he had a valid reason for being mad at me. I should have called to let him know I was going AWOL for a couple days. But then, I'd have had to tell him why, and he'd have wanted to see and then we'd be in a bigger fight.

Still, I made a mental note to pick up a pint of his favorite ice cream and stash it in the fridge out back as an apology.

In the meantime, I might as well survey the damage. Today was the first day I could honestly say I didn't love my job. Starting with the top left corner, I worked at deciphering the notes Flix had left for me. Slashed in his distinct handwriting, the first few were terse and to the point.

Call Harry Tart.

Mona Katz: Still on for Thursday?

Call Harry Tart.

Call Harry Tart.

Tom says thank you.

And then the frustration began to creep in.

For the love of Danu, call Harry Tart.

Harry Tart will die if you don't call him.

If you don't call him soon, I will kill Harry Tart myself.

Harry Tart is a hairy tart.

Who wants a tart with hair anyway?

Screw you, you disappearing bint. I gave Harry Tart your private number.

Well, that explained the twenty-seven texts. I use an answering service that forwards all my calls to my private number when I'm out working in the field and gets turned off when I need a break.

That Flix had appointments on a day I wasn't in the office, and more, that he broke a cardinal rule about giving out my cell number to Harry spoke volumes about how worried and annoyed he had been. The ice cream wasn't going to be enough. I sighed. I'd probably have to let him dye my hair or something.

Another frantic text from Harry rounded the number up to thirty and when I glanced at the message, I saw he had written in all capital letters.

I'M FREAKING OUT. WHERE ARE YOU?

Instant headache.

Picking up my phone, I made the dreaded call. Harry answered before the end of the first ring.

"Lexi. Where have you been? I don't know what to do. You have to help me."

I'm not proud of it, but I snapped for a minute.

"Why do I have to help? There's no warranty on what I do. I put people together, but the rest is up to them. Happily ever after isn't a given, it takes work. You are the ones in charge of your future, not me." As soon as the words left my lips, I regretted them. The choked sound from the other end of the line only made it worse.

"I'm sorry, Harry. Of course, I'll help you. Tell me what's happening."

"A tattoo. Lemon got a tattoo." He made it sound like getting a tattoo was the next best thing to being caught cheating.

"Okay. Lots of women get tattoos, it's a popular form of self-expression. Some men find them sexy. I take it you're not one of them?"

"I'm not that narrow-minded, Lexi. Give me a little credit." At least the whiny pitch was gone from his voice. Maybe the key to helping Harry was to bring out the pissed off side of him a little more often. "She got…a guitar." His voice lowered at the end to make the word guitar sound ominous. I didn't get it.

"Work with me here, Harry, because I'm not seeing the problem. So Lemon likes music. What's the big deal?" A frustrated sigh came through the connection loud and clear.

"It's that guy. You know. The one that plays at that club."

"What guy at which club? I need more information." I suspected I knew the answer already and it was one I really didn't want him to confirm.

"The guy with the weird name. Mackinaw or something."

"Mackintosh Clark?" A stone dropped into the pit of my stomach and splashed acid up like a fountain. "Plays at Driven on Wednesday nights?"

"Yes. That's the one. It's not just Wednesdays anymore. He's there three nights a week now, and so is Lemon. I'm losing her and I don't even know how it happened. It's like she has some kind of fever or something. Everything changed so fast."

I did the best I could to get him calmed down and resolved to have a conversation with Lemon as soon as possible. The rest of my day would be spent playing catch up and placating Flix over his sense of abandonment. My gut told me there was nothing fundamentally wrong with Lemon and Harry, but I wasn't sure if given the current circumstances, I should trust my instincts. They could be as wonky as everything else in my life right now.

I'm a witch, right? Shouldn't that make my life easier instead of harder? I should be able to cast a spell that would fix all my problems so I could float along on a pink cloud eating bonbons and ice cream.

Too over the top? Probably, but shouldn't there be a few perks? So far the experience of coming into my majority as a witch had been anticlimactic. Not only had nothing changed for the better, certain areas of my life had gotten worse.

With nothing better to do on my walk home, I set my feet on autopilot and pondered the events of the last couple weeks.

The detente with the godmothers had been too easily achieved for me to rate the experience as a success. There was a Jimmy Choo hanging over my head just itching to drop on that score. I'd bet everything I had on it. One day of pancakes and platitudes did not a pattern make. Trust me, I've been there before.

Vaeta's reappearance upset the balance in ways that caused alliances between the four sisters to form and reform over the past few months. My life had morphed into that of an extra on the set of a faerie version of a reality TV episode. Whispers and promises flowed like the silken threads of a spider web and were just as sticky and just as easily torn away. Even the simplest questions seemed fraught with subtext that changed levels so fast it made my head spin to try and follow along.

I also noticed their roles were changing. Terra, the most affectionate of the three, took on the motherly role. With me, and sometimes with her sisters—whether they needed it or not. She had been the one I ran to when I fell off my bike, the one who baked my birthday cakes, the one who taught me how to handle the changes in my body as I grew into a woman. For motivation, I turned to Soleil—the sun, the maker of light, the restless champion of justice, Soleil was a creature of passion.

And finally, there was Evian with the strength and relentlessness of an ocean wave. She gave me the gift of logic. She taught me that when things went south, sometimes it was best to just chill.

Every single one of their strengths, though, went poof when the sisters found something to fight about. Terra still maintains it was a dream, but I distinctly remember being turned into a mouse one time when I got into the middle of one of their tantrums. My family, in all their dysfunctional glory.

The memory put a half smile on my face that fell right back off when I realized I'd taken a wrong turn and ended up right in front of Athena's Attic.

Or not, actually. The place was closed. Not just for the day, but gone. Like it never existed.

Confused, I cupped my hands around my eyes to shut out the glare of the setting sun and pressed them to the window to peer inside. From what I could see, the shop was barren and dusty—way too dusty to have been the home of a thriving business just days before. A wave of regret washed over me and I understood that I had come here to beg Athena to give me some guidance regarding what my next step should be. With her gone, it looked like I was on my own. Again.

Chapter 16

"Don't you recognize me?" I looked up from my barely picked-at chicken Caesar salad, noticing Mona Katz for the first time. I tried to cover my surprise with a wide smile, but I saw her stifle a giggle. "Bad day?"

"Oh, you have no idea." Absolutely none. If my professional life wasn't in enough of a shambles already, I had spent the entire morning attempting to locate a new client's soul mate—whose energy or essence or whatever it was I tapped into—had been clicking on and off of my radar like a strobe light. Not a normal situation for Lexi Balefire: Magical Matchmaker.

Getting my magic hadn't been all that useful. Ever heard the saying *be careful what you wish for*? Well, they ain't lying.

"Can I sit?" Mona asked. "Or, If you're meeting someone I can come back later."

When I first met Mona, I had known exactly where the man of her dreams was located. Since then, the feeling compelling me toward him had lessened, and now the shrapnel from my new powers was confounding the one thing that had never steered me wrong before. I was beginning to wonder if I had finally tapped into my full potential but just wasn't smart enough to work the controls.

"Of course. How's it going? I'm sorry I've been MIA for the past few days. Family emergency." A blanket statement used exclusively by people who aren't original enough to come up with a better lie.

Mona didn't seem to notice, and instead of prying into my personal life like I expected her to do, simply leaned over and gave my hand a friendly squeeze, offering condolences I couldn't even hear because I was too fascinated with watching the stream of glowing hearts that popped up over her head. The same type I'd seen in the coffee shop the day I'd almost passed out, only purple this time.

It seemed the experience was not the one-time occurrence I'd been hoping for. I needed more complications in my life. Not.

"...so sorry." I pulled my gaze back down to Mona's earnest face in time to see her puzzled expression and realized I'd been frowning at her. "What? Do I have something in my teeth?"

"No. You're fine. I was..." *Trying to see if I could*

slow down the light show coming out of your head seemed like the wrong thing to say. *Trying to figure out if I need to refund your money* wasn't much better. "…just caught up in thought." Mona patted my hand again.

The familiar feeling of just knowing returned all at once for the brief second her skin touched mine; some of the noise from inside my head quieted, and I could feel Dream Boy's signal ramp up in intensity. As Mona pulled her hand away, the connection faded completely to be replaced by the sneaking sensation someone was watching me.

Trying not to look like I was looking, I let my eyes track over the area around me but didn't see anyone who appeared overly interested in my activities. Still, the feeling remained.

This new development was going to put a crimp in my day.

"Do you want to come with me? I'm just going to run some errands, but I wouldn't mind some company. Unless you're busy…" The words spilled out of my mouth before I really had time to think, but somehow I knew the only way I was going to find Mona's guy was to stick close to her.

Poor thing, it was taking a lot longer than normal to get her settled and I really liked the woman. She was the kind of person I could be friends with if not for all the necessary secrets I would have to keep.

If anyone did, Mona deserved a great meeting

story, and at this point, I'd be lucky to get her matched at all.

Her eyes lit up. "Sure, it's my day off, so I'm free as a bird."

"Perfect. Let me pay for my lunch, and then I was thinking about heading uptown to check out a new bookstore I haven't had a chance to visit yet." Conveniently, right toward your destiny, Mona.

By the time we made it to The Novel Hovel, I had found two more excuses to make physical contact with Mona, and was starting to worry that she might think *I* was interested in *her*—worse, the signal coming from her match had moved to an entirely different part of town. A few more books I probably didn't need provided a tiny silver lining, and I was imagining an evening in my PJs, curled up next to a roaring Balefire with my purchases as we exited onto the street.

With each touch, the tremulous hold on the connection to Mona's sweetie strengthened. Not to anything like a normal level, but a workable one, and I didn't waste any time pulling her into a merry chase that lasted several blocks at a breakneck pace.

I was beginning to wonder if her guy was a cab driver or a bicycle messenger considering how he seemed to keep just ahead of us but managed to pop up everywhere. I had a short but satisfying fantasy of nailing some faceless guy's foot to the floor.

"Wow, you really do get around," Mona's breath came out a little puffy, her cheeks pinked with exertion.

Somehow, telling her we were on a city-wide manhunt to track down her perfect match while trying to identify the source of the creepy stalker vibe that wouldn't quit didn't seem like a great idea. So I lied. Again. Not my finest moment, but it was for a good cause. I hoped that was enough to stave off any negative karmic effects.

"Keeps me out of the gym, right?" I nudged her with my elbow as though punctuating the joke when what I really wanted was to give my intuitive process another boost.

"So what happened to you the other night? Did you ride home with that guitar player? He seemed totally into you. Was he a decent guy? Did he ask you out?"

My face grew hot at the mention of Kin, and the memory of the kisses I still hadn't stopped dreaming about. "Kin? Yes, he did give me a lift..." Before I could tell her about our time spent alone in the office closet, she cut me off.

"I hope the night didn't end badly because he's right over there." Sure enough, there Kin was, leaning up against the side of a brick building, his guitar case resting on the sidewalk. He stopped, his back to me, and lifted his head as if he were a dog who had just caught a whiff of a porterhouse steak, and turned around slowly to look me right in the face.

It was only then that I noticed the group of coffeehouse patrons crowded around him like adoring groupies. There were more women than a simple afternoon street-side, one-man performance really warranted, and all of them practically writhing in ecstasy with every move he made. We must have stepped into the middle of his act because Kin winked at me and introduced his next song.

"This one I wrote for the girl on the pink scooter." Jealousy over the women hanging on his every word fought a quick war with an onslaught of romantic feelings strong enough to speed my heart rate.

He began to pluck at his guitar, and the soft acoustic notes wafted toward us in a visible—at least, visible to me—haze. The same type of sparkling symbols I had been seeing around Mona all day now danced around Kin. Not hearts this time. Moons. Bright yellow moons. Flipping appropriate given the way all the women were mooning over him.

Turning back to my companion, I saw Mona's eyes trained on Kin, her face set in an expression identical to those worn by every female in the vicinity. Not a single symbol appeared around her now. Why hadn't my powers come with some kind of training manual?

"Oh wow, he's so...wow." Mona breathed. "If you're not going to go for it with him, I'm definitely going to take a shot." Well, that was certainly a quick change of tune. Seconds ago, she had asked me about Kin without any trace of desire; in fact, I had the distinct impression she'd been acting as a friend, looking out for me.

"Uh, well I…" Finishing the sentence was pointless. Mona had stopped listening. To me, at least. Kin commanded her full attention.

Seriously, what was it about this guy that turned women to mush whenever he played guitar? Granted, he regularly turned me to mush, but it took more than a song and I didn't think he'd spent time making out in his car with all these women. I work with people every day; rarely would a man fool me like that, and Kin was not that kind of man.

He was the kind of man who kissed you like you were the only woman in the world. It's hard to fake that level of interest and I consider myself a good judge of kisses. No, not because I indulge in that many of them myself, but I sure do engineer plenty of them. Never underestimate the importance of a good first kiss.

A hard nudge brought me back to the present and to a scorching look from Mona. A look I saw repeated on a number of faces.

"Lexi. Come over here." I would rather have undergone a root canal without anesthesia. I shook my head. How could he be so clueless? Maybe he planned to plaster a target on my back. No, wait, he already had.

I'm not proud of it, but I shook my head and literally dragged Mona behind me as I ran away. She struggled a bit at first, but as the proximity to Kin decreased, her resistance drained away. I needed to think about that in detail at some point, but not right now.

At this moment, Mona's man was finally close. If we hurried, I might have a chance to put together a meet for her. Not one up to my normal standards, but at this point, I'd settle for what I could get.

"Lexi, slow down. I'm…wait, are we going in circles?" Mona yanked on my arm. "And you forgot to finish your story about your ride home with that singer guy."

Surprise slowed my steps. "You mean the man you just spent ten minutes drooling over? That singer guy?" Jealousy barbed my tongue.

"I did not," Mona retorted. "Did I? My memory is a little hazy." Mona frowned.

Before I could formulate an answer I heard my name being called. Harry Tart. Just what I needed right now. A testimonial to impending failure. Lexi Balefire the un-matchmaker.

Or maybe not. Lemon hung off Harry like…well, she was a lemon and he was a tree. She let go of him long enough to give me an overly enthusiastic hug.

Surreptitiously rubbing the sore spot where her handbag had jabbed me in the ribs, I said, "You two look happy today." I gave Harry a searching look which he answered with a little nod. Matching symbols sprouted from the pair of them. I wish I could say they were hearts or flowers, but they weren't. A backward C shape with a hashtag in the center bobbled along just about a foot over the couple's heads. Hearts I could understand, even a moon made sense to some degree. This was just weird.

I grunted my way through two minutes of conversation while trying to work out the hidden meaning and finally gave up when nothing came to mind. At least they both had the same symbols; that had to be a good thing, right?

"Say you'll do it." Lemon gushed.

"Er…okay," I replied.

"I'll call you," was her parting comment as Harry gallantly opened the car door and waited to usher her into the seat like a true gentleman.

After Harry and Lemon drove away, I said to Mona, "What did I just agree to do?"

She gave me a raised eyebrow and answered, "You're giving a toast at the wedding. Is everything okay? You're very distracted today."

If she only knew. I tuned back in to find her intended was out of range again.

"To tell you the truth, I'm not feeling all that well. I think the rest of my errands are going to have to wait. Can I call you a cab?"

Mona gave me another perplexed look. "Lexi,

we're almost back to the cafe. My car is parked right over there. Maybe I should be the one calling a cab for you. Better yet, let me give you a ride."

"I'm fine. Really. You go on. I'm staying with a friend tonight. It's just around the corner." I hurried away against her protests and didn't even go back to the office.

Chapter 17

My first response when I saw a face peering in through the parlor window was to shriek like a girl. Okay, I am a girl, but you know what I mean. My second response, when I recognized the face, was similar, but a bit more primal.

"Serena," I stalked to my front door like a rampant lion leaping to confront an encroaching enemy. "Why are you peeking in my windows? That's trespassing. Give me one good reason why I shouldn't call the cops." I took a wide stance, folded my arms, and gave the stupid cow my best stank face.

"I was just trying to get an idea of how big the place is. You know, for when I move in to take care of the Balefire. I wanted to see if my couch would work in the space."

If you look up the term batcrap crazy in the dictionary, you'll find a photo and a full description of

Serena. It came down to either laughing at her or beating her to death with her own arm. I chose the former and dissolved into giggles.

"Haven't you ever heard of a deed?" Blank stupidity wrote itself all over her face. "You know, a legal document that proves ownership of a piece of property. A deed." I exaggerated the word with every bit of condescension I could summon. "Say it with me, Serena. A deed."

"I'm familiar with the concept." She ceded dryly.

"Then you'll know that this is my house and your sofa or the ass that owns it will never have the slightest chance of finding out whether or not they fit in my living room."

"Don't try to fool me with fancy talk," she retorted while I ran my mind over the conversation to figure out where I had gone all fancy on her.

"It's no secret that you're woefully inadequate for the job. When you can no longer keep the Balefire going, I'll need to live here to take over and bring it back to life." Poor deluded moron, she actually believed this pile of steaming stupidity.

"You know that the Balefire doesn't actually own the house, don't you? This place has been in my family since the land was bought and paid for by my great grandmother. Even if you had a cotton candy's shot in a bucket of water of taking over the Balefire duties, it would not be from within these walls, because the house does not go with the job. Honestly, Serena, your mother must be so proud of your deductive reasoning skills."

"Leave my mother out of this," at least an octave higher than normal, Serena's squawk sounded like it could cut glass.

"Don't start measuring for curtains just yet. I'm going to give you a one-time offer to come inside and look at what you'll never have."

Serena's nose shot up far enough for her to try out her best intimidating stare, which had about as much effect on me as a soap bubble breaking against my skin. She sailed triumphantly into the foyer, then stopped when she caught a glimpse of the merry flames whooshing up the chimney in the room beyond.

"But that's…how did you do that? What happened?" Serena sputtered.

I moved forward the two steps it took to bring us nose to nose. "If I see you on my property again, I'll turn you into a perpetual boil on a frog's butt."

"That's right," I continued when her eyes widened, "I can do that because I've been Awakened. So stick that in your cauldron and boil it, you half-witted twit." Actually, I probably couldn't have done that yet. I mean, I hadn't had a lot of time to memorize spells, and my power was still raw and untamed.

Then there's the whole reciprocity thing. I'm not entirely clear on how it works, but, unlike my grandmother, I do respect the law of threes enough not to send out too many bad vibes.

Mouth working like a fish off the hook, Serena's gaze tracked from me to the fireplace and back several times. "You can't have done that. Everybody knows your grandmother…" She broke off there and I wondered what, indeed, it was that everybody knew, because I had no idea what she was talking about.

"What, Serena? What does everybody know?"

"That Clara Balefire was a stone killer and unlike her, you don't have enough power to stop me doing this." Serena's face took on an air of concentration. My first instinct was to giggle because her casting face looked a lot like a bathroom face. The air around me turned dry and crackled with energy.

"Hah, you wish." hoping it would work, I made up a quick rhyme in my head, infused it with the intention of creating a protective barrier against her spell. No one was more shocked than I to see a huge pink bubble form around me just as whatever she conjured would have made contact.

For a split second, the bubble's wall bowed inward, then the whole thing rebounded and shot back toward Serena. The sweet scent of bubblegum filled the air and the ball of chewy, gooey stickiness plastered itself all over her, along with the spell she had tossed at me. Green warts sprouted on her hands and arms. At least they looked green through the haze of pink.

Is it petty to admit I pulled out my phone and

recorded Serena's shocked fury for posterity? Sorry. Sometimes I am just that big a jerk. Plus, payback really was a witch.

"Curse you, Lexi Balefire. I'm going to…"

"Watch your tone, Miss Snodgrass. You're a guest in this house." Vaeta appeared out of thin air between us. "I suggest you conduct yourself accordingly."

"Look what she did to me." A bony finger pointing at me accompanied the accusation. "Aren't you one of her keepers? You need to do something about this right now. I can't go out in public this way."

"Correct me if I'm wrong, but this was entirely your own doing. Lexi merely cast a defensive shield that rebounded your own spell back at you. In the future, I'd suggest you stick to trying to intimidate witches at your own level of power and leave alone those who are your better in every way."

Vaeta's tone was mild, but the rebuke was clear and I didn't even try to hold back a triumphant smile. "Get out, Serena."

"I can't leave looking like this. I'm human flypaper." She whined.

"It's not my fault bugs are attracted to you. Flies do seem to like piles of…"

Vaeta murmured my name as a warning before I could finish the satisfying comparison, then said to Serena, "It would serve you right if I let you leave like that. It's no more than you deserve." Still, with little more than a flickering of her eyes, the faerie lifted the shroud of goo, leaving my nemesis clean and dry.

"What about these?" Serena brandished a wart covered arm and glared at me as though the blemishes had been my idea.

"You're the hag who sent them out," I shot back, "they're your problem now."

"Get out," Vaeta repeated and clapped her hands. A little puff of wind nudged old wart-face toward the door. Serena took the hint and stalked across the foyer.

"Nice job, fate weaver." A glint in her eye and a grin on her face, Vaeta congratulated me. "First time I've seen chewing gum used as a defensive mechanism."

"I'd like to take credit for all the brilliance, but I can't. I had no idea what was going to happen or if anything would. My spell casting skills are spotty. Half the time nothing happens and the other half it's like I tried to move a feather using a hurricane. I can't seem to find a happy medium."

Something fell in the foyer, causing Vaeta and me to exchange a look.

"Serena," we said in unison and rushed to make sure the vile witch had left the premises. I'd rather she not know how vulnerable I still was.

An umbrella lay on the floor near the open door.

Chapter 18

I pushed a purple satin sleep mask off my face and blinked a few times at the light shining through my window. It was well past noon and, blessedly, I couldn't hear a peep coming from downstairs. Salem was curled up at the foot of my bed, in his cat form for once, and he hopped up guiltily as I poked at him playfully with my toe, then pounced on my foot and began to kick at it with his hind legs. Five seconds later, when my wiggling toes were no longer enticing, he exploded in a ball of fur and smoke. When it cleared he was sitting, fully clothed, on the edge of my bed.

"It's your birthday, it's your birthday. It's Beltane, it's Beltane." Salem sang, bouncing up and down and tickling my ribs until my face hurt from laughing too hard.

"It's my birthday, it's my birthday." I did a little dance and moonwalked across the hardwood floor and into the bathroom. Too bad I hadn't mastered that glamour spell yet; it would make getting ready in the morning so much easier. Just as I had every birthday I could remember, I found a tiara resting on the top of a stack of clean towels, the words "Birthday Girl" emblazoned across the front in glitter.

If there was one thing my godmothers were good at, it was birthdays. When I picked the tiara up, I realized this was not the plastic novelty item of years past; this was the real thing: some type of unbelievably shiny metal that probably hailed from the Faelands.

Glittering gems caught and reflected the light; aquamarines, a personal touch from Evian flanked a flawless diamond that had Terra written all over it. A polished carnelian screamed Soleil and I could only assume that the luminous moonstones were Vaeta's contribution. It touched me that Vaeta cared enough to have a hand in the beautiful, priceless gift. The second I put it on my head, I felt a rush of pure love and protection that brought tears to my eyes.

"All hail Alexis, Queen of the Balefire," Salem announced as I descended the staircase with my nose in the air and a huge grin on my face.

"My loyal subjects, I pronounce this day "Lexi Day" and command thee to party as though it were the year nineteen-ninety-nine!" Waking up without the annual sense of dread had turned me giddy.

"Oh, it's on," Soleil pressed a hot mug of coffee

into my hand, and the scent of vanilla tickled my nose. "We pulled out all the stops." After a tense couple of days, a party might be just the thing to clear the air and it seemed like the faeries wanted the same thing.

In the kitchen, I saw she'd been telling the truth about going all out.

The kitchen counters groaned under the weight of everyone's favorite brunch dishes; complete with some sort of fishy-smelling paste for Salem, a mimosa fountain, and a cinnamon roll decorated to resemble a birthday cake.

Something told me that today they would break the twelve-cake record set the year of my 21st birthday.

Lush grass carpeted the downstairs and flowers sprang up behind me at every step. A nice touch from Terra, but I had to admit my favorite thing was the fountain in the backyard. Jets of colored water arced and played over an ice sculpture of me dressed as Marilyn Monroe in that iconic scene where her dress billows up over the steam grate.

"I love it," I squealed and hugged Evian who blushed.

"Vaeta helped."

The last of the distance that had existed between us since my Awakening faded like mist under a summer sun. Not because they'd heaped birthday surprises on me. I might collect shoes like a charged surface collects dust, but I've never been the kind of person driven by things. Everything my family had done, even the wacky, came from a place of love.

Nothing, not space, not time, not even magic could come between us now.

And it was not the mimosas talking when I made a speech to that effect, either.

The tension broken, we moved the party into the dining room, an interior space with no windows that was reserved for company and thus rarely used. Fairy lights, courtesy of Soleil, lit the room like fireflies inside glass jars. A four-tier cake covered in multi-colored fondant occupied the center of the table.

Vaeta sent our loaded plates, coffee mugs, and champagne flutes through the door on a gust of wind, and everyone settled around the table. Salem skirted the edge of the group until Terra scratched him behind one ear, and with a fond smile instructed him to take human form and sit down with the rest of us.

Evian raised a glass, her silver-tipped fingernails shining in the firelight, and toasted me. "To Lexi! I wish you light, love, and magic." Everyone cheered, I blushed pink under all the attention, and then we dug into our meal. I knew from experience that today would be a marathon, and justified the extra carbs as fuel for the duration.

"We have an hour, maybe two before the onslaught." Terra waved a blini in the air and addressed the group, "Everything is set for the Beltane celebration.

The fire is burning at full power, and I think we can expect a much more enthusiastic turnout this year. This will be Lexi's coming out party, and I think we should plan to make it one hell of a night!"

The wicked edge to her tone boded ill for anyone who disagreed, but mostly for any witch who hadn't heard my good news and showed up looking to take over the Balefire duties.

"So basically I'm going to be on display, like some animal in a zoo?" I asked, not having taken the time to think about what would actually happen once I came face to face with half the witches on the east coast.

Vaeta's musical laugh echoed across the room. "No. Well, maybe a little. Next year it will be old news, but when a Balefire comes into her powers, it's usually on the chair."

"You mean off the chain?" I couldn't help riffing on Vaeta's limited knowledge of today's vernacular. At least she'd stopped saying she was going to nip a problem in the butt.

"Whatever. You know what I mean." I wanted to laugh out loud, but pressed my lips into a line and nodded sagely instead. Salem covered a less-than manly giggle with a large cough and made a show of snagging a piece of bacon, refusing to make eye contact with Vaeta.

"What my sister means is," Terra tossed Vaeta the kind of stink eye that on any other day might have meant the opening salvo of a tiff, but my birthday was a no fight zone. "You have a strong family history to live up to, and that comes with a level of extra attention. Just be yourself, and don't worry about what those other witches think."

I'd put my money on Terra to win in a witch-on-faerie confrontation, and that was without considering she had backup, so I listened to her advice and tried not to think about what would happen later.

The first round of presents—yes, I said first round; don't judge—included a gorgeous Zac Posen party dress I had circled in last month's Vogue and left open on the kitchen island, and another set of jewels so lavish I felt like I should write a check to a children's charity ASAP.

When you can create diamonds and gold on a whim, money becomes a non-issue, but I have enough crazy in my life that lavish living would be too over-the-top. Besides, I love my work and the satisfaction of being able to pay my own way. With my birthday falling on the one day a year where a magical party was not only accepted, but expected, we went over the top with Beltane festivities.

I noticed a gift from Flix in the pile and wondered why he hadn't shown up this morning. I'd missed him even if I hadn't needed him to talk me out of my failure funk this year, and I was a little hurt at the thought that he didn't want to share in my happiness when things had finally turned around. The box felt like it was filled with absolutely nothing, but inside I found a photo of Flix holding a pair of Manolo Blahnik strappy sandals that matched the dress perfectly in one hand and a note that said "Bliss" in the other.

"Go meet him at the spa, Lex, we've got the Beltane preparations covered. All you have to do is show up." Soleil practically pushed me out the door before I could finish my second mimosa.

"How do they make mud feel so luxurious?" I asked Flix sleepily. Wrapped in a cocoon of wet dirt I felt more relaxed than I had in weeks.

"It's the peat mixed with the mineral water. It has healing properties." He responded languidly before lapsing into silence again.

"Why didn't you come wake me this morning?" I asked, still a little hurt despite the expensive shoes he had splurged on for my big day. He'd been as scarce as two dollar bills for months.

"Your house is a bit on the insane side lately, so I figured I'd stay away. Not all faeries take kindly to halflings; your godmothers are an exception, but I haven't been able to get a real sense of Vaeta's position on the matter. She's hard to pin down. I take it you made up with Terra."

"I guess. We never talked about the problem, but she seems to have moved past the anxious stage. The truth is, nothing much has changed with me. I still can't do magic." I took a sip of my cucumber-mint water and wiggled down deeper into the tank to let the mud ooze up to my chin. "Except for one spell, but that was an accident."

The memory of Serena's face peeking out of a bubblegum cocoon occupied a special place in my heart. Was that mean? I didn't care. I spent a long moment enjoying it again before noticing Flix was giving me his best you're-an-idiot look.

"What?" I frowned back at him and waited while one of the spa staff refilled our glasses. When she'd gone, I asked. "What did I do, now?"

"Nothing. Just talk to Terra and find out the true reason behind her reaction. I have a feeling it's important."

Back at the house, I dodged up the stairs. I didn't want to get sidetracked, and I had business of my own that needed doing.

Besides, walking head-on into a faerie party with no expectations is pretty spectacular; I preferred to wait until I made my official entrance to take it all in. A dozen mice skittered in front of me on their hind legs, carrying a box of what looked like tulle and glitter over their heads. Over the years, I've wondered if Terra took her cues from traditional fairy tales or was the inspiration for them.

One of these days, I should ask.

Out of the corner of my eye, I could see four blue jays busily covering the windows with some kind of shimmery fabric I knew would block the view of the inside from the street; if they were enlisting the help of woodland creatures, this party was sure to impress.

I hightailed it to my bedroom, shut the door and enjoyed the calm before the storm while I applied a drugstore's worth of lotions, balms, and cosmetics, taking care not to completely ruin the complicated updo Flix had tortured my hair into after we left the spa.

The din from below was audible enough now to set my nerves tingling, so I took a moment to center myself before venturing downstairs. I pulled a purple candle from my stash, anointed it with lavender oil, and sent up a prayer to Brighid, the goddess of eternal flame; Hestia, the goddess of the hearth; and Ma'at, the goddess of balance.

"Grant me balance, and the ability to preside over the hearth and flame as my fore-mothers did. Grant me peace, Goddesses."

With a whisper of a breath, I extinguished the flame and felt a surge of power as a blanket of calm enveloped my body. I don't know if it was because it was my birthday, or because it was Beltane, or if it was simply because I performed the ritual with more confidence and intention than ever before, but I knew in my bones I had completed my first successful spell.

Okay, maybe the second, but the first one I meant to do, anyway.

I carried that feeling with me into the hallway, where I paused for a breath at the top of the stairs.

The dining room was a ghost town, but I could hear laughter and bright voices in the parlor. My throat tightened. If you've ever felt like an outsider, you'll understand why. Women say more with a look than men do with a song. A tilt of the head, eyes that slide away, bright smiles paired with subtle frowns all show that pity and sympathy are close cousins.

No one can convince me the godmother's interpretation of the Beltane ritual bears more than a nodding acquaintance with witchly traditions. The departure is probably one of the reasons for the intense dread I felt every year as I stood in this spot, steeling myself against the set shoulders, the forced warmth that reminded me I would never fit in. *Never fit in.* Those words played in my head even now when they were no longer true.

Get over it, Lexi. I gave myself a little pep talk. Go in there and give this a chance.

Chin high, shoulders squared, and spine straight, I followed my own advice.

The Balefire burned so bright it hurt my eyes to look at it, so I directed my attention toward the sea of faces that turned my way. Smiles, wide and warm and real, wreathed faces reflecting the fire's glow. I barely cleared the doorway before being swamped by hugs and pats of congratulation.

I know it's a little small-minded to dwell on the past, but a hint of bitter came with the sweet.

Only two faces carried guarded expressions. Serena Snodgrass looked like someone had bottled her up in a fart jar with no way out. It was the pained look on her face that brought my first tentative smile. The second sober countenance belonged to none other than Athena, the missing shopkeeper.

And what was that all about?

For the span of a few heartbeats, our eyes met and I felt a pull as if something in me recognized something kindred in her. It wasn't that far different from my matchmaking mojo, and I knew I had to talk to her. If I could get to her in time, that is.

"Excuse me, won't you."

I kept one eye on her while I tried to extricate myself from the clutch of happy witches, but they were on me like fur on a familiar. At one point, I saw Athena and Serena in a discussion that looked heated. Athena leaned in close and whispered something in the younger woman's ear and I saw Serena's face blanch before becoming more pinched than ever.

Marvita Walthrop harnessed me for a kiss on each cheek, "You must be on top of the world," she said. "I remember how I felt when my Awakening came after being a year late."

Why she waited until now to regale me with a tale that would have made me feel more connected to my peers in years gone by was a mystery to me.

By the time the story ended, so had Serena and Athena's conversation. With a series of jerky motions, Serena selected a willow stick from the basket we provided and thrust it into the flame. The last I saw of her, the half-witted witch was marching toward the door with a flickering twig in her hand and a look on her face that was blacker than the soot in the fireplace.

By that point, Athena was nowhere to be found.

I spent the rest of the evening getting to know my sister witches and learning how much of the distance between us had been imagined or created by my own insecurities. Wine flowed, music played, and we sang and danced—danced to honor the gods and goddesses. We danced to honor our own mortality. We sang songs of unification and I think I might have even made a few friends.

All in all, it was a good night.

Chapter 19

Did I mention I'm not a morning person? Is that something you can grow out of? Because I remember being young and waking with the sun, the excitement of a new day coursing through my veins. But that was before sunshine gave way to a caffeine-induced alertness that never lifted me as high or for as long.

The morning following my first Awakened birthday started out like every day had when I was a six-year-old. I woke to feel energized and ready for anything. Okay, it could have been a residual wine buzz, but I didn't waste a lot of time worrying about it. For once, I would get downstairs in time for the first wave of breakfast.

To my surprise, I found Salem hunched over the breakfast bar with a cup of milk and a plate of smoked salmon, practically purring as Soleil, Terra, and Evian bustled around the kitchen making good use of all the party leftovers.

"Morning Lexi." They all chimed in unison.

Soleil reached for a coffee mug, spun around in a perfect pirouette to avoid Evian, who ducked beneath her arm and grabbed a carton of cream from the fridge. She let go, sending the carton through the air, where it hovered over an old, slate blue Fiestaware creamer and, without spilling a drop onto the granite counter top, floated back to its cold cavern and stilled. Sugar cubes danced across a napkin and deposited themselves into the cup, and Soleil rotated her finger at a tiny spoon, ordering it to stir my coffee.

Watching the three of them together was like having a front row seat to The Nutcracker—starring Harry Potter. They worked in perfect unison, spinning and ducking and twirling in time to an unheard tune.

Soleil's affinity with fire allowed her to brown, toast, and char to perfection, and I inhaled the scent of crisp, but still chewy bacon.

Evian pointed to a pot of water on top of the stove, which immediately bubbled to a perfect simmer as two eggs slipped in and began to poach.

Terra danced over to the sunny bay window and I watched as a tiny potted plant grew two feet tall and hung heavy with three types of sweet peppers. After picking, the plant returned to its previous size. She whisked them to the counter where a large butcher's knife began chopping the fragrant peppers into pieces and then, with a wave of her hand, they flew into a sauté pan and started to sizzle.

I stuffed an egg, some bacon, and a piece of cheese between two halves of a buttery croissant, sipped my coffee and spent a pleasant hour hashing over highlights of the party the day before.

Times like these, when all of the elements of my household were working in perfect harmony, I felt like I could overcome any obstacle. I basked in the glory for about three-tenths of a second before I heard the unmistakable sound of my phone ringing. Crap, I'd left it upstairs.

A mad dash ensued.

Blessedly, it stopped before I could answer. Six missed calls starting yesterday afternoon, all from Harry Tart. I'd like to get off this see-saw, please. What could possibly be wrong now, and when did I become Harry's personal love coach, anyway?

Of course, I should have known my birthday cake-induced good mood wouldn't last. I debated calling him back immediately and instead decided to take a shower first. I had a feeling it was going to be one of those days. Check that—another one of those days.

"Lexi!" came Harry's emotion-roughened voice over the line. "You've got to fix this. I can't live without her!"

"Slow down, Harry. Tell me what's wrong." I tried

to remain calm, figuring this was another bout of panic that would dissolve as quickly as it had formed.

His voice echoed with pain, and my heart wrenched for him. "She left me. Lemon left. Canceled the wedding. She says she's in love with that singer and they're going to be together."

My heart stopped beating for a millisecond, and when it began again I could feel the pulse of blood throbbing in my temples at an alarming pace. Somehow, I had convinced myself that Lemon was just acting out, sowing her wild oats before the wedding.

Had I been blind to just how far over the edge she had gone? Harry hadn't, and I had basically ignored him because I didn't want to admit Lemon might actually have a connection with Kin.

Hurt, anger, and a few other emotions roiled to the surface, but I tamped them down with Harry's distress in mind. "There's got to be a reasonable explanation, Harry. Try to calm down, and let me see what I can do."

"You keep saying that, but nothing you've done has helped. You said we were meant for each other, and I believed you. Everything was perfect, and now I wish I had never been born. Do you have any idea what it's like to finally find your soul mate and then have them walk away, just like that? It's worse than never having found her at all." Harry's despair flowed through the phone line so palpably it made the hair on my arms stand at attention.

No, I didn't know what it felt like to lose my soul mate, but the strength of the emotion roiling inside me at the thought of Lemon and Kin becoming an item told me whatever Harry was experiencing must be a hundred times worse.

I had to get to the bottom of this or, something told me, I'd be making a huge mistake that could hurt my business. My professional pride was on the line.

I knew Lemon and Harry belonged together as surely as I knew my own name, and I wasn't about to let their relationship get derailed by the man who might hold my future in his hands. My own love life would have to be put aside. Or, so I thought.

"I'm sorry, Harry. Really. I'll get in touch with you as soon as I can."

My heart tripped over itself again as another image of Lemon and Kin floated in front of my eyes, and I quickly shook my head to clear it while I dialed Lemon's cell number.

"Hi, Lexi, what's up?" She answered cheerfully. Okaaay.

"What do you mean, what's up? I just spoke to Harry, and he says you've canceled the wedding! What in the world is going on with you?" I demanded.

Lemon's voice turned husky. "I'm in love with another man. Kin Clark. He's a musician, maybe you've heard of him?" Apparently, it was a rhetorical question because she kept jabbering on without giving me a chance to answer. "If you haven't, you will soon enough; I'm going to make him a star! I can't believe how lucky I am."

I threw up a little bit in my mouth.

"And this Kin is fine with the fact that until yesterday you've been engaged to another man?" I retorted.

"What difference would that make to him? I know he's the one for me; I know we're a better match than Harry and I will ever be. I mean, come on, Lexi. Lemon Tart? It felt whimsical at first—meant to be—but now that I've experienced real love…I can't walk away from that. I'm putting in my notice at the firm; I'll start my own company, with Kin as my first client. He'll be a huge sensation, and soon we'll leave this one horse town and Harry will never have to see me again."

One horse town? Who talked like that? Whatever was messing with Lemon's head was making her even more theatrical than normal. It didn't seem like I was going to get anything else out of her, and I had a pretty good idea where I would find the next target for my irritation.

"All right, Lemon, I'll be in touch."

For the love of all that is good and holy.

Chapter 20

Sometimes I miss having a plain old house phone; the kind with a cord, and a cradle to slam the ear piece into when the person on the other end pisses you off. Jabbing at a touchscreen "End Call" button is far less satisfying, and the alternative is much more expensive. Instead, I paced back and forth across my bedroom, white rage rolling off me in waves.

No, Kin and I didn't have any kind of arrangement.

No, we hadn't even gone on an official date yet, so why was I hearing chirping birds and wedding bells every time his name popped into my mind?

But I hadn't expected him to just pick up with some other woman without at least letting me down easy. I mean, he was the one who pursued *me*. And an almost married woman, no less. How could I have been so blind to his true nature? What kind of a witch was I, anyway? For that matter, what kind of woman was I, not to have read the signs correctly?

Whenever I saw Kin out and about, he was covered with adoring women. Somehow, I had brushed the fact away, focusing on the way he acted when we were alone. Dr. Jeckyll and Mr. Hyde would have been proud.

Well, he was sure to get a rude awakening the next time I saw him. My pacing continued, and I could feel the power welling up inside me, searching for release. And there was only one person I wanted to unleash it on. I stabbed at my phone until Kin's number appeared, and hit "Send" before I had fully prepared my opening line.

"What the hell kind of person poaches a married woman from her fiancé?" I shouted into the line before Kin could finish saying hello. "And one of my clients? Really? How dare you come between soul mates! And what was I, collateral damage? If you wanted to run off with Lemon then why did you pretend to be interested in me?"

"Lexi?" Kin sounded a little bit scared, and it made my blood boil and brought power surging up from the heat pooling in my belly.

"Of course, it's Lexi. Although it doesn't surprise me that you don't know who I am—just another one of the herd of idiots following you around like a puppy. Let me just tell you this right now, Mackintosh Clark, you will steal Lemon away from Harry over my dead body!"

Silence stretched on the other end of the line for a moment longer than I would have expected, and I almost hung up before Kin collected himself enough to respond.

"You know, this kind of suspicion and accusation isn't going to help us in our relationship." Not the retort I was expecting.

"What relationship? You're starting a new life with another woman. If you think I'm some kind of trollop who's content with being someone's mistress, you clearly know nothing about me."

"Lexi, calm down. I don't even know a Lemon. Or a Harry, for that matter. Where are you getting this information from?" He spoke with the even, measured pace of someone trying to talk a nutjob off the rails.

"You most certainly do know a Lemon!" I screeched, "I've seen her practically strip naked in front of you during one of your little shows. She's always in the front row, and she's already told Harry and me that you two are running off together. What more do I need to know? Lemon isn't a liar, but I don't know you well enough to say the same."

"Are you talking about that short little blond woman who's always dressed in yellow? She certainly looks like a Lemon, and she's always trying to touch me. But I've never even had a full conversation with her! Please, Lexi."

Something about the pleading tone of his voice rang true to me and, trusting my instincts, I stopped my tirade mid-expletive. "Then why? I don't understand."

"Come to my house. We can talk; sort this all out.

Please?"

I'm embarrassed to say, I crumbled. Could I have been wrong? Lemon had been acting a little nutty lately; maybe there was more to the story.

"Fine, I'm on my way."

Kin answered the door before my knuckles made contact, and ushered me inside without a word. I stood, taking in my first peek at his home with my arms crossed in front of my chest and refusing to make eye contact.

It wasn't your typical bachelor pad, that was for sure. Deep-toned wood paneling covered sections of the ceilings and the bottom half of the walls in the entryway and great room, the spaces between painted a medium blue-gray that reminded me of the sky on a stormy summer day.

An overstuffed armchair and a couch with a couple of pillows and a fuzzy blanket looked cozy and inviting. I could see the spines of many books peeking through the glass doors of a craftsman-style built-in shelving unit that surrounded a mosaic tiled fireplace.

Pushing away the urge to explore the rest of the house, I took the proffered seat on the couch, and turned to Kin with an expression that clearly said *this better be good.*

"Lexi, please." Kin pleaded. "Tell me what's going

on. I swear I don't know why this woman would say these things. Are you sure she was talking about me?"

I sighed, my anger draining by the second. I looked into Kin's face and searched it for signs of dishonesty. Years spent avoiding jerks who came to my office for nothing more than a cheap thrill had honed my lie-detection skills to top-notch, and I suddenly realized I'd let my feelings for Kin affect my common sense.

"Honestly, I don't know why I freaked out. We're not together; it's your life; you can do whatever—whoever you want. Lemon's fiancé, Harry, has been in a panic for the last few weeks, and when I saw you play at Driven the other night, she was there, acting nothing like a doting wife-to-be." I relayed all the calls from Harry, all of my encounters with Lemon while Kin listened.

"Maybe I was wrong about Harry and Lemon after all." I didn't add that it wouldn't surprise me if I had been, given the way things were going since my powers ramped up and I'd lost access to any sort of happy medium.

"Anyway, Harry called me this morning and told me that Lemon had left him a note saying she had met a musician, that they had a future, and the wedding was off. I called Lemon myself, and she confirmed that you two were in love and that she was going to quit her job to follow you around on tour. She thinks she's going to use her PR background to make you a star."

Kin jumped out of his chair and started pacing. I let him ramble because, well, you can learn a lot about a person watching them melt down. "Seriously, this is the most ridiculous thing I've ever heard! I have a day job; I just moved into this house—does it look like I'm planning on packing up and leaving anytime soon? I'm renovating the upstairs, for crying out loud. I told you about my business plan."

He speared fingers through his curls, brushed them back away from his face and took things up to near-rant level. With every word, I felt calmer.

"Look at my phone; nothing from a Lemon. Or a Lime, or a freaking Orange, or from any other woman. What reason would I have to lie? You're right, we're not together, but that's not how I was hoping this thing was going to go down."

My calm gave way to a frisson of excitement. He'd had hopes for us? Well, so had I.

"Yeah, when I play, women tend to get a little overly excited. I honestly have no idea why; nobody even notices me without a guitar in my hand, and to be perfectly honest, I'd like to keep it that way. I know we just met, but I've been nothing but honest with you."

Excitement turned to dismay as my emotional roller coaster dipped down another hill. Too bad I couldn't say the same to him. Telling someone you're a witch these days is like telling them you're the tooth fairy. Not that I'd ever try to pass as that crazy bitch.

I closed my eyes and felt for my intuition, or my power, or whatever it was that showed me other people's soul mates. And, for the life of me, I didn't get so much as a tingle as I searched for Kin's. If he did have one, it wasn't Lemon, or I would have been able to tell. Furthermore, unless he'd been trained by the CIA, Kin was telling the truth.

"She did sort of skirt my questions about how you felt about all this." I looked into Kin's pleading eyes and I caved. Or gave in to common sense, I'm not really sure which. He wasn't planning on running off with Lemon, of that much I could be sure. What I most wanted to know was what his intentions were with me, other than the carnal ones I could see floating around in the deep brown of his irises.

A split second later we were in each other's arms, and he was kissing me, pushing any doubt from my overworked mind. It didn't matter, as long as I got to revel in this feeling for as long as possible.

It's a little difficult to fully let go with a man when you can sense his soul mate in the vicinity, and Kin's lack thereof was both a blessing and a curse. I didn't know what it meant, but for now, it didn't matter; I could pretend he was mine, even if he wasn't destined to be, without that nagging truth hanging over my head. I'd cross that troll-infested bridge when I came to it.

My hands explored Kin's muscled body; clawed hungrily at his shirt buttons until his corrugated chest and abs were exposed, and let out a sigh. He moaned in response, lifted me gently, and carried me, my legs wrapped around his waist, into the bedroom. The sun was barely peeking through the trees by the time we came up for air and settled into a giddy state of post-coital bliss, my head on Kin's bare chest.

"I fully intend to repeat that many times, but right now, I have to get ready for the show tonight." Kin apologized while gently stroking the small of my back. "I wish I could cancel and just stay right here. You'll come, won't you?"

I rolled onto my stomach and wiggled closer, in no mood to end the perfect afternoon. "Definitely. Wouldn't miss it. Besides, I have a mess to clean up."

Kin's eyes crinkled into a smile. "Come to think of it, what kind of rock star shows up on time. I think we've got a few extra minutes…"

Chapter 21

Pinky's tiny headlight hardly pierced the fading light of dusk when I tooled into town. Trading helmet hair for a slim chance of being on time had seemed like the smarter thing to do when I left, but I'd rather walk than drive my baby at night. I parked her in front of my office, knowing full well even witchcraft wouldn't make a parking space magically appear in front of the club.

Plus, with the way my magic worked, I'd probably wreck a few cars and I didn't need that kind of attention.

The shortest route between FootSwept and Driven had my boot heels clicking down a couple short alleys, one of which only looked like a dead end if you weren't as familiar with the area as I was. A sharp rap in just the right spot clicked the gate latch open and when I slipped through, I could already hear the steady hum of excited voices ahead.

Stepping out of the alley entrance, two buildings

down from Driven, I found myself in the middle of a winding line of women waiting for an empty table. Kin's voice floated over the excited chatter like a balm on the wind. Only a balm would have been calming, and these ladies were anything but. Their tension vibrated against my senses and set my teeth on edge.

Dodging left, I ignored the angry protest when I cut through the line and approached the bouncer, a hulk of a man whose nickname, naturally, was Tiny Tim.

"Lexi." Tim's face lit up.

"Busy tonight." My dry comment pulled a quick grin as he lifted the thick velvet rope so I could pass.

A wall of protesting females slammed against my back and Tim shouted in my ear, "You think they're going to rush the door?"

"I'll see if Brock can send someone out to help." I patted him on the arm and made my way into the club where I quickly learned why Tim had been left alone to handle the door. His counterparts had their hands full inside. A line of burly men was all that held a horde of frantic women back from rushing the stage where a single spotlight shone on Kin plucking the final note of a song on his guitar.

Shrieks, catcalls, whistling, and thunderous applause echoed as the spotlight winked out and the stage lights came back up. The adoration thrown at him from the audience felt like a living thing. A monster, if I had to put a name to it.

Weaving my way through the crowd, I dodged more than one elbow to the ribs. These women were pumped—too pumped, really. Like they were high on something. Tuning into a few snippets of conversations, I quickly realized what that something was: they were high on Kin.

A sea of those weird moon symbols floated above the crowd, taunting me with the puzzle of a hidden meaning that had to be connected, somehow, to the fever pitch of the energy buzzing around the room.

"Over here." Large hands grasped my arm and gently led me toward the darkened area near the back of the stage. Hale, one of the bouncers playing bodyguard for Kin, whisked open a door painted black to blend into the shadows and practically shoved me through.

Kin waited on the other side and pulled me into his arms for a kiss that shot electricity right down to my toes.

"Did you see what's going on out there? It's crazy." His tone suggested he meant crazy in the bad sense. "Just before you got here, they had to toss one woman out for flashing me."

"So there are some perks to the crazy, then." My tone was dry enough to kill a cactus and earned me nothing more than a slight twitch of his lips.

"If I didn't know better, I'd say these women were under some kind of spell." Kin twitched the curtain aside just far enough to survey the bar. "See? I didn't do anything to make them act like that." Together, we gazed at the crowd. With him safely out of sight, the whole vibe of the place returned halfway to normal, but Kin's chance statement got me thinking.

I wasn't the only witch in town. Heck, I probably wasn't even the only witch in the club that night. What if someone really had been using Kin to mess with women's emotions? That kind of spell would carry a lot of karmic debt, and I couldn't think of a reasonable motive for it being cast, either. Someone would have to be really powerful or really stupid to even try.

"Can I stay back here and watch you play your next set?" I wanted to keep an eye on the audience, observe their reactions more closely. I might even spot the culprit.

"Sure." Kin picked his guitar back off the stand and tossed a vintage guitar strap printed with 1940's-style pinup girls over his shoulder. "I almost don't want to go back out there. Will you promise to be here when I'm done?"

"I promise." He laid warm lips against mine again and was gone.

Everything after that happened so fast it's hard to remember clearly.

While I sidled into the darkness cast by a stack of speakers, Kin stepped onto the stage, strummed the strings, and launched into a song. I couldn't tell you which one because the normalcy evaporated with the first note. Moon shapes written in light hovered over the guitar and over the crowd in an undulating wave.

A mask of feral attraction fell over every female face in the room and I knew. Absurd as it sounded, Kin had been correct. These women were under a spell, and he was the one casting it. Boy, I sure know how to pick them.

I was all ready to leave him to the fate he deserved—because if I had to watch any more of this, I was going to throw up—when he shot a panicked look my way. White skin and pleading eyes said he probably hadn't brought this on himself. A fact I knew deep down already, but the confirmation didn't hurt. Sigh of relief. The angle of his body gave me a better look at the guitar in his hands.

The moons popped out from between Kin's fingers and flew a few feet before fading away. The last time I'd seen this happen, the color had been different. I clutched the edge of a speaker and closed my eyes to bring back the memory more clearly.

Hazy at first, the image cleared. Kin sitting on the back of a metal bistro chair, his feet resting on the seat. A smile on his face, the guitar held in those long-fingered hands while he plucked at the strings. Yellow. The symbols were yellow that day, not red.

Yellow for caution; red for danger seemed like a reasonable assumption based on the fact that the women tonight looked like they were one step away from turning into a mob—with Lemon leading the way. And there she was, right in the front row, waving her arms and screaming out her love for a man who had never said two words to her. Danger didn't half describe it.

The estrogen in the room was running at a fever pitch and aimed right at my man. Do something. My inner voice sounded loud given how noisy it was in the place.

Adrenaline running high, I propped open the back door just enough to give my fingers purchase when it came time to get back inside, and ran to assess the getaway situation. Kin's car sat in its usual spot around the corner, but judging by the number of women draped all over it, we wouldn't be speeding away in the Corvette tonight.

That left calling a cab or the worst-case scenario for this time of night: Pinky.

A taxi rolling up behind Driven would be about as discreet as sending up a flare, so I took the shortcut back to FootSwept as fast as I could go and retrieved the pink scooter from the vestibule where I left it. Pushing a scooter is a lot harder than it looks when you're trying to be stealthy.

By the time I snugged my baby up next to the stage door exit, I was sweaty and sore. No one saw me slip back inside or sneak my way to the hidden alcove I'd left a few minutes before.

In that short time, the situation had worsened. The

bouncers faced away from the stage, arms linked to keep the screaming horde from taking Kin down. It looked like the burly men wouldn't be able to hold out much longer.

Kin's shoulders slumped with relief when he glanced back and saw me standing there. I absolutely suck at charades, so it came as no surprise that Kin didn't seem to get my pantomimed message about Pinky being right outside. I finally had to show him my helmet before his frown cleared. I gave him the circling hand wave to indicate he needed to move things along, and that one he understood.

At the end of the song, he shouted, "Goodnight everyone" into the mic and leapt off the back of the stage to land lightly next to me.

"Come on," I tossed him my spare helmet and dragged him out the door. "Hurry."

We hit Pinky like a force of nature, fired her engine, and pulled down the narrow access to the employee parking area that formed a dead end behind the club.

"Go left. Take Dolman to Hastings," Kin shouted in my ear. Was he crazy? I'd have to drive through the mob of women forming outside the club to get to Dolman Street. I put our chances of getting through without them yanking him off the back of the scooter at somewhere around nil.

Before I could answer, the side door to Driven burst

open to release a horde of women with lust on their minds and blood in their eyes. The effect of the guitar now outlived Kin's playing it.

"Trust me." I steered Pinky past the group and cranked a sharp right hand turn onto Snyder.

"There he is. Kin. Come back. I love you." I heard shouting from not that far behind me and poured on the gas. Pinky did her best, bless her little aluminum heart, but two full grown adults are more than she was built to carry. We soared off at a pace just slightly faster than a woman can run in a pair of heels, followed by what looked like twenty or so ladies trying to test that theory.

They chased us for three blocks before the less determined ones fell away to leave the die-hards behind. I banked right onto Fellows and left a few more women in the dust before I had a chance to take a glance behind me. Lemon, short legs flashing, led the charge. Who knew she could run that fast?

"Lexi." Kin warned, "Look."

Brake lights ahead. I should have remembered they started nighttime roadwork this week. I slowed down to think for a moment, which let the three women still chasing after us get too close. A hand latched onto the arm of Kin's shirt just as I gunned the engine again.

Kin clutched hard at my waist and I heard a tearing sound, but Pinky didn't let me down. We picked up just enough speed to make a clean getaway as I dodged down the line of idling cars looking for a gap big enough to get to the sidewalk. If I could make it another half a block or so, there was a bike trail leading through Tidewater Park and from there, I could get back to Hastings Street and head home.

Horns blared behind me and I heard Kin say, "Huh," in a bewildered tone, but I caught a break and got us to the park without further incident.

"It's okay, you can stop now." Kin shouted in my ear, so I pulled over under one of the old-fashioned looking street lamps lining the edge of the trail and killed the motor. "There's nobody following us."

Yanking off my helmet, I inspected Kin for signs of damage. His sleeve was torn from the shoulder to the wrist and he had a long scratch down that arm and a spot where his guitar strap had rubbed some skin raw, but otherwise, he looked okay.

"What the hell just happened? Do you know? Because I don't, and this whole night has been…I can't even describe the level of strange. It's off the charts." Leaning the guitar against the side, Kin slumped onto the park bench conveniently located next to a street lamp and raked a hand through his hair. In a few weeks, there would be flowers growing in the box behind the bench, and I would take this route home several times a week so I could sit and watch the waves.

Or maybe I wouldn't, because this was about to become the scene of my most recent relationship failure. I'd probably avoid the place for the next year. I wondered if I could talk him into postponing this discussion until we got back to his house.

The pause during the time it took me to work through that bit of logic tipped Kin off to the fact that I might actually have an answer to his purely rhetorical question.

"Lexi?"

"What? I have no idea what happened." The lie could only have been more obvious if it had waving flags, fireworks, and a marching band to announce it.

"Yes, you do." He insisted.

"Let me take you home first. Then we'll talk."

"No. I'm not going anywhere until you tell me what you know. Nothing about this night has been normal and I need to know why."

I ignored his plea, "Where did you get that guitar?"

Frowning, Kin said, "I bought it when I was in New Orleans right after Christmas. From a guy that deals in musical memorabilia. Cost me a pretty penny, too, since it belonged to Skip Stark back in his heyday." I caught a hint of nostalgia and a dash of hero worship in the way he spoke the rock legend's name. "Guy I bought it from told me the wildest story, too. Stark was into the spooky New Orleans counterculture in a big way."

"Tell me the story," I urged.

"Not until you tell me what you know." Kin's fingers speared through his curly blond hair again. As irritated as I was, I couldn't help wishing it was my hands tangled in the strands.

Ignoring his suspicion, and my compulsion for physical contact for the moment, I said, "I'm guessing the story had something to do with the guitar being enchanted, right?"

Comprehension dawned. "But that's…it's not *possible*. It was just a sales tactic by the dealer. Give the rube a good story so he'll pay more."

"Tell me," I urged gently. "And then I'll explain how I knew, okay?"

"There's not much to tell. Basically, it went down like this; Stark's career was on a downswing. His last album hadn't been selling all that well, and he wasn't booking tours, so…there's two versions of the story. One is that he went to the crossroads and made a deal with the devil to get back on top. The other is that he found someone, like a Voodoo priestess or something, and asked for a spell that would make him popular again. Next thing you know, he's selling out stadiums and has a string of number one records. Total comeback."

I raised an eyebrow, "And you thought a little of that success might rub off on you?"

"No." Kin scuffed a toe across the pavement in front of the bench and avoided looking at me. "Maybe. To be honest, I'd rather be gifted with a touch of his song writing skills rather than any large measure of his fame. Especially if what happened tonight is the end result." Even under the dim streetlight, I could see his face was paler than normal. "It was fun for about a minute, right before it turned into something out of a hokey teen movie."

"It can't be all bad. At least you got to see some boobs." Teasing him put some color back into his face. I love a man who blushes. Like, I mean like.

Expectation lingered on the silence between us and I sighed.

"What have the neighbors told you about me?" Like a lover who hogged the bed, the city had sprawled its way into my neighborhood and driven most of the rural right out of the area. Suburbia had marched up to our insulated community and stopped just short of swallowing it whole.

Within that small town core were neighbors who probably knew more about my family than I ever would. It was a sore spot with me, given the fact that while they seemed delighted to discuss my history behind my back, I had never been able to pry a single story from any one of them.

"Nothing."

Too hasty; I wasn't buying the denial, so I let a short silence and a raised eyebrow speak for me.

"Fine. I might have heard some things about you and your family. Sue me, I was interested in knowing more about you, but I know better than to believe everything I hear." His eyes slid from mine and he looked guiltily away.

"Which parts did you choose to believe? That I've never had a steady boyfriend because I drive away men? That three really strange but gorgeous women who might or might not be gay live in my house? That weird things happen there all the time? That my grandmother and my mother got into a fight and they both disappeared? Or that I am the last living member of a long line of witches?"

Family skeletons rarely remain safely in their closets after a couple of generations have lived in the same house, and even if my lineage hadn't been common knowledge, the pilgrimage at Beltane was hard to ignore.

"You've touched on the highlights." The wood slats creaked under Kin's weight as he crossed one leg over the other. There wasn't enough inflection in his voice to give me a clue what he was thinking, so I just blurted out the first sarcastic thought that ran through my head.

"Did they also tell you those women are my faerie godmothers and I am the protector of the sacred flame? A fire that has burned in my hearth for hundreds of years?"

"Well, I'm sure it keeps the Easter Bunny warm." Kin matched his tone to mine. I rose to pace in front of him.

"I knew the guitar was the source of the problem because I saw...well, I can't exactly explain what I saw because this is all new to me. Symbols or runes. I don't know what they mean because I've only seen them a couple of times. Being a witch doesn't come with any sort of training manual. Well, I guess it does if you have someone to train you, but it didn't work that way for me. I only just got my powers the other day, and you came along at about the same time, and I'm in over my head."

At that point, I knew I was mostly babbling to myself simply to keep talking, because the minute I stopped, Kin would get a chance to speak, and that would be bad. I forced my mouth shut and waited.

After an hour-long minute it was Kin's turn to stand and pace while I sank back onto the bench.

"Did you just tell me that you're a witch? I think that's what I got out of all that. Unless I've lost my mind, which actually makes more sense to me than anything else I've heard tonight."

"I'm sorry," I started to say, then stopped, "No, I won't apologize. This is who I am. The real me. Lexi Balefire, the raw and uncut version. Matchmaker. Orphan. Spinster. Witch. They're all just words. You know my heart, or at least I think you do, but I won't apologize for who I am. Not anymore. You can either accept me or not."

"I need some time. Please, don't follow me." Kin walked away into the darkness while I stood, stunned, and listened to his footsteps until the sounds faded away into the night.

Chapter 22

Insistent hammering knocks and a ringing doorbell sent me into full alert mode about two minutes after I finally fell asleep. The clock said it had been three hours, but what does a piece of plastic and computer chips know?

Practically flying over Salem, I landed on the floor in some sort of morning ninja crouch. Hair sticking up on one side, raccoon makeup smudged over puffy eyes, and pale skin went ignored as I tossed a robe over shorty pajamas I didn't remember donning.

"Salem. Did you undress me last night?" The tears had waited until I got Pinky safely into the garage and turned to a deluge by the time I landed face down on my bed. The rest of the night I remembered as one long sobfest followed by a restless sleep. No personal hygiene had been involved, and that included changing into a silky tank over matching shorts in a floral pattern.

"And how many times do I have to tell you, if you are naked on my bed, you'd better be wearing fur." That sounded better in my head.

"Me-*ow*," he said.

"Boundaries, Salem. Seriously."

"Lexi. Open up." The front door muffled Kin's voice. What on earth was he doing here? I'd spent hours the night before resigning myself to the fact that I'd probably never see him again. Not even the logic of him living only a few doors down had factored into my delusion.

"Please, I need to talk to you. Open the door."

Already racing from the adrenaline rush of my abrupt awakening, my heart zoomed a little faster. What did he want? Salem, now in cat form, dashed between my feet and nearly tripped me in the hallway. I stopped short, and he blinked back into his human form. A handy trick, that.

"Don't you dare open that door. It took me hours to get you calmed down enough to sleep last night; nothing good can come from seeing that man right now. He'll only hurt you again."

"He might be in trouble. I can't just leave him out there."

"Sure you can," Salem assured, "just tell him to go away."

"I can hear you through the door," Kin said. "Who's the guy?" A tiny thrill shot through me when I detected a hint of jealousy.

I moved toward the door.

"Oh, I *am* done here." Salem turned his tail and stalked back up the stairs. Not all the way, though. Just far enough to eavesdrop.

"It's Salem." Stretching up on tiptoes, I peered through the high glass pane shaped like a cobweb.

Kin looked like he'd been run through a shredder. His hair stood on end, his face was haggard and sleep deprived, but it was the look in his eyes that made me open the door. They had the same expression as an abandoned puppy, and while I wasn't sure I could fully trust him, I couldn't leave him standing out there, either.

The first thing he did was try to take me in his arms, but I dodged far enough away to keep several feet of distance between us. Walking away like he had was the one thing that played into every one of my biggest relationship fears. Rejection because the chemistry isn't right, or from a lack of common interests is one thing.

Being rejected just for being me is what strikes my heart like a hammer. It's not rational and I know whatever cataclysmic event ended my family most likely had nothing to do with me, but rejection hits every feeling of loss I carry from that time.

"What do you want, Kin?" I asked, masking my pain by removing all emotion from my voice, with effort, "We're not going to talk about personal things right now, because I'm not ready for that, so unless something else happened after you left last night, I think you should leave."

The puppy eyes got worse. Great goddess, I wanted to make that look go away almost badly enough to forget the night of tears he had caused. Almost.

Eyes glittering against black fur, Salem padded over to Kin and rubbed against his legs until the man bent to scratch the cat under his chin. Bloody stripes across the back of his hand came as an unexpected result.

"Ow, what in the world got into him?" Kin exclaimed.

"I'll tell you what got into me." Salem at least had the common sense to be clothed when he turned human in front of Kin. The black turtleneck over black slacks against inky skin combined with a lithe body gave him an appropriately cat burglar-ish appearance. Only the white hair would have given him away.

Kin's eyes bugged out and I hid a tiny smirk. "Hush now, Salem."

"I will not. He's a jerk." To Kin, he said, "Actually, you're an idiot. I might even feel sorry for you if I was a charitable sort. Lexi is too good for you anyway. I don't know what I was thinking when I brought the two of you together."

I gasped.

"What? You thought my little spate of breaking and entering was a random moment?"

"You…he's…" Kin looked from the man standing next to him back to me with wide eyes.

"My familiar. It came as a shock to me, too. Now I find he's been meddling in things that are *none of his business*." I emphasized the last four words with a narrow-eyed glare.

"I thought he was a good guy." Salem defended himself.

"Can't I be a good guy who turned into an ass for a little while and then realized what he'd done was incredibly stupid? Lexi, I'm sorry. It didn't take me long to figure out I'd made a mistake and I tried to come back and tell you that last night, but you'd already gone. So, I sat on that bench for hours and just thought it all through. The guitar, all the success I've been having lately, and you. The miracle of having you come into my life." The words caught, turned his voice hoarse with emotion. "I was a fool."

A snort from Salem netted him another dirty look from me. "Go back upstairs. I can handle this myself." He went, but not without treating Kin to a deliberate stare while he rubbed his cheek against mine in a gesture of possession.

"Gee, why don't you just pee on her leg."

"Lexi wouldn't like that, and unlike you, I prefer to give her what she wants." Salem sailed down the hall, gave Kin one last glowering look, and marched up the stairs.

"Is there something going on between you and…"

"Don't." I held up a hand. "Don't even go there. I might be able to forgive you for last night. In time. But if you put that image in my head, we're done."

Kin gave me a quick grin that I did not return. "Is that everything you wanted to tell me?" I asked.

"It was the most important thing, but there is something else. Can I come in?" Curiosity drew Kin's gaze past me toward the bit of kitchen he could see at the end of the hall. He actually leaned his head over to see beyond me.

"You are in."

"Come on, Lexi. I really need to tell you what happened. I think I need help. The magical kind." I blinked at him and wrapped my arms around my waist in a protective gesture. My mind raced through a short argument about whether or not to help him—especially if that meant exposing him to the godmothers in all their glory. The devil on my shoulder snickered at the mental image.

"Fine, but I need to get cleaned up first. I look like death warmed over."

"You look perfect to me."

"Stop trying to suck up. It's beneath you. You'll have to…" I looked around in desperation. There was no safe space for him downstairs. Sigh… "Come upstairs. Follow me." Over my shoulder I said, "There will be no further discussion of us or our relationship." I didn't make air quotes, but I'm pretty sure he got the point. "Those are the rules. Follow them or leave now."

"I'll try."

"And no comments about the decor, either." I swung open the door and pulled it back closed just as fast. "Salem. For the love of all that's holy."

A faint sorry drifted through the closed door. Waiting an extra second to make sure I wasn't about to get another unwanted peep show, I popped the door open a crack to see a fully-dressed Salem sprawled on his favorite beanbag bed. Kin followed me into the room.

"You two stay here, I'll be just a few minutes. No fighting." Wagging a finger at my familiar, I grabbed clothing from the dresser and hit the shower. It is a total myth that women are incapable of taking a quick shower, and I think I qualified for a land speed record that day. Ten minutes later, I walked back into a tense silence, which I ignored.

"Okay, tell me," I said to Kin and sat down to put on enough makeup to cover the last residual puffiness around my eyes.

"After I got done with my little pity party, I decided that I didn't want the burden of owning something that could affect women that way. Despite my actions last night, I'm not that kind of guy. Sure, it was fun for a little while, but I would never intentionally take advantage of anyone like that." His distaste went some way toward softening my heart, but not far enough to make me trust him with it again.

"So, I figured I'd just destroy the guitar and that would be the end of it. I filled it full of rocks and tossed it off the bridge." Gingerly, he sat on the edge of my bed, amid the sheets rumpled from a night of tossing and turning. Kin's face was troubled. "Lexi, I stood there and watched it sink."

Keeping one eye on him and the other in the mirror, I took another two minutes to pull a comb through my hair and yank the wet strands into a slicked back tail.

"And…" I prodded when he fell silent.

"And then I went back to the club to pick up my car. When I went backstage to grab my things, the guitar case was still there." I had to strain to hear the next part. "The guitar was in the case." Kin's eyes met mine in the mirror, worry rode his expression. "How could that have happened?"

While I fished in the closet for a pair of ballet flats, Salem warned, "I'll go tell the family we have company."

"Be nice." Depending on what he said to them before they met Kin, the next hour could be a total disaster. "Or I'll get the vacuum cleaner out."

Kin stood in the middle of the room with a look on his face that I couldn't quite read. "You said faerie godmothers last night. Did I hear that right?" The man looked nervous. Who could blame him?

"About that. I'm sure Salem is waking them up right now. They get cranky when that happens." Another sigh, "And they're drop dead gorgeous. Even in their everyday glamour. Try not to stare."

"Give me a little credit, Lexi. I'm not a total dog." That sent my eyebrows toward my hairline. "Okay, maybe I am a little dog. But I'm trying."

"Relationship talk. Against the rules. If Salem tells them you made me cry, they'll be even more cranky. Things could get hairy." I paused. "Literally."

"What does that mean? Literally?"

"Let's hope you never have to find out." The devil was back and whispering things about how funny it would be if he did. I'm pretty sure my godmothers are at the heart of every single one of the Bigfoot rumors. Hair growth is one of Terra's favorite curses.

Salem met us at the foot of the stairs, his body humming with contained excitement. "They're in a good mood. No need for the vacuum." Just saying the dread word made him whisper.

By good mood, what Salem really meant was playful, which had the potential to be almost as bad as angry. Kitted out in their best glamour, my faerie godmothers couldn't pull off normal even when they tried. Bustling around the kitchen wearing a pastel fantasy number from the Disney princess collection—belled skirt, nipped waist, snug bodice with a sweetheart neckline—Terra was halfway done cooking breakfast for twenty.

"Come in, come in. It's been so long since we've had guests. Sit right down, Kin is it?" She picked up a glitter covered, star-tipped wand to match her dress and I almost died trying to hold back a snort.

"Kin, Terra. Terra, this is Kin." Terse, but all I felt up for in the way of an introduction.

Since I turned six, I've been able to see past even the best glamour. Under hers, Terra watched Kin like a hawk.

"Just you? Salem said he told everyone to come," I said to Terra.

"We're here." Three voices chorused from three faces of supermodel caliber beauty. They were dressed the same as Terra, save for color. Salem's snort sounded distinctly catty and not in a feline way. I risked a curious glance at Kin, who was so determined not to stare he barely dared to look up from the empty plate in front of him. And now they were going to think he was shifty.

Well, what did I care? I might never forgive him anyway, so his veracity was a moot point.

Right.

Following the second round of hasty introductions, I bypassed the smaller coffee mug sitting at my regular spot at the table and grabbed one of the over-sized ones from the cabinet, because slurping down the entire pot in one gulp would have been rude.

"Was all this really necessary?" Dry doesn't begin

to describe my tone.

"What? You're the one who decided to let him in on our secrets, why not give him the full experience?" Goddess forbid if that ever happened. I decided to cut my losses and go with the mild version of life in the Balefire house.

"I'd really like to get this over with. Kin, eat something, or Terra will be offended. She really is a good cook." And then, while he did, I repeated his guitar story.

"Where is the instrument now?" I detected more than curiosity from Evian.

Kin flushed. "It's outside."

"What? You thought if you brought it inside I might go all braindead fangirl on you?"

"No. I was so concerned with apologizing to you I forgot."

"I'll get it." Salem darted from the room and returned seconds later carrying the familiar case. Instead of handing it to Kin, he laid it at the other end of the massive table. Carefully, like it might go off if he jostled it. Then he backed away. "Strong magic around that thing. Comes off it in waves and makes me dizzy."

"Odd. It normally only affects women." Kin's comment was innocently meant.

"Are you calling me a girl?" Salem bristled.

"Salem," I growled. "Give it a rest."

The four faeries crowded around the instrument,

poking it, tweaking a string here and a string there. Kin gasped when Soleil took her smaller form and flew into the sound hole for a better look.

"Play it for me." Vaeta handed the guitar to Kin. He struck a chord, then played a few bars of something with a boogie beat. "Okay." She held up a hand. "Stop."

Chapter 23

Kin, Salem, and I sat in awkward silence while the faeries indulged in a short, whispered discussion. The weight of each sidelong glance from Kin fell on me like a blanket. I ignored them all and stared straight ahead.

"Put the guitar back on the table. We have an idea," Vaeta said.

"It's a stupid idea, but apparently we're going to go ahead with it anyway," Terra cast a hard look at her sister.

"Don't start." I pushed back my chair and pinned the two of them with a pointed finger. "We don't have time for one of your fights right now. Kin, do as Vaeta says." He did, and I felt the prickle of magic across my skin.

"*Reveal.*" Vaeta stepped forward to whisper into the sound hole while we waited to see what would happen next. Shimmering motes rose from the hole to form the vague shape of a man standing next to the table and I heard Kin's quick intake of breath.

"*Crystallize.*" A complicated wave of Evian's hand accompanied the command and the motes formed into a solid outline that reminded me of the way they make things look invisible in movies. It looked like a man made from liquid.

"*Solidify.*" Terra's contribution was some next-level stuff. The man-shape flickered as bits of matter appeared. In under a minute, the lifelike figure of Skip Stark stood there.

"*Animate.*" Soleil laid a hand on the figure and lightning shot from her fingertips to jolt into Stark's body. He opened his eyes.

"It's alive." I quelled Salem's mutter with a hard look, even if I could see the humor in it. Later we could have a good laugh about Frankensinger, but for now, seriousness was the order of the day.

"Unbelievable." Kin's voice came out on a quavering note. "Love your music, man."

"You're not bad yourself, kid." Stark's voice sounded a little rusty and he cleared his throat.

Before this turned into a love fest, I interrupted. "Mr. Stark…"

"Call me Skip, Sweetheart."

"Skip. Can you tell us how you ended up in that guitar?" This might be a simple haunting that the dealer had embellished into a more complicated backstory in order to sell the guitar to Kin.

Stark quelled that faint hope with a word, "Wizard." He pulled out a chair, flipped it around and sat straddling it with his arms resting on the back. A blur of pastel at the corner of my eye had me turning my head in time to see the faeries leaving the room, and I was torn between following them and listening to what Stark had to say.

Okay, that's not true. Wild horses couldn't have dragged me from my chair, and I knew that whatever happened while they were gone, they'd hear anyway. If they wanted to, that is.

"All I wanted was to get my mojo back, you know? Another shot at the big time. Hell, at that point, I would have settled for a permanent gig singing in a bar. I was broke—my own fault for throwing money around like confetti. Take it from me, son, you got the chops, don't let this business go to your head. That'll get you all kinds of messed up."

Kin only gulped and nodded. I think he was having trouble forming full sentences.

"Anyway," Stark snagged a piece of bacon off the platter and crunched with evident pleasure before he continued. "I shoulda known the guy was up to no good. He had shifty eyes." A second piece of bacon went down his maw. "He did his mumbo jumbo, nicked my thumb with a little knife and scattered the blood onto my guitar."

"Blood magic. A powerful binding spell from the sounds of it. He probably bound your soul to the guitar so that whenever you played, it was your amplified essence and intention that went out to the crowd." Privately, I thought his intentions toward women were not remotely honorable, but there wasn't anything I could do about that now, and a discussion of his skeezy ethics would be counterproductive.

Now Kin spoke up. "You know it wasn't my intentions that made those women act like that, don't you, Lexi? I would never…"

"I know." I cut off that line of discussion because it smacked of the out-of-bounds relationship topic. "What else can you tell us, Skip."

"Things were pretty quiet for a while there. Then, this young fella bought the guitar and played it so pure and clean that I felt the dark hold on it slipping away." Skip turned to Kin, "You had me halfway to the light. I thought I was finally going to go to my rest. Stupid wizard never told me I'd be stuck in that thing forever."

"What happened next?" Normally clothed now, the four faeries suddenly appeared. Kin jumped about a foot.

"We were outside a coffeehouse, and this one was playing so sweet I was halfway home when something grabbed me and yanked me back. Next thing I know, there's some guy with a funny looking beard and a heart-shaped scar on his face talking about breaking true love's hold on the world, and I got sucked right back inside. Dude was a real freak. He got so keyed up he sprayed spit all over the place."

Vaeta made a choked sound at the mention of the heart-shaped scar, but I ignored her for the time being and circled a hand to indicate Skip could continue his story.

"That's when all the crazy started. I'm not a bad guy, I swear I'm not. Sure, I liked women in my day; as many as I could get. What's not to like, I mean, come on. Boobs. Right, man?" Skip looked to Kin to back him up. Kin flushed red and zipped it. I admired his restraint.

"What can you tell me about last night? Do you remember being thrown in the water?" The question came from Kin. "I'd like to know how the guitar got back in the case."

"Don't know anything about that. When you're not playing, I kind of go to sleep."

Evian clapped her hands, "I think we have learned everything we could from Mr. Stark. Would you all agree?" When there was no word of dissent, she gestured to her sisters. "Shall we?"

"*Sleep*," Soleil reversed her spell.

"Dissolve."

"Shatter."

When Vaeta uttered the final command, nothing remained of Stark but a few motes of light. "*Release*."

"No," Evian cried out. "What have you done?"

Stark's essence coalesced into a column of light that sucked upward from the bottom and disappeared.

"You let him go before we had a chance to reverse the original spell on the guitar. What is wrong with you?"

"I'm sorry. I thought we were finished with him, and he wanted to move on to the next plane so badly." Even to my ears, Vaeta's protest sounded weak.

"Kin, think hard. Have you ever cut yourself on or around your guitar? All it would take is a trace of your blood to transfer the spell to you." Terra picked up on an aspect of this whole debacle that no one else had even considered.

"Well, sure, I guess. E strings are thin and can be sharp on the ends. Nicks during restringing are common."

While her sisters questioned Kin more thoroughly, I pulled Vaeta out onto the patio.

"What's his name?" Birds chirped in the trees, but Vaeta remained silent for a beat, then another. "You thought I didn't notice your reaction to Stark's description. You know the man who put the whammy on Kin's guitar, and if you try and pawn off one of your half-truths on me, I'm going to tell your sisters about it."

"Tattletale." Gone was the slightly spacey demeanor that Vaeta tended to present in public. For a split second, I saw the crafty faerie in her truest light.

"And proud of it. Spill it, Vaeta."

"It's Striker. Jett Striker."

"And…" Knowing there was more, I prodded.

"He has…" Vaeta searched for the right word, "…ties to two different worlds."

"Dangerous?"

"When he wants to be—which isn't often. He's a trickster. Gets his laughs mostly by pulling lovers apart."

"Like what? An anti-matchmaker?"

Vaeta's eyes widened slightly. "Something like that."

Chapter 24

"A simple location spell is all we should need." I said and watched the look on Kin's face as the wall popped open and my hand emerged unharmed. From stricken to disbelief in under a second. Probably a harbinger of things to come if we stayed together.

Yeah, I was considering it. You know, if whatever Jett Striker had done to the guitar didn't kill Kin, or consume his soul, or something worse. Nothing like a little grievous peril to put your priorities in the right place.

This time when I approached the book of magic and touched the spine, it opened to a page in the middle all by itself, as if it knew exactly what I needed. There, in delicate calligraphy were the words "To Locate An Enemy" and below it, a description and a list of ingredients for a simple spell. I scanned the items, picked up the ritual broom, and started the process of cleansing the circle, all while barking out orders.

"Evian, I need a goblet of water; Terra, sandalwood and myrrh incense; Salem please tell me there's a mugwort infusion in those supplies; Soleil, four blue candles at the four corners; Vaeta, a map of the city—we'll assume he's nearby and start there—and the clearest quartz crystal pendulum you can find."

Kin's eyes were wide as he looked around the room, and if it weren't his soul on the line I might have found his incredulity cute—or his fear a bit funny, considering how he had been acting over the past twenty-four hours. I vowed to harden my heart just as soon as we were out of this mess.

"What do I do?" He asked.

"Just sit there and be quiet." I snapped, and Salem chuckled from across the room, earning an irritated glare from Kin. "Enough, you two. It says we need a part of Jett's essence to solidify the connection. We have to hope some of his spit remained in or on the guitar." Kin passed it to me quickly and wiped his palms on the front of his jeans as soon as he let go. I didn't blame him for feeling the heebs.

"Forensic science meets magic." Kin observed. "It would make a great TV show."

I carried a low table into the center of the pentacle, pretending to struggle a little in order to avoid making eye contact with Kin. He squirmed and his face gave away the internal struggle over whether to remain seated, or give in to his chivalric instincts and insist on helping me. I think it was something about the upward tilt of my nose or the infinitesimal narrowing of my eyes that kept his butt firmly planted on the sofa.

Carefully, I laid the guitar across the middle of the table, the map spread out on one side, the goblet of water on the other and anointed each of the four candles with the mugwort infusion. Then I sat down cross-legged, facing west.

"Soleil, if you would, please." She lit the candles with a flick of her wrist, and each faerie took her place at her respective corner: Vaeta and Terra to the east and the north; and Soleil and Evian to the south and west.

If there was ever a moment of truth, this was it.

"Goddesses of the east, bless this water. Imbue it with the power to locate the demigod Jett Striker. Help us find our foe, and bring him to justice." I dipped my right index and middle fingers into the goblet of water, swirled it in a clockwise direction seven times, then picked up the pendulum with dripping fingers and swung it seven times counter-clockwise over the city map.

As soon as the droplets of water hit the map, it promptly burst into flames. Red smoke curled up from the spreading fire. I grabbed the goblet and poured the contents on top, which only made the hungry fire reach toward my bare fingers. I wound up a scream, but Terra was on top of the situation and immediately doused the fire with a pile of sand, so there was no need for it, and I awkwardly shut my mouth and stepped away from the circle.

"Was that what was supposed to happen?" Kin asked, and I nearly bit my tongue in half trying not to shout at him.

"No, genius, it wasn't," Salem spoke the words for me and directed his next snarky comment in my direction. "You're still adding too much power; this spell is delicate, and it's like you're using a meat cleaver when you should be using a fillet knife. Let me think."

"It's because…" Vaeta broke off when I glared at her. "Never mind."

"I'm trying to hold back, but this kind of thing keeps happening." It wasn't a whine, but it was close. "Aren't you guys supposed to do something? Isn't it your job to help a witch in trouble?"

"Well, we're really more of a clean-up service than a preventative one," Soleil chirped. Sometimes her sunny nature got on my last nerve.

"That's rich given the number of times I've had to put the house back together after one of your battles. I'm starting to think someone got the Cinderella story wrong and it was the faerie godmothers who worked her fingers to the bone."

"Lexi, come look at this. I think it might help." Salem interrupted from the Grimoire's pedestal.

To Balance Power I read from an entry written in a

different hand than the one for locating an enemy. This spell was closer to the end of the book where the pages were less tattered and worn.

You have Seen
And now you know
Where the Balefire burns
Your powers grow

You listened well
And braved the flame
But still must work
To earn your name

When at last
You know your way
This spell you cast
Shall fade away

If balance be
Your heart's desire
Then speak your wish
Unto the fire

"What kind of cryptic nonsense is that?"

"Clearly, it's a balancing spell. For your fledgling powers. Apparently, someone thought you might experience this phenomenon, and wrote a spell to help you control your magic. It's worth a shot. But this one is all you; the rest of us can't help."

"I bet it was my mother and this was her last gift to me." When I noticed the handwriting looked a lot like mine, I ran a finger over the text to see if I could pick up any residual energy. "I'll give it a shot."

Everyone took a step back from the circle, and Vaeta magicked a collection of supplies onto the altar in front of me. I rang the tiny bell, anointed the white candle in Bergamot oil, and whispered my wish for balance into the flame before blowing it out.

For a moment the wick sizzled, and the bell began to tinkle all by itself as a warm breeze enveloped my body. I could smell fresh laundry, the salty scent of the ocean, and the crisp odor of cut grass. A golden glow of light surrounded me, and I floated off the floor as stimuli flooded my senses.

Just as quickly as it began, it was over, and I was seated back on the floor as if nothing had happened. "Did it work?" I asked, looking around at the six people who were staring at me like I had sprouted a second head, or a couple of extra limbs.

"I don't know, dear, you tell us." Terra gestured to the candle and I leaned in, focusing all of my attention on reigniting the wick using only my will and a breath of air from my lungs. I blew gently, and the candle flared to life once more. We were all silent, expecting some sort of fallout, but nothing happened.

"I did it! I finally did it!" I shouted, relieved that I had hit another milestone on the path to controlling my powers. If we were going to go up against this Jett Striker, I would need every ounce of discipline I could muster.

He had experience on his side, and probably more than one wild card, but I had four elemental faeries on mine. It's my job to match souls, and I'd sooner eat a whole plate of live beetles than stand around and let some jerk tear them apart. Plus, there was no way I was going to let Kin's soul be anchored to an inanimate object, whether he was the one for me or not.

"Quick, let's try the location spell again," Terra exclaimed, and everyone rushed back into motion, resetting the candles, guitar, and the goblet of water. Last time, I had been in the dark, but now, with my head clear and my brain working at full potential, I could sense that something was missing.

I turned to Kin and motioned for him to enter the circle. "I think you need to be playing the guitar. By itself, it's just an object; the magic is released when you play."

Kin looked as though he'd rather walk through a snake pit than step inside the pentacle, but he resolved himself, stepped across the line, and picked up the cursed instrument. I called to the goddesses of the east once more, and as I dipped my fingers into the water Kin began to play.

The scrying crystal hummed with energy, and I felt it touch down heavily and then still, but I couldn't tear my eyes away from the guitar. At Driven, the symbols wafting from the strings were red, but now they had turned black and had a nearly solid quality that seemed to be growing in intensity. What that meant, I couldn't say, but it didn't seem to point toward anything good.

"You've got to be kidding me." I breathed after finally checking Striker's location on the map. "The pendulum is resting right on top of Serena Snodgrass' house."

"Who is Serena Snodgrass?" Kin asked, laying the guitar back inside the case and closing the lid with a bit more force than necessary.

Vaeta stepped out of the shadows from where she had been watching me work the spell, and let her opinion be known. "Of course that little wench is involved. I knew she was bad news the minute I laid eyes on her. Let's bring this fight to them. You all take care of Jett Striker; I call dibs on Serena. Nobody messes with my goddaughter and gets away with it!"

Utter silence followed Vaeta's proclamation, and I felt a tear form in the corner of my eye; I was touched that Vaeta had referred to me as her goddaughter. I strode across the room and hugged her, hard. Vaeta stiffened and patted me awkwardly on the back. A small smile twitched across her face, and when I let go everyone except Kin got a little teary-eyed.

"That's really sweet of you, but the witch is mine. Clearly, she's afraid of me if she had to enlist extra help to mount some kind of sneak attack." I'd already decided she was the force behind this whole thing. "Going after Kin was a big mistake." I might be mad at him now, but nobody attacks my possible boyfriend. Nobody.

Vaeta was all for marching right up to Serena's door and big bad wolfing it down with a mighty wind. There was only one problem with the plan—Serena wouldn't be there alone.

"Vaeta, what else do you know about Striker?"

"Not a lot. I've seen him around," her shrug was noncommittal.

"Around where? I'll admit I've been curious about where it is that you flit off to when you're not here." Evian threw down the challenge. "Why don't you tell us, because I know you're not going home; I'd smell Faelands on you."

"You're not the boss of me. I have friends in this world. At the edges of it anyway."

"Aha." A flicker of flame arced from Soleil's pointed finger. "The Fringe."

"The TV show? Didn't that get canceled?" Kin's question made him the object of exasperated looks and he held up both hands in surrender. "Never mind."

"It's the place where worlds meet. Not everyone can pass through the in between. I'm not even sure if I can, and I'm of the blood, which means Striker has more magic than me."

"Who is Serena Snodgrass?" Kin asked for the third time, clearly in the dark and not happy about it.

"I'll explain on the way."

"On the way where?"

"To the scene of the crime, of course."

"What crime?" He squeaked.

My answer was a dark look.

Chapter 25

There was nothing more that Vaeta could tell us about Striker. He hung out in the Fringe, had exceedingly poor taste in women, and had warped the enchantment on Kin's guitar into something sinister. Those facts remained undisputed; his motivations for tampering with the instrument were something only he could explain, but all I could see was Serena's mocking face, and nothing would sway me from believing she was at the bottom of everything.

Fury carried me right up to her doorstep, Kin trailing along behind with the guitar slung across his back. When the four faeries had taken their smaller form, he'd gone silent and wide-eyed.

"Get your game face on," I shot the terse order at him. Deer in headlights was not his best look. "If things get ugly, you walk away. Run if you have to." The worst Serena could do was cover him in warts. Striker might do a lot more.

Vaeta settled on my shoulder and used her power to amplify my voice, "Serena Swampgrass. Get out here now." Terra added a localized ground shake to the effect.

A curtain twitched aside to show Serena's sharp features and beady eyes. I cocked an aggressive pose and crooked my finger at her in the come here signal. When she didn't move immediately, I flashed her a different gesture, using a different finger. That one did the trick.

The curtain swished closed about a second before the front door discharged not much more than a hundred pounds worth of spitting witch.

"How dare you come to my house and threaten me, Lexi Balefire. I'll…" Serena marched down the steps, strode right up to me, and leaned in close.

"You'll what?" I took a step toward her. "I'd really like to hear just what it is you're planning to do."

The answer was a low growl and her hand reaching for my hair, only to stop short when Kin's fingers closed around her wrist.

"Don't even think about it," he gritted out from between his teeth.

"Who are you? Lexi's lapdog?" Serena yanked her hand from his grasp and took a step back to tilt her head and look up at his face. "You don't look like the biggest idiot in the world, so I know you can't actually be involved with her."

"Don't play dumb, swamp thing. I know you had something to do with the curse on Kin's guitar." Power gathered in me like a crouching panther waiting to pounce. It prickled across my skin, leaving every tiny hair standing on end. Beside me, Kin shivered but stood strong. Serena ran one hand up and down her other arm as though remembering the aftermath of the last time she had faced me. I saw indecision on her face and a measure of fear that sent a dark thrill through me. My wicked nature?

"You are completely delusional. I never laid a finger on that guitar." The slight emphasis on the word *I* condemned her. "Now get off my property."

"Oh, I don't think so," I said and gave a subtle nod. Four tiny streaks buzzed past Serena's head. Seconds later, a male voice loosed a string of naughty words inside the house. Flashes of light and booming sounds echoed out the front door while Serena shrieked.

"You leave him alone. Get out of my house." The gangly witch turned to dash back inside, but before she got to the steps, a dark-haired man shot out the door. A puff of smoke billowed out behind him. Good grief, had Soleil set his pants on fire? It looked like it. She zapped him again, I think just for the fun of it, and he yelped.

"You little bitch, you have no idea who you're messing with." The man, Jett Striker, I presumed, picked up a stick and took aim at Soleil. The blow, meant to knock her out of the air, never landed. Instead, she and her sisters shot from dragonfly size to their normal height—at least a foot taller than Striker, and she set the stick ablaze. With another oath, he tossed it away and glowered up at her.

Soleil responded by wagging a finger at him, "Naughty, naughty."

Blue eyes blazed from under beetled brows tweezed to sharp arches. Paired with the black goatee, I think he was going for evil, but mostly he just looked surprised. Hair blacker than coal flopped over one side of his head; the other was shaved to a stubble.

"Don't you know who I am?" Arrogance curled his lips to a sneer and warped the heart-shaped scar on one cheek.

I bit my lips hard to keep back the smile when four pairs of sardonic eyebrows raised. "Loki wannabe?" Vaeta queried.

"Captain Jack Sparrow come to life?" Was Terra's guess.

"No, it's Gruber from Die Hard." Soleil giggled while Vaeta frowned. I believe monthly movie nights might have corrupted the faeries.

"Well, if we're going with Alan Rickman references, he's really closer to Snape, only without the redeeming value," Evian added her opinion.

As did I. "No. No. No. Depp comparisons are fine, but you can't taint Rickman's memory by comparing this…this…*thing* to him. I simply won't allow it."

"My father is a God, he will smite you if you screw with me." It didn't sound as though Striker was sure of his facts at this point, but who doesn't love a good *I'll tell my daddy on you* coming from an adult?

"Really? He's welcome to try." Terra sent a waft of butterflies circling his head. When Striker batted at them, the delicate, water-colored cloud morphed into a swarm of bees that angled right for him until Terra flicked a finger and they veered away and over my head. The unintended effect of her action served to draw his attention to me.

"You," he spat venomously. "If it isn't Lexi Balefire." He sing-songed my name. "And her entourage. Didn't dare to face me by yourself?"

"Until two hours ago, I didn't even know you existed. Am I supposed to know who you are?" I would have thought I'd remember meeting someone who looked like him, but when I searched my memory it came up blank.

Waves of hatred swamped me, and I wondered how I had managed to so thoroughly piss off someone I'd never even met. Apparently, I was gifted. That kind of animosity was usually reserved for mortal enemies like Serena and me. Or for family. Jett Striker fit neither definition.

"Wait, let me guess. You were in love with one of my clients and I matched her…" at his nasty look, I revised, "…or him with someone else."

"You really don't know who I am, do you?" Striker's eyes burned against skin artfully paled with makeup. I nudged Kin closer toward Evian for protection.

"I've got better things to do than stand around on Serena's front lawn having a spitting contest with some dude who bears a grudge against me for something I don't even remember doing. What are the chances you're going to be decent and remove the curse from Kin's guitar?" It was a mystery to me why I bothered asking. Striker was hell-bent on making me pay for whatever it was he thought I'd done to him.

Serena draped herself over Jett, who largely ignored the toothpick with a head. Honestly, the woman lacked so much as a thimbleful of dignity. I've got shoes with more brains. My matchmaking mojo kicked in to show me what I had already figured out. This man was not Serena's perfect match. Information I absolutely didn't need at that particular moment.

"Nice manners, Sis. I'll make sure to tell Dad you welcomed me with open arms."

I goggled at him. The words were all ones I knew, but in that configuration, they made no sense to me.

"Dad? I don't understand."

"Lexi." Kin came up behind me and snaked his arms around my waist. "Walk away. Whatever is going on here isn't worth it. We'll find another way. Please."

I shrugged off the attempt at emotional support. Alarm bells clanged in my head as I searched Jett's face for any sign of a resemblance. The box labeled Father on my birth certificate was empty. For all I knew, Striker really might be my brother. And wouldn't that just be my luck? I really crapped out in the family department.

"Explain. Now." Magic built inside me, its raw energy just waiting for me to shape it into a weapon and for the first time, I understood how my grandmother might have given in to the temptation to do harm to a family member.

"Wow, I expected you to be a little quicker on the uptake. Didn't your mother tell you about how she used her youth and beauty to steal our father away from my mother? Oh, wait, you've never even had the displeasure of speaking to her, so it's not surprising you have no idea who you are." Jet sneered, his no-punches-pulled words hitting me right in the gut.

"That's right, little sister, your mother was a home wrecker."

"She was not," I started to defend her hotly, then realized I might be wrong. My mother could have been exactly the kind of person he accused her of being. My mind raced through the possibilities and landed on the obvious. If Striker's statements were true, he could tell me more about my family than I'd ever known before.

My thoughts must have shown on my face because Jett's next words were giddy with triumph. "Not so sure about that, are you, little orphan? And now you're just dying to know, aren't you?" He melted out of Serena's grasp, approached me so swiftly there was no time to dodge and grabbed my wrist.

A shock ran through me at the point of contact. Somewhere in the background, I heard voices calling my name, but at that moment, all I could see was what Striker needed to show me—his life passing before my eyes, in reverse.

Not every detail, mind you—just the highlights that applied to this situation blurred past my mind's eye.

Jett following me around last week with Mona—which confirmed my feeling of being watched that day.

Kin leaning his guitar against the side of a building and turning away to speak to someone. Jett's hands moving over the instrument. I could even see the darkness that flowed from them to sink deep into the wood.

Hatred. Hot and black and fierce. Jett had felt my magic uncurl from where it slept deep inside me. That was the moment I had become a threat. How or why was something he would have to explain.

After that, the images sped up. I saw Jett's hand throw withered flowers down next to a headstone.

Another whirl and the harshly lined face of a contemptuous woman screaming insults grew clear.

Back and back it went in a wash of color and light

until the rush of images slowed down to show a shining man who loomed straight and tall. Based on the perspective, I'd have guessed Jett to be no older than three. Pudgy arms shot into my field of vision. The boy begging to be held. The weightless moment when the man obliged.

From inside the boy, I experienced the sense of safety and peace in his father's arms and I'm ashamed to say a lick of jealousy took root in my heart.

My father's face was chiseled perfection. Full lips, wide brow, blue eyes with more than a hint of mischief in them. The fond smile for his son flitted when confronted by the boy's mother. Younger now, and without the bitter lines, her face was lovely. Like a TV being turned up, I heard the escalating sound of fighting. Of Jett's mother begging for more attention, for the man not to leave her. It went on for only a few minutes, but felt like more, before the man set Jett gently on his feet and turned away.

The woman, his mother, called out a name as the door closed behind her love for the last time, "Cupid, no."

Cupid? Like God of Love, bow and arrows, hearts and flowers? *That* Cupid?

Jett released his hold on my arm, taking the images with him.

"Your father was Cupid?"

"Our father, you mean. He dumped my mother and

moved on to be with yours." Jett's contempt for me made a little more sense now, given the context.

I closed my eyes; this was a lot to take in. More than I could accept if I'm being honest. "I had no idea." My throat closed and only a whisper came out. "I'm sorry." For what, I couldn't say, but it felt like an apology of some sort was warranted, even if none of this had been my fault.

No wonder Jett was bitter. "Why now? You must have known about me all along, so why are you only just coming out of the woodwork now?"

"Oh little sister, you weren't worth my time. Playing at being a Child of Cupid without ever knowing the true power at your disposal? How could I take you seriously when you held yourself back from the one thing that feeds everything you are? How you ever managed to create true love's kiss a few times is beyond me."

"True love's kiss? Isn't that a fairy tale?"

Jett turned to Serena, "She lives with faeries and still thinks fairy tales are fiction. You were right, she is a backward fool."

The spell on the guitar, I could see now, had been aimed at me, not at Kin. He was just a casualty in a battle I never even knew I was fighting.

Ever get that feeling that you're standing on the edge of a precipice and the least little thing can send you tumbling down? Then you know what I was feeling at that moment.

"My father has not returned to this world since the day your mother died. With him gone, love is slowly seeping away. Watch the news, you can see it happening. Soon everyone will feel as desolate as I do, and when that happens, my father will have to return to put things right."

Meet my half-brother, the cartoon villain, ladies and gentlemen.

"Jett, please. It doesn't have to be this way. Let me help you." I reached out to him.

"Stay away from me. It isn't bad enough that whatever happened with your *mother*," he spit the word at me, "made my father turn away from me and the rest of the world, but then you go and do father's work for him. I think that's why he won't return. He doesn't need to with the Fate Weaver here to step in and handle things."

Fate Weaver. Harder than the possible truth that my matches were not as fated as I thought, those words falling from his lips hit me. I had heard them before. From Vaeta.

Still tightly wound, Jett continued his tirade. "Well, I'm going to put a stop to it. Every time you set up a match that will end in true love's kiss, I'll be there to screw it up. Love took my father from me. Hate will bring him back."

With a flourish that could only have been more

melodramatic if he was wearing a cape, Jett stalked back toward Serena's house.

I felt faerie magic building behind me and said, "No, Terra. Let him go."

Chapter 26

I don't remember the trip home; all I could think about while the godmothers, Kin, and Salem tried to rouse me from my near catatonic state was the movie reel of Jett's life that wouldn't stop playing on a loop.

Cupid. The God, Cupid, was my father. *My father.* The word felt strange on my tongue. Does it make sense that throughout my entire life, the question of my paternity had played such a small role in my innermost thoughts and dreams, that I had barely recognized the hole that his lack of presence drilled into my heart?

Given the circumstances, looking for my father should have been the obvious route for me to take; after all, he was the only one of my family left alive. And yet, I'd never had the inclination—or the means, for that matter. I didn't know thing one about my mother, so where would I have even started the process of learning who my father might be?

If I thought of him at all, I assumed it'd be up to him to find me if he ever wanted to. As the years went by, I figured he didn't, and drove the thought from my mind.

This must be how Terra, Soleil, and Evian felt about Vaeta for the last hundred years. We all thought someone had intentionally left us, and we had also learned a hard truth: that person's reason for staying away wasn't that cut-and-dried.

When I finally came back to the present, I was seated on one of the sofas in the sanctum and there was chaos all around me. Salem had reverted to his cat form and was curled up in Kin's arms.

Kin had retreated into the furthest corner of the room and pressed himself into a recess between two windows. Frightened didn't begin to describe his expression, and I could detect a hint of something else.

Finally present enough to notice the arms around me belonged to Flix, who I assumed had sensed my distress and flitted in to provide assistance, I could see little flickers of jealousy coming from Kin. This was not the time for misplaced emotions.

I forced my gaze back to the casting circle where Evian, Terra, and Soleil stood in a group facing Vaeta. Insults hurtled back and forth and threatened to whip up a storm that was sure to tear the roof from the rafters if I didn't get involved.

"Stop," I whispered, and the room turned

completely silent. Terra rushed to my side and Flix stepped away, patting my arm to let me know he wouldn't venture far.

"Are you all right?" she asked, attempting to wrap her arms around me lovingly. I pulled away, and even though the hurt that crossed her face felt as real to me as it did to her, I couldn't bring myself to be touched by any of them until I got some answers.

"I want to know everything. Now." I looked past Terra and fixed my gaze on Vaeta. "Is this why you called me a Fate Weaver before? You knew, didn't you." My gaze now shifted, piercing the others each in turn. "Did *all* of you know?"

The four of them all started yelling at each other at once, and I realized why the energy in the room was so volatile. They had been having this fight since we left Serena's. It seemed like a million years ago now.

"Silence. That's enough." Vaeta stepped forward and spoke at a volume that could have shattered glass. "Don't take it out on them. They had no idea. But I knew exactly who you were from the moment I laid eyes on you."

"How could you?" Soleil stepped from the fray toward Vaeta with a look of malice more fierce than any I had ever seen her display. "Six months. You've been back for six months, lecturing us on the many *many* reasons we should have come looking for you. I fought for you; I went nearly to hell and back to bring you home, and the very first thing you do is lie to all of us? I understand why you might not have wanted to tell Lexi about this, but keeping a secret so big from your own *sisters*…you know what Lexi means to us. What explanation do you have?"

Evian practically spit, "None. She never has an explanation. Airy Faerie, just running around not caring how many truths she has to twist to get what she wants. Always leaving us to clean up after her. This is her M.O. I told you both she'd ruin everything if she stuck around."

"Your sisterly love is touching, Evian," Vaeta screeched, "So sorry it was such an inconvenience to your perfect little lives to come rescue me! Did it ever occur to you that maybe the world doesn't revolve around you? Of course not, this planet is 70% water, so you get 70% of the attention—it's always been like that!"

Terra stood to her full height, stretched out her arms, and shook the earth beneath the house until everyone fell silent.

"Vaeta, answer the question." Terra crossed her arms and waited while Vaeta muttered under her breath and finally, with a toss of her head and a roll of her eyes, agreed to explain her motives.

"I know none of you ever agreed with my lifestyle or the company I chose to keep, but I've come across many types of beings over the years. Some good, some bad, some downright evil. There are plenty of halflings out there, as you probably realize." She turned to face Flix as she continued. "I don't like that term; never have. It's offensive and closed-minded."

Flix nodded, and I could tell he appreciated the sentiment, but wouldn't be letting Vaeta off quite that easily.

"When I first came here, I thought you all knew about Lexi. I didn't understand your relationship, or why you were still here when she clearly didn't need you anymore. And then I realized it wasn't just Lexi who didn't know her own heritage; you were *all* in the dark and seemed content to keep it that way. So I didn't say anything." Vaeta sighed. "I didn't want to do anything that would disrupt your lives. You were already so angry with me."

Vaeta looked down at the floor, her toe tracing an invisible shape on the weathered wood planks. "I thought I would hate Lexi. I thought she was a replacement for me, but as it turns out I understand why you love her so much." Vaeta turned to me. "Lexi, my sisters and I can hash this out on our own. It's more about us than you, anyway. I want you to know that I didn't mean any ill will toward you. I wanted to tell you, but I just...*couldn't*."

Vaeta's words, save for the way she said "couldn't" at the end, rang true. I didn't have time to parse the meaning, and I realized I didn't care. Vaeta had no way of knowing what kind of minefield she had walked into, and as long as my family hadn't deceived me, I could process the rest at a much, much later date.

"I can forgive you, Vaeta. But that doesn't mean I'll forget, or fully trust you. At least not yet."

Vaeta nodded, a painful smile etching the contours of her face; for a moment, she looked older and more drawn than I had ever seen a faerie look before, and I realized I might have misjudged the toll of a long existence. A thousand years of pleasure came with a thousand years of pain. I somehow doubted there was a faerie psychiatrist out there, and vowed to be a little easier on them from now on.

"I understand," Vaeta replied quietly and turned toward her sisters. "We can discuss this later. Right now we need to help Lexi break Jett's spell on that guitar."

I excused myself with a lie about needing to use the bathroom, trusting the faeries to keep the peace between the three men in my life while I took a much-needed few moments for myself. Gazing into the mirror at my windblown hair and tear-stained cheeks, I searched for some resemblance to the face that was now seared permanently into my memory; perhaps the line of my jaw or even the shape of my earlobes would provide physical proof of my lineage. Nope, I still looked, for all the world, exactly like my grandmother.

Inexplicably, I was overwhelmed with the desire to cleanse myself and decided the others would just have to wait a few more minutes. I turned the tap to the hottest setting, got undressed save for the bloodstone pendant hanging heavily around my neck, and willed the water to wash away all of my fear and pain.

Be careful what you wish for is a cliché or a maxim, I supposed; one I'd never understood fully until my deepest wish came true. Sometimes, when the universe says *yes*, there's a giant, annoying *but* at the end.

Yes, you can have your magic, Lexi…but it comes with a few caveats and surprises. Well, thank you fate for tossing me a curveball.

The pendant around my neck hung warmer than the water against my skin, its heat reminding me of the balancing spell I'd done earlier in the day and the feeling of peace returned. There were enough blessings in my life to make up for today's sudden turn of events, and I counted them on water-pruned fingertips.

My family, odd as it was—and really, isn't every family strange in some way or another? My work. My job as keeper of the flame. Flix. Kin. So what if I had a half-brother---oh my goddess, I had a half-brother—who hated me for no good reason. I wasn't any worse off than a lot of other people. It was time to suck it up and move forward.

When I finally pulled the lever and returned to the sanctum, my head was clearer than it had been in weeks.

Salem, having returned to his human form in favor of the opposable thumb, was flipping through a stack of dusty volumes belonging to the shelves above the dais. Where he had plucked them from exactly, I couldn't be sure; no spaces in the stacks stuck out like missing teeth, and I vowed to clean and organize the space as soon as possible.

"Lexi, it says here that Cupid is the God of both true love and passion, and that he manipulates and enhances the connection between two people in order to bring soul mates together." Salem read from one of the books.

Vaeta snorted. "What's that you've got, a Valentine's Day card? Cupid does more than just bring soul mates together; he is the ultimate Fate Weaver." A glance at everyone's confused faces prompted an eye roll before she continued.

"So while you have no problem whatsoever accepting that some people are destined to be together, it never occurred to you that there might be other couples out there who shouldn't be? That sometimes, love is volatile and that certain matches might affect the fate of the world itself?"

Everyone started talking at once, and I began to pace, finally shouting for quiet while I processed Vaeta's revelation. So that was how Jett and I could be cut from the same cloth, but use our gifts in entirely different ways. It was becoming abundantly clear to me that what little power had been at my disposal until recently was only distantly related to my witch genes; it had been Cupid's influence providing my matchmaking abilities.

That revelation was more than I could deal with at the moment, so I focused on the problem at hand. What to do about Kin and the guitar.

As I continued pacing, I talked—my way of working out the problem while the others let me stew.

"This wizard—the one who cast the original spell—just meant to amplify Skip Stark's talent by adding the power of attraction to the guitar. The fact that Stark was able to move on to a place of light tells me it wasn't malevolent in nature. Jett took that energy and twisted it into a love spell—or rather, a lust spell; his intention to screw with the hands of fate turned the magic dark."

"Just like his heart." Kin spat, his voice touched with bitterness. "I can feel it seeping into me. Lexi, I'm scared. We don't have much time."

"Just like his heart. Just like *his* heart." I repeated, stopping dead in the middle of my pacing.

"That's it! Jett has only known sadness, anger, and hatred, so that's what he uses to fuel his power. Misery loves company. But I've had you all in my life; I've known happiness and love, and fostering love has always been my objective. So if I can figure out how to infuse the guitar with my own magic, it should negate

Jett's curse and cancel out the spell entirely!"

I grabbed the guitar and shooed everyone else away from the casting circle. "I saw what he did; I think I understand it, but I need a little boost." Jett might have years of knowledge on his side, but he was still less than I—I was as much a blood witch as I was a demigod, and if there was any way I could use that to my advantage, it was worth a shot.

Sliding a finger up the spine of the Grimoire, I watched as the pages flipped, noting that more spells had appeared on the once-blank sheets. I caught the name of one in particular, and shoved a finger in between two pages to get a better look: *To Awaken the Initiate* was scrawled across the top.

This must have been the original version of the spell I had been toting around for years; my eyes flicked through the list of familiar ingredients, but before I could begin to read the instructions the pages flipped and fell open to the spell I needed now.

"Here, this one says it will amplify the intention bound to any spell." The ritual called for several ingredients, and again everyone pitched in to bring me what I needed. With a light breath of air, each of the five candles blazed with white light, symbolizing the pure, benevolent intention in my heart.

Standing in the center of the flickering flames, I laid my hands against the body of Kin's guitar and thought about every pair of soul mates I had ever brought together.

Symbols, the same ones I had been seeing around people since the bakery, blazed against eyelids I didn't remember closing. Heat followed the path they traced down my arms, through my fingers, and into the polished wood.

I felt a surge of power and heard a chorus of gasps that caused me to open my eyes, and a quick glance down at my hands offered ample explanation. The symbols had merged into a golden glow that made my skin shine brightly with the same light I had seen in Jett's shared memory.

This was it; my father's essence—the very thing I had been looking for in the mirror less than an hour ago. The experience lasted a few seconds, and then everything—the candles, my skin, the ringing in my ears—returned to normal.

"Kin, you need to play it now. We need to know if it worked." I held my breath as he entered the circle, slung the strap over his back, and began to pluck away. The room filled with the notes of the song Kin wrote for me, but I couldn't enjoy the music. Moons of dark fire floated into the air.

As my eyes widened, so did Kin's. "Lexi, I can't stop playing. Help!" His fingers began to move faster, his eyes tearing up as each string sharpened into a tiny blade, cutting into his flesh and drawing blood that spattered onto the floor. His gasps of pain were like needles piercing my heart and, without thinking, I sprang to my feet and rushed forward, throwing my arms around his neck and kissing him with all of the abandon of a woman in love.

The second our lips touched, my body began to hum, and the same pure light from before enveloped us both. In a rush, the black moon symbols streamed out of the guitar along with the last of Jett's twisted magic, and the white light of my benevolent intention coursed into the void left behind. Kin finally stopped playing.

When he raised his arms to embrace me, his hands were clean and the cuts had faded to white lines.

"Wow, what happened?" Kin sighed with relief and tossed the guitar aside to pull me closer to him. I fit against the contours of his body as if intention had shaped me that way. His or mine made no matter to me. I felt the beat of his heart against my still glowing hand—strong and steady, just like Kin. When I dared raise my eyes to his face, there were tears. Not from the momentary pain of his brush with darkness, but from knowing how close he had come to losing me.

If I had had any doubts before, they were gone now along with the last of those pesky symbols—washed away in the dark fire of banished magic. Jett had told the truth, I was a Child of Cupid with the inheritance of love running through my veins.

"Lexi." Kin breathed my name. "What happened?" His hands lifted to cup my face and he leaned close.

"Tell me."

"True love's kiss."

"You mean like the happily ever after, fairytale kind?" Kin seemed entirely too pleased with the notion.

"Don't get too excited. The kiss always happens there, but it's not the end of the story; it's just the beginning."

And then I burst his bubble. "And I'm still mad at you."

Chapter 27

For the love of designer shoes, can't I just have one day to sleep in? I thought as the sound of my personal phone ringing dragged me out of sleep.

"Hello?" I tried to keep my voice even and mildly pleasant, even though I had wanted to answer with as rude a "what?" as I could possibly manage.

"Lexi? It's Lemon. You won't believe what I've gone through over the last twelve hours!"

Wanna bet?

"I woke up in the middle of the night and it was like I had been trapped in a nightmare. I don't know what got into me, but I can't live without Harry. The wedding is back on!" She practically shrieked into my still-half-asleep ear.

"That's wonderful, Lemon." What did this have to do with me?

"Well, it would be, if I hadn't canceled the venue. Or the caterer. Or the cake." I had a feeling there was more. "You know absolutely everybody. You're my only hope!" Lemon cried.

Part of me wanted to tell her to go take a flying leap. I was just about done dealing with the soon-to-be Tarts, and would really love to wash my hands of the whole situation, but something—probably the Fate Weaver in me—compelled me to help.

If Harry hadn't been a client of mine, I might never have found out about Kin's guitar, and his soul might not be safe and sound at the moment, so in a way I owed Lemon more than she knew. Besides, it would take the faeries and me one-tenth of the time it would take Lemon and Harry to put an entire wedding together.

"Text me a list of what hasn't been canceled; you're in charge of those elements. I'll take care of the rest, but it's going to cost you." I warned.

"I'll pay anything, just name your price."

"Let me out of giving the toast."

"Done."

It turned out all Lemon had retained was the photographer, the dresses and tuxedos, and the favors and decorations she hadn't had time to shred. I told her to bring the lot over to the office, called Flix to meet her there, and then demanded he pop over to my place for a much-needed pow-wow.

In the meantime, I made a few calls, got dressed,

and grabbed a cup of coffee before rallying the troops. By the time we all settled around the kitchen island, I was fresh as a daisy and my head was clear of the stuffing that had been all but coming out of my ears.

The biggest shocker of the morning was Kin showing up and being greeted by the faeries like he belonged there.

I'm not going to pretend I had processed a fraction of what had transpired the evening before, but somehow the revelation that I was a Daughter of Cupid—and yes, it seemed more like a title than a family connection—filled a hole I hadn't even known had been present. I felt like the Grinch; like my heart had grown two sizes and if I tried to stuff anything else inside I'd blow that little measuring device to smithereens.

My entire life had been full of unanswered questions. Adding another to the list wasn't exactly devastating, even if the implications were life-changing. Maybe dealing with strange and unusual things was part of my gift, but something also whispered that I'd barely scratched the surface and there were plenty more land mines ahead of me.

"Okay, everyone, here's the deal. We have T-minus 48 hours to whip up a fabulous wedding for Harry and Lemon. Stop snickering, Salem, or I'll turn you into a cater waiter, force you to serve tuna tartare, and hex you so you can't eat any." Salem blanched and shut his trap.

"Obviously, Flix, you're on hair, makeup, and

tending to the bridal parties. Does that work?” Flix stood at attention and aimed a sarcastic salute and a *yes, ma'am* in my direction.

"How many lovely ladies in the bridal party?"

"Five, counting the bride. If you need help, I can reach out. Remember that really sweet cut-and-color specialist I matched back in September? I ran into her last Tuesday and she's between jobs because Antonia decided to retire." Maybe if it worked out, he'd hire her full time.

Checking his watch, Flix replied, "I know the one you mean and I have her number. I'll handle it, but I have to go." Tossing Kin a grin, he planted a kiss on my cheek and flitted off to do whatever it was he needed to do.

I turned to the faeries. “I've already contacted most of the event directors across the city, and nobody has an opening. It's the first weekend of the warm season, and even *I* don't have enough clout to bump another event at the last minute like this. That means we have no venue, so I'm counting on the four of you to get creative. The guest list has been whittled down to only about 150, and the weather is supposed to be sublime. That should give you plenty of options. You'll be handling the decor, too. Simple but elegant.” It was a warning, not a suggestion.

Evian and Vaeta exchanged a glance that I interpreted as hurt over my lack of trust. Too bad, I've seen their handiwork in the past. Over-the-top is their baseline.

"Leave it to me," Terra assured, "We'll give your friends a wedding to remember."

And that was exactly what I was afraid of.

"Kin, I need you to call that DJ friend of yours and make him an offer he can't refuse. Whatever it takes."

"Is that it?" He asked, his expression hopeful. I knew he was itching to discuss our relationship, and even though I knew it wasn't fair to be mad that a regular guy had needed more than two seconds to process the idea that his girlfriend was a witch, and even though we had shared true love's kiss, I wasn't ready to make up just yet.

"Can you make sure he plays "Can't Help Falling In Love?" I asked. "It's their song."

"Why don't you let me play it for them; I'll brush up on my Elvis Presley impersonation." He suggested.

"I'm sure you would do a bang up job, but I doubt Harry would appreciate the gesture." I tossed him a small smile and sent him on his way looking slightly more hopeful than he had when he entered.

I finished handing out assignments while Terra ran through a mental list. "What about the cake?" She asked hopefully.

"I know you'd do something fantastic, but I have it covered." I tossed her a wink. "I think that's it. Let's get to work."

"Lexi, wait." Kin caught me at the front door and

pulled me outside. "Can we talk?" Loaded question much?

"Of course." We both sat down on the front stoop and were quiet for an awkward moment.

"So, that kiss…" Kin finally broke the silence.

"Yeah." I replied, thinking I couldn't sound any more lame if I tried.

"True love's kiss. That was real? Because it sure felt real to me."

I nodded my agreement. "But are you really sure you want to get involved with someone who could get your soul sucked into an inanimate object?"

This time he didn't hesitate. "How am I supposed to be with someone who *can't* now? I know too much. Unless you have some way to wipe my memory, I think I'm sort of stuck in this world."

He had a point even if he made it in the worst possible way. "Stuck? That's an attractive way to put it. I want this to work as much as you do. But I don't want you to get hurt. Being with me comes with a significant amount of baggage; I mean, four faerie godmothers are a lot to deal with on a regular basis. To say nothing about my cat/man familiar, and a whacked out half-brother who is hell-bent on destroying everything I hold near and dear. That includes you; I don't want you caught in the crossfire again."

Part of me hoped Kin would walk away; the part that had no idea how to be in a committed relationship, especially an honest one. I had never been able to be honest with anyone in my whole life, and that's where the flip side of my feelings came into play. How desperately had I hoped for someone just like Kin, and now here he was and I was this-close to throwing it all away over a little fear.

I laid a hand on Kin's bare arm, closed my eyes, and reached out for the power to See our future. At the point of contact, my skin lit up bright and golden. I also felt that old tug of intuition telling me that if I let Kin go it would be the biggest mistake of my life.

"As long as you understand that nothing with us will ever be simple…"

"Nothing worthwhile ever is." Kin murmured, and then pressed his lips to mine.

While necking on the steps sounded like a lot more fun than putting together a wedding on short notice, I knew we needed to get to work.

Mona gave me a bright smile when I walked into Crumb—one I knew I hadn't earned. I felt like the world's biggest heel asking her for a favor, and this wasn't an ordinary boon, it was major.

"You must hate me and I don't blame you. I've been distracted and full of wonk this whole time. I promise I'll make it all up to you." She deserved more than I'd been able to give.

Picking up a twisted cone full of icing, Mona resumed piping a delicate lacework pattern onto a cookie that looked too beautiful to eat. When she glanced back up at me, her eyes were bright.

"Do you have any idea what you've done for me already?" She asked.

"Let's see…I implied you weren't attractive enough by giving you a makeover, then I hauled you all over town and dragged you into my own personal apocalypse. At the least, I owe you an apology and probably a spa day."

Mona shook her head. "That's not how I see it. You gave me confidence and reminded me that the first person who needs to care about me is *me*. Don't get me wrong, I'd love to meet my match, but I wasn't ready before."

"Are you ready now?"

Out of reflex, Mona squeezed the icing tube a little too tightly and ruined the careful pattern on her cookie. "Like this minute? Why? Is he outside?" She leaned to look past me.

"No. He's not."

"Well, that's okay." Mona smiled again. "I'd prefer to meet him when I'm not covered in icing and flour anyway."

"Mona, I have to ask you for a favor. Lemon and Harry are getting married on Saturday and it's a long story, but they don't have a cake. Do you think you could…"

"Done." She smiled. "How many guests?"

"150 and I'll pay double your usual fee." Mona waved the suggestion away.

"Colors?"

"Gray and yellow. Can you make gray icing? Maybe just yellow."

"Not to worry, I'll keep it simple, but elegant." Mona said. "Three tiers, each one a different flavor. I keep a few in the freezer for just such occasions. Don't worry, I've got this. Is there anything else I can do?"

"Come to the wedding; I'll let you know where as soon as we iron out that tiny detail. Weddings are a great place to connect with new people." I gave her a wink.

At some point during the previous couple of days, the glitches in my matchmaking radar had cleared up. More than that, I knew exactly who her intended was and on Saturday, Mona would finally meet her match.

My next stops were the docks, where I talked to my favorite fishmonger, and the east side of town to talk my favorite butcher out of his entire stock of chicken.

Terra could conjure up fruits and vegetables, but it would be easier all the way around if I had certain menu items delivered. Okay, so I wanted to avoid a flock of chickens being magicked up in my backyard.

Can you blame me? Cliché wedding fare, I'll freely admit, but Lemon would have to deal. Besides, Soleil could turn a pig's ear into a four course gourmet meal;

the food would be spectacular.

Next I cleaned out both party supply stores in town of anything gray or yellow, and hit Hardy Rental for chairs, tables, and the only party tent they had left. Lemon had better appreciate this; I'd called in favors all over town.

By the time I pulled Pinky back into the drive, she looked like the Beverly Hillbillies' pink pack mule with so many boxes and bags strapped on there was barely enough room for me. He must have been watching for me, because Salem opened the door before I could.

"Wait until you see what's been going on here. I think you started something with the faeries and this party planning thing." By his tone, I couldn't tell if that was a good or a bad thing. "They're bringing in reinforcements."

"Tell me it's not going to be like my birthday."

"Your birthday?" I hadn't heard Kin coming up behind me. "When was that?" He swooped me in for a kiss before I had time to answer and when it was over, I wasn't sure I could formulate one.

"How cute are you?" Salem managed to dial down the sarcasm to a faint level. "I think I'll call you *Lexikin* like one of those Hollywood power couples."

"Shut up and help me carry this stuff inside."

Walking into the kitchen felt like walking into ground zero at party central. Soleil, deep in her element, had every pot and pan we owned pressed into service.

Trays of canapes were lined up on the counter and when I reached out to nip a sample, a wooden spoon swatted my fingers away.

"Ow, Soleil. I just wanted to try one."

"Over there," she pointed to a platter on the table. "Taste those and tell me what you think."

"What I think is that you're overdoing it. I said keep it simple, remember?" I admonished without any actual malice. Everything looked gorgeous, and Lemon wasn't exactly low-maintenance to begin with.

"This is the best fun I've had in years, so just taste those crab puffs and tell me if I've used too much crab."

"I don't remember ordering crab. Where did this come from?" I wondered.

Soleil pointed a thumb toward Evian, who gave me a how-dumb-are-you look, and I knew I'd lost control of the wedding the minute I asked them to help.

"So help me Goddess, if I have to do some kind of memory wipe charm on the entire guest list because you've gone overboard, I'll..." what could I threaten them with that would make a difference? "...be cranky." Lame and entirely useless.

Because they were there, and because to ignore Soleil was entertaining disaster, I tried a crab puff. "Okay, fine. This is a bite of heaven. Did you find a venue?" I changed the subject.

"Well, don't get mad, but we figured it would be easiest to just have it here. In the backyard." Terra wasn't actually seeking my approval.

"I said 150 people. You heard me, right? How are we supposed to cram a crowd that size in there?"

"It's big enough." Terra insisted and I shot her a doubtful look. "Now," she grinned. "Go look. It's almost ready."

I stepped out the sliding doors and into wedding wonderland. Yellow and white flowers bedecked an arbor made from twined branches. I doubted anyone would notice the trees were actually rooted in the soil, so artfully had they been grown. Terra's influence at work—as was the fact that the area had tripled in size and could easily accommodate Lemon's guest list.

"The chairs will go here. You got the tent, right?" I nodded. "We'll have them set it up over there. What do you think?" I'd never heard Terra so eager to please before.

"It's perfect. Lemon will love it. She'd be a fool not to." My praise brought a smile to Terra's face. "I couldn't scare up one of those portable dance floors, though." I sighed. It was the only item on my list that I had failed to find.

"I've got it covered." Terra walked to the spot she had designated for dancing and bent to lay her hand on the ground, which rumbled under her touch. Flat stones seethed up out of the soil and spread into a perfectly level surface.

"Now for the lighting." The other three faeries

appeared next to me. "What do you think of this?" Soleil shot sparks from her fingertips, Evian encased them in icy bubbles, and Vaeta used a breeze to waft them gently into place over the dance floor. At night, the effect would be magical. "We're doing these on a smaller scale in all the trees, too."

The sting of tears in my eyes surprised me and I couldn't decide if they were coming from the perfection before them or from the fact that my godmothers, all four of them, had tried so hard to please me.

"It's perfect."

And it was. The wedding went off without a hitch. The reinforcements Salem mentioned before turned out to be a faerie string quartet who played so beautifully that half the guests were in tears before the bride made her entrance. Glowing with love, Lemon walked down the aisle, or in this case, the carpet of tiny flowers Terra had coaxed into bloom, and stood beside Harry to take her vows.

"Do you, Lemon Piel, take this man…" I stifled a burst of laughter. How had I not known Lemon's last name all this time? No wonder becoming a Tart had been no big deal to her.

I don't know about the rest of the crowd, but I breathed a hearty sigh of relief when the deed was done and the pair were pronounced husband and wife. Beside me, Mona wiped away a tear.

"Weddings, you know?" She sniffled and smiled

while I watched Lemon and Harry exchange true love's kiss with a sigh of my own.

While the photographer did the formal shots, I went with Mona to add the finishing touches to the cake. Rounding the table, I tossed an arm around her and gave her a squeeze.

"That cake is gorgeous. It's a shame we have to cut into it." White fondant blanketed each layer to form a smooth base for a riot of lemon-hued flowers. The sides Mona had piped in a charcoal gray latticework pattern accented with silver and white. I knew Lemon was going to love it. "Your work here is done, and so is mine. What do you say we enjoy the rest of the festivities?"

Mona squeezed back. "It's a beautiful wedding. Thanks for letting me be a part of it." Then she grinned. "Lemon Piel? Did you know?"

I shook my head and locked arms with her. Something told me Mona was going to become a part of my life from now on. Navigating the separation between my home life and the one spent in public might get a little more complicated with her in it, but she was worth it. Getting her together with Mark today was going to be a personal achievement as well as a business-related one.

I'd lied to Mona, though. There were two more hurdles before I could fully relax. If the meal went off without a hitch, I would be able to breathe freely for the first time since Lemon had pulled me out of sleep with that phone call.

"Can you wait here while I check on the final details. I'll be right back." I dodged around the back where all the activity was hidden from the crowd. Our history had me prepared for almost anything except for what I found—four perfectly polite faeries working in harmony. It even looked like they were enjoying the work. Terra waved me away.

"Go. We're fine."

I went. I'd heard that tone in her voice before. Still, it looked like they had everything well in hand, and I wanted to be out front to see the look on Lemon's face when she caught a glimpse of the ice sculpture. I'd given Evian a peek at the engagement photos splashed all over Lemon's social media, and she'd chosen one of them kissing to immortalize in ice. The heart shape surrounding their heads had a wing along each side that would flow with champagne when everything was ready.

The last detail of the day revolved around Mona and Mark. It was finally time for them to meet and I really wanted to give her an epic moment she would never forget. Too bad I had no concept for what that might be.

Keeping them apart until the optimum moment wasn't difficult; Mark, in his capacity as DJ and emcee, was busy with his duties.

I got the shock of my life when he played a musical

flourish as the side of the tent whooshed open to reveal the food—partly because the tent wasn't constructed to open that way—but mostly it was the vision of my gorgeous godmothers dressed in chef whites and their most nondescript glamour.

"The caterers; do you have their card?" Mona waved a forkful of food at me. "I'd love to talk to them about one or two events they'd be perfect for." I choked on a bite of delectable chicken.

"I think they're booked through the end of the year, but I'll talk to them and see," I lied right to her face. How good a friend did she have to be to learn all my secrets? I knew we weren't there yet. We chatted through the rest of dinner, watched the Tarts dance their first dance as husband and wife, and I knew the moment was finally upon me. I had to give Mona her happy ending.

"Come with me." I pulled her to her feet and toward her destiny.

Chapter 28

I waited for the fireplace to close behind me before I slumped onto the sofa and enjoyed a few quiet moments of peace. Processing everything that had happened over the last few days was taking a lot out of me, and the pandemonium had my nerves set on edge.

Lemon and Harry had ridden off into the sunset, Mexico-bound for what was sure to be a romantic, relaxing honeymoon, and I couldn't help but wish I could take a vacation, too. My business was secure, at least for now, but I had my work cut out for me with a mischievous half-brother to worry about.

My sanctum was a mess, and a little mindless cleaning seemed just the thing to set me to rights. I retrieved the ritual broom from the floor, tucked a few loose twigs into the binding, and placed it back on its display mount above the fireplace. With a flick of my wrist, the unnecessary warmth from the roaring Balefire dissipated, while the flame continued to burn just as brightly as before. No sparks, nothing exploding, no backlash.

I could feel the power thrumming below the surface of my skin, and with a healthy amount of respect instead of trepidation, practiced adjusting the intensity. This was going to be fun.

Pointing to a pile of cleaning supplies littering one of the long hardwood tables, I set my intention and allowed a small amount of magic to flow from my fingertip. A swirling, glittery cloud curled lazily until it came into contact with a bottle of furniture polish and a rag, both of which rose into the air and began carefully dusting a set of shelves filled with corked bottles of who-knows-what.

The mop and broom danced a waltz across the floor, sweeping the dust and debris into the fireplace on the 1-2 count, and twirling backward to apply a coat of wax over the ancient wooden planks. I felt like a character from Fantasia, the sounds of spraying and wiping and sweeping singing a tune of their own. There, in the middle of my odd victory dance, I noticed the Grimoire resting on its pedestal, and remembered the empty pages that teased with spells still inaccessible to me.

I flipped idly through the pages, some still blank but far fewer than before, until I came across the one that had unlocked my ability to See; the one that had allowed me access to my powers and the courage to reach into the Balefire flame.

There, in bold lettering, was a passage that hadn't been copied onto the loose page I had carried around for years. I read aloud, "The Stone of Blood contains the key to the power of the witches of the Balefire. It must be passed directly from mother to daughter and protected at all costs."

I reached automatically for the amulet hanging at my throat. Athena's gift. A sudden and overwhelming urge to vomit slammed into the back of my throat. This was no ordinary necklace; no regular bloodstone, and certainly no innocent gift. This was the Stone of Blood, and it had been consecrated by every Balefire witch before me.

A scene began to play through my mind, over and over again as a fog lifted from my memory. I remembered Athena and the magic shop; her interest in my life and my command of the ritual flame. I recalled how she had removed the amulet from her own neck and fastened it around mine. I felt her fingers sear across my nape, heard the sound of her throaty laughter, only this time, the scene had a different ending.

When the Stone of Blood fell heavy between my breasts, I looked Sylvana in the eye and said, "Thank you, Mother."

-The End-